"Addictive and hypnotic."
—The Eternal Night

Praise for the
Morganville Vampires Series

Lord of Misrule

"Ms. Caine uses her dazzling storytelling skills to share the darkest chapter yet.... In the midst of death and destruction brought to this well-built world, there's always strong friendship and the touch of romance to add light and warmth to the story line.... An engrossing read that once begun is impossible to set down." —Darque Reviews

"Filled with delicious twists that the audience will appreciatively sink their teeth into.... Rachel Caine provides a strong young-adult vampire thriller, and not a Weather Warden in sight." —Genre Go Round Reviews

Feast of Fools

"Fast-paced and filled with action ... fans of the series will appreciate *Feast of Fools*." —Genre Go Round Reviews

"Thrilling.... In sharing her well-imagined world, Ms. Caine gives readers the danger-filled supernatural moments they crave while adding friendship, romance, and teen issues to give the story a realistic feel. A fast-moving series where there's always a surprise just around every dark corner."
—Darque Reviews

"Very entertaining ... I could not put *Feast of Fools* down.... There is a level of tension in the Morganville books that keeps you on the edge of your seat; even in the background scenes you're waiting for the other shoe to drop. And it always does." —Flames Rising

continued...

"I thoroughly enjoyed reading *Feast of Fools* . . . it was fantastic. . . . The excitement and suspense . . . is thrilling and I was fascinated reading about the town of Morganville. I greatly look forward to reading the next book in this series and catching up with the other books. I highly recommend *Feast of Fools* to paranormal readers for a delightful and fun read that you won't want to put down."

—Fresh Fiction

Midnight Alley

"A fast-paced, page-turning read packed with wonderful characters and surprising plot twists. Rachel Caine is an engaging writer; readers will be completely absorbed in this chilling story, unable to put it down until the last page. . . . For fans of vampire books, this is one that shouldn't be missed!"

—Flamingnet

"Weaves a web of dangerous temptation, dark deceit, and loving friendships. The nonstop vampire action and delightfully sweet relationships will captivate readers and leave them craving more."

—Darque Reviews

The Dead Girls' Dance

"It was hard to put this down for even the slightest break. . . . Forget what happens to the kid with the scar and glasses, I want to know what happens next in Morganville. If you love to read about characters with whom you can get deeply involved, Rachel Caine is so far a one hundred percent sure bet to satisfy that need. I love her Weather Warden stories, and her vampires are even better."

—The Eternal Night

"Throw in a mix of vamps and ghosts, and it can't get any better than *Dead Girls' Dance*." —Dark Angel Reviews

THE MORGANVILLE VAMPIRES NOVELS

FADE OUT

THE MORGANVILLE VAMPIRES

RACHEL CAINE

A SIGNET BOOK

SIGNET
Published by New American Library, a division of
Penguin Group (USA) Inc., 375 Hudson Street,
New York, New York 10014, USA
Penguin Group (Canada), 90 Eglinton Avenue East, Suite 700, Toronto,
Ontario M4P 2Y3, Canada (a division of Pearson Penguin Canada Inc.)
Penguin Books Ltd., 80 Strand, London WC2R 0RL, England
Penguin Ireland, 25 St. Stephen's Green, Dublin 2,
Ireland (a division of Penguin Books Ltd.)
Penguin Group (Australia), 250 Camberwell Road, Camberwell, Victoria 3124,
Australia (a division of Pearson Australia Group Pty. Ltd.)
Penguin Books India Pvt. Ltd., 11 Community Centre, Panchsheel Park,
New Delhi - 110 017, India
Penguin Group (NZ), 67 Apollo Drive, Rosedale, North Shore 0632,
New Zealand (a division of Pearson New Zealand Ltd.)
Penguin Books (South Africa) (Pty.) Ltd., 24 Sturdee Avenue,
Rosebank, Johannesburg 2196, South Africa

Penguin Books Ltd., Registered Offices:
80 Strand, London WC2R 0RL, England

First published by Signet, an imprint of New American Library,
a division of Penguin Group (USA) Inc.

First Printing, November 2009
10 9 8 7 6 5 4 3 2 1

To Alan Hanna, who got me going.
To Nina Romberg, who got me out there.
To P. N. Elrod and Carole Nelson Douglas, who showed
me the ropes.
To my dear friends Jackie and Bill Leaf,
Heidi Berthiaume, Glenn Rogers, Sharon Sams,
Christina Radish, ORAC, and so, so many
more, who keep me climbing.
To my dear husband, Cat, who's always there when I
come back.
Special thanks to Aviva and Aziza, who helped me with
specific issues.

Acknowledgments

To my wonderful bosses, Sondra and Josefine, who truly make this whole balancing act work.

To my fantastic agent, Lucienne Diver.

To Excellent Editor Anne and the entire staff of NAL, who make these books a delight to write.

INTRODUCTION

WELCOME TO MORGANVILLE. YOU'LL NEVER WANT TO LEAVE.

So, you're new to Morganville. Welcome, new resident! There are only a few important rules you need to know to feel comfortable in our quiet little town:

- Obey the speed limits.
- Don't litter.
- Whatever you do, don't get on the bad side of the vampires.

Yeah, we said vampires. Deal with it.

As a human newcomer, you'll need to find yourself a vampire Protector—someone willing to sign a contract to keep you and yours safe from harm (especially from the other vampires). In return, you'll pay taxes ... just like in any other town. Of course, in most other towns, those taxes don't get collected at the blood bank.

Oh, and if you decide *not* to get a Protector, you can do that, too ... but you'd better learn how to run fast, stay out of the shadows, and build a network of friends who can help you. Try contacting the residents of the Glass House—Michael, Eve, Shane, and Claire. They know their way around, even if they always end up in the middle of the trouble somehow.

Welcome to Morganville. You'll never want to leave.

And even if you do ... well, you can't.

Sorry about that.

1

Eve Rosser's high-pitched scream rang out through the entire house, bouncing off every wall, and, like a Taser applied to the spine, it brought Claire out of a pleasant, drowsy cuddle with her boyfriend.

"Oh my God, what?" She half jumped, half fell off the couch. Mortal danger was nothing new around their unofficial four-person frat house. In fact, mortal danger didn't even merit a full-fledged scream these days. More of a raised eyebrow. "Eve? *What?*"

The screaming went on, accompanied by thumping that sounded like Eve was kickboxing the floor.

"Damn," Shane Collins said as he scrambled to his feet, as well. "What the hell is wrong with that girl? Was there a sale at Morbid R Us and nobody told her?"

Claire smacked him on the arm, but only out of reflex; she was already heading for the hallway, where the scream echoed loudest. She would have moved faster, but there wasn't panic in that scream after all.

It was more like . . . joy?

In the hallway, their roommate Eve was having a total fit—screaming, bouncing in hoppy little circles like a demented Goth bunny. It was made especially strange by her outfit: flouncy black sheer skirt, black tights with neon pink skulls, a complicated-looking corset with buckles, and her clunky Doc Martens boots. She'd worn her hair in pigtails today, and they whipped wildly around as she jumped and spun and did a wiggling victory dance.

Claire and Shane stood without saying a word, and then exchanged a look. Shane silently raised a finger and made a slow circle at his temple.

Claire, eyes wide, nodded.

The screaming dissolved into excited little yips, and Eve stopped randomly bouncing around. Instead, she bounced directly at them, waving a piece of paper with so much enthusiasm that Claire was lucky to be able to tell it *was* a piece of paper.

"You know," Shane said in an entirely too-calm voice, "I kind of miss the old Morganville, when it was all scary monsters and dodging death. This would *never* have happened in the old Morganville. Too silly."

Claire snorted, reached out, and grabbed Eve's flailing wrists. "Eve! What?"

Eve stopped bouncing and grabbed Claire's hands, crushing the paper in the process. From the jittery pulse of her muscles, she still wanted to jump, but she was making a great effort not to. She tried to say something, but she just couldn't. It came out as a squeal that only a dolphin would have been able to interpret.

Claire sighed and took the paper from Eve's hand, smoothed it out, and read it aloud. "*Dear Eve*," she began. "*Thank you for auditioning for our production of* A Streetcar Named Desire. *We are very pleased to offer you the role of Blanche DuBois*—"

She was interrupted by more bouncing and screaming. Defeated, Claire read the rest silently and handed it on to Shane.

"Wow," he said. "So, that's the town production, right? The annual?"

"I've been auditioning *forever*," Eve blurted out, dark eyes as wide as an animé character's. "I mean, *for-*

ever. Since I was twelve. Best I ever got was one of the Russian dancers for the Christmas performance of *The Nutcracker.*"

"You?" Shane said. "You dance?"

Eve looked offended. "You've been to parties with me. You know I dance, jackass."

"Hey, there's a difference between shaking your ass at a rave and *ballet.*"

Eve leveled a black-nailed finger in his direction. "I'll have you know I was good on pointe, and, anyway, that isn't the issue. I got the part of *Blanche.* In *Streetcar.* Do you know how wicked huge that is?"

"Congratulations," Shane said. He actually sounded like he meant it, to Claire's ears at least, and she was pretty sure he really did. He and Eve yanked each other's chains hard enough to leave marks, but they really did care. Of course, Shane was a guy, and he couldn't leave it at that, so he continued. "Maybe I should go out for it. If they picked you, they'll love my Marlon Brando impression."

"Honey, nobody likes your Brando. He sounds like your Adam Sandler. Which is also terrible, by the way." Eve was calming down, but she was smiling like a lunatic, and Claire could tell she was on the trembling verge of another jumping fit—which was okay, really. Eve excited was quite a show. "Oh my God, I've got to find out about rehearsals. . . ."

"Page two," Claire said, and pointed at the paper. On the back was a neatly printed schedule of what looked like an awful lot of dates and times. "Wow, they're really working it, aren't they?"

"Of course they are," Eve said absently. "The whole town turns out for—oh, damn, I'm going to have to call my boss. I'm going to have to switch shifts for some of these. . . ."

She hustled off, frowning at the paper, and Claire sighed and leaned her back against one wall of the hallway while Shane took the other. He raised his eyebrows. She did, too.

"Is it really that big a deal?" she asked him.

Shane shrugged. "Depends," he said. "Everybody does go, even most of the vampires. They like a good play, although they're usually not so hot on the musicals."

"Musicals," she repeated blankly. "Like what? *Phantom of the Opera*?"

"Last one I saw was *Annie Get Your Gun*. Hey, if they'd put on *Rocky Horror Picture Show*, I'd definitely go, but somehow I don't think they'd have the guts."

"You don't like musicals? Unless they involve transvestites and chain saws?"

Shane pointed both thumbs back toward his chest. "Guy? In case you forgot."

That made Claire smile and tingle in deep, secret places. "I remember," she said, as indifferently as she could, which was not very. "*And* I'm changing the subject, because I need to get to work." A glance at the window told her that it was an ice-cold spring afternoon, with the freezing Texas wind whipping old leaves down the street in miniature tornadoes. "And so do you, soon."

Shane pushed off and crossed the distance fast, pinning her in place with his hands flat against the wall on either side of her. Then he bent his elbows and leaned in and kissed her. The warmth spread from his lips to hers, then out in a rushing summer heat that moved over her entire body in a wave, and left her feeling as if she were glowing inside.

It went on a long time, that kiss. She finally put her palms flat against his chest with a wordless (and mostly weak) sound of pleading.

Shane backed off. "Sorry. I just needed something to get me through another eight hours of the exciting world of food service." He was working at Bryan's Barbecue, which wasn't a bad gig as jobs in Morganville went. He got all the barbecue he wanted, which meant a lot of free brisket and ham and sausage for the rest of them when he carted home a goody bag. The job also brought decent money, according to Shane, and as a plus, he got to use a sharp knife most of the day, carving meats. Apparently that was cool. He and some of the other guys practiced throwing them at targets in the back when the boss wasn't looking.

Claire kissed him on the nose. "Bring home some brisket," she said. "And some of that sauce. I've had enough chili dogs this week to last me a lifetime."

"Hey, my chili dogs are the best in town."

"It's a really small town."

"Harsh," he said, but he was smiling. The smile faded as he said very seriously, "You be careful."

"I will," she promised.

Shane played with knives, but she had the dangerous job.

She worked with vampires.

Claire's job was lab assistant to a vampire mad scientist, which never made sense when she thought of it that way, but it was still accurate. She hadn't *meant* to become Igor to Myrnin's Frankenstein, but she supposed at least it was a paying, steady job.

Plus, she learned a lot, which meant more to her than the money.

She'd been on job leave, with permission, for a couple of months while the vampires got themselves back together and fixed the damage that had been done—at least the physical damage—by the tornado that ripped through town. Or by the vampire war that had burned down part of it. Or by the rioting by the human population, which had left some scars. Come to think of it, the construction was going pretty well, all things considered. So she hadn't been to the lab for a while—today was, in Myrnin's words from his note, the "grand reopening." Although how you had a grand reopening of a hidden lair beneath a tumbledown shack, Claire had no idea. Was there cake?

The alley next to the Day House—a virtually identical twin to the Glass House where Claire lived, only with different curtains and nicer porch furniture—looked the same. The Day House was a shining white Victorian structure, and the alley was narrow, dark, and seemed to get narrower as you went along, like a funnel.

Or a throat. Ugh. She wished she hadn't thought of that.

The shack at the end of the alley—a leaning, faded wreck, tired and abandoned—didn't look any different, although there was a shiny new lock on the door. Claire sighed. Myrnin had forgotten to give her a key, of course. That didn't present much of a problem, though; she tested a couple of boards and found one that easily slid aside enough for her to crawl through.

Typical Myrnin planning.

Inside, most of the space was taken up by a set of stairs that went down, like a subway station. There was a bright glow coming up from it.

"There'd better be cake," she said, mostly to herself, and hitched her backpack higher on her shoulder as she headed down into the lab.

The last time she'd been here, it had been totally destroyed, with hardly a stick of furniture or a piece of glass left intact. Someone—most likely Myrnin himself—had gotten busy with a broom and maybe a dump truck to sweep out the mounds of shattered glass, scrapped lab equipment, broken furniture, and (worst of all, to Claire's mind) ravaged books. The place had always had a mad scientist–meets–Jules Verne flair to it, but now it *really* did—in a totally good way. There were new worktables, many of them wood and marble, and a few shiny metal ones. New electric lights had been installed to replace the odd collection of oil lamps, candles, and bulbs that Thomas Edison might have wired together; now they had indirect lighting behind elegant fan-shaped shields. Modern, but retro-cool.

The floor was still old flagstone, but the hole Myrnin had punched in it the last time she'd been here had also been repaired, or at least covered with a rug. She hoped there was something *under* the rug, but with Myrnin, you really could never tell. She made a mental note to poke it before she stepped on it.

Myrnin himself was shelving things in a new book-case that must have been ten feet tall, at least. It came with its own little rolling ladder—no, as Claire looked around, she realized that the entire room was surrounded by the same tall bookcases, and the ladder was on a metal rail so it could slide all around. Neat. "Ah," her boss said, and looked down at her through the little square antique glasses perched on the end of his long, straight nose. "You're late." He was five feet up in the air, on the top step of the ladder, but he hopped off as if it were pretty much nothing, landed light as a cat on his feet, and straightened his vest with an absentminded little tug.

Myrnin wasn't especially tall, but he was just ... strangely cool. Long, curling, lush black hair that fell to his shoulders. His face was vampire-pale, but it suited him, somehow, and he had the kind of sharp features that would have made him a star if he'd wanted to be in the movies. Big, expressive dark eyes and full lips. Definitely cover-model material.

If the lab was neater, so was Myrnin. He was still favoring old-timey clothes, so the coat was black velvet, and flared out and down to his knees. The ensemble also included a white shirt, bright blue vest, a pocket watch chain gleaming against the tight black satin pants, and ...

Claire found herself staring at his feet, which were in bunny slippers.

Myrnin looked down. "What?" he asked. "They're

quite comfortable." He lifted one to look at it, and the ears wobbled in the air.

"Of course they are," she said. Just when she thought Myrnin was getting his mental act together, he'd do something like that. Or maybe he was just messing with her. He liked to do that, and his dark eyes were fixed on her now, assessing just how weirded-out she was.

Which, on the grand scale of zero to Myrnin, wasn't much.

"I like a good bunny slipper. I'm surprised you didn't get the ones with fangs," she said, and scanned the room. "Wow, the place looks fantastic."

Myrnin's eyes brightened. "They have some with fangs? Excellent." He got a faraway look for a moment, then snapped back to the here and now. "Thank you. I've had quite a time ordering all the instruments and alembics I need, but did you know that you can find almost anything on the new computer network, the Interweb? I was quite amazed."

Myrnin hadn't paid much attention to the past hundred years or so. Claire wasn't too surprised he'd discovered the Internet, though. *Wait until he finds the porn.* That would be a very uncomfortable conversation. "Yeah, it's great; we like it a lot," she said. "So, you said you needed me today . . ."

"Yes, yes, of course," he said, and walked over to one of the tidy lab tables, one laden with boxes and wooden chests. "I need you to go through these, please, and see what we can use here."

"What's in them?"

"No idea," he said as he sorted through a stack of ancient-looking envelopes. "They're mine. Well, I think they are. They might have once belonged to someone named Klaus, but that's another story, and one you don't need to worry about just now. Go through them and see if there's anything useful. If not, you can throw it all away."

He didn't seem to care one way or another, which was another odd mood swing from him. Claire almost preferred the old Myrnin, when the illness he (and the other vampires) suffered from had made him genuinely loony, and desperate to regain control of himself. This version of Myrnin was both more in control, and less predictable. Not violent or angry, just—never quite where she expected him to be. For instance, Myrnin had always struck her as a keeper, not a tosser. He was sentimental, mostly—more than a lot of the other vamps—and he seemed to really enjoy having his things around him.

So what was this sudden impulse for spring cleaning?

Claire dumped her battered canvas backpack in a chair and found a knife to slide through the ropes that held the first box closed. She immediately sneezed, because even the *rope* was dusty. It was a good thing she took the time to grab a tissue and blow her nose, because as she was doing that, a fat, black spider crawled out from under the cardboard flap and began to scuttle down the side of the box.

Claire gave out a little scream and jumped back. In the next fast heartbeat, Myrnin was there, bending over the table, examining the spider with his face only inches from it. "It's only a hunting spider," he said. "It won't hurt you."

"*So* not the point!"

"Oh, pish. It's just another living creature," Myrnin said, and put his hand out. The spider waved its front legs uncertainly, then carefully stepped up on his pale fingers. "Nothing to be frightened of, if handled properly." He lightly stroked the furry back of the thing, and Claire nearly passed out. "I think I'll call him Bob. Bob the spider."

"You're insane."

Myrnin glanced up and smiled, dimples forming in his face. It should have looked cute, but his smiles were never that simple. This one carried hints of darkness and arrogance. "But I thought that was part of my charm," he said, and lifted Bob the spider carefully to take him off to another part of the lab. Claire didn't care what he did with the thing, as long as he didn't wear it as an earring or a hat or something.

Not that she'd put that past him.

She was *very* careful as she folded back the old cardboard. No relatives of Bob appeared, at least. The contents of the box were a tangle of confusion, and it took her time to sort out the pieces. There were balls of ancient twine, some coming undone in stiff spirals; a handful of what looked like very old lace, with gold edging; two carved, yellowing elephants, maybe ivory.

The next layer was paper—loose paper made stiff and brittle and dark with age. The writing on the pages was beautiful, precise, and very dense, but it wasn't Myrnin's hand; she knew how he wrote, and it was far messier than this. She began reading the first paper.

> *My dear friend, I have been in New York for some years now, and missing you greatly. I know that you were angry with me in Prague, and I do not blame you for it. I was hasty and unwise in my dealings with my father, but I honestly do believe that he left me little choice. So, dear Myrnin, I beg you, undertake a journey and come to visit. I know travel no longer agrees with you, but I think if I spend another year alone, I will give up entirely. I would call it a great favor if you would visit.*

It was signed, with an ornate flourish, *Amelie.* As in, Amelie, Founder of Morganville, and Claire's ultimate—although she didn't like to think of it this way—boss/owner.

Before Claire could open her mouth to ask, Myrnin's cool white fingers reached over her shoulder and plucked the page neatly from her hand. "I said determine if we can use these things, not read my private mail," he said.

"Hey—was that why you came to America? Because she wrote to you?"

Myrnin looked down at the paper for a moment, then crumpled it into a ball and threw it in a large plastic trash bin against the wall. "No," he said. "I didn't come when she asked me. I came when I had to."

"When was that?" Claire didn't bother to protest how unfair it was that he wanted her to not *read* things to figure out if they needed them. Or that since he'd kept the letter all this time, he should think before throwing it away.

She just reached for the next loose page in the box.

"I arrived about five years after she wrote to me," Myrnin said. "In other words, too late."

"Too late for what?"

"Are you simply going to badger me with personal questions, or are you planning to do what I told you to do?"

"Doing it," Claire pointed out. Myrnin was irritated, but that didn't bother her, not anymore. She didn't take anything he said personally. "And I do have the right to ask questions, don't I?"

"Why? Because you put up with me?" He waved his hand before she could respond. "Yes, yes, all right. Amelie was in a bad way in those days—she had lost everything, you see, and it's hard for us to start over and over and over. Eternal youth doesn't mean you don't get tired of the constant struggles. So . . . by the time she wrote to me again, she had done something quite insane."

"What?"

He made a vague gesture around him. "Look around you."

Claire did. "Um . . . the lab?"

"She bought the land and began construction on the town of Morganville. It was meant to be a refuge for our people, a place we could live openly." He sighed. "Amelie is quite stubborn. By the time I arrived to tell her it was a fool's errand, she was already committed to the experiment. All I could do was mitigate the worst of it, so that she wouldn't get us all slaughtered."

Claire had forgotten all about the box (and even Bob the spider), so focused was she on Myrnin's voice, but when he paused, she remembered, and reached in again to pull out an ornate gold hand mirror. It was definitely girly, and besides, the glass was shattered in the middle, only a few silvery pieces still remaining. "Trash?" she asked, and held it up. Myrnin plucked it out of her hand and set it aside.

"Most definitely not," he said. "It was my mother's."

Claire blinked. "You had a—" Myrnin's wide stare challenged her to just *try* to finish that sentence, and she surrendered. "Wow, okay. What was she like? Your mother?"

"Evil," he said. "I keep this to keep her spirit away."

That made ... about as much sense as most things Myrnin said, so Claire let it go. As she rummaged through the stuff in the box—mostly more papers, but a few interesting trinkets—she said, "So, are you looking for something in particular, or just looking?"

"Just looking," he said, but she knew that tone in his voice, and he was lying. The question was, was he lying for a reason, or just for fun? Because with Myrnin, it could go either way.

Claire's fingers closed on something small—a delicate gold chain. She pulled, and slowly, a necklace came out of the mess of paper, and spun slowly in the light. It was a locket, and inside was a small, precise portrait of a Victorian-style young woman. There was a lock of hair woven into a tiny braid around the edges, under the glass.

Claire rubbed the old glass surface with her thumb,

frowning, and then recognized the face staring back at her. "Hey! That's Ada!"

Myrnin grabbed the necklace, stared for a moment at the portrait, and then closed his eyes. "I thought I'd lost this," he said. "Or perhaps I never had it in the first place. But here she is, after all."

And just like that, Ada flickered into being across the room. She wasn't alive, not anymore. Ada was a two-dimensional image, a kind of projection, from the weird steampunk computer located beneath Myrnin's lab; that computer was the *actual* Ada, including parts of the original girl. Ada's image still wore Victorian skirts and a high-necked blouse, and her hair was up in a complicated bun, leaving wisps around her face. She didn't look quite right—more like a really good computer generation of a person than a person. "My picture," she said. Her voice was weirdly electronic because it used whatever speakers were around; Claire's phone became part of the surround sound experience, which was so creepy that she automatically reached down and switched it off.

Ada sent her a dark look as the ghost swept through things in her way—tables, chairs, lights.

"Yes," Myrnin said, as calmly as if he spoke to electronic ghosts every day—which, in fact, he did. "I thought I'd lost it. Would you like to see it?"

Ada stopped, and her image floated in the air in the middle of an open expanse of the floor without casting a shadow. "No," she said. Without Claire's phone adding to the mix, her voice came out of an ancient radio speaker in the back of the lab, faint and scratchy. "No need. I remember the day I gave it to you."

"So do I." Myrnin's voice remained quiet, and Claire couldn't honestly tell if what they were talking about was a good memory, or a bad one.

"Why were you looking for it?"

"I wasn't." That, Claire was almost sure, was another

lie. "Ada, I asked you to please stop coming here, except when I call you. What if I'd had other visitors?"

Ada's delicate, not-quite-living face twisted into an expression of contempt. "Who would visit *you*?"

"An excellent point." His tone cooled and hardened and took on edges. "I don't want you coming here unless I call you. Are we understood, or do I have to come and alter your programming? You won't thank me for it."

She glared at him with eyes made of static and ice, and finally turned—a two-dimensional turn, like a cardboard cutout—and flashed at top speed through the solid wall.

Gone.

Myrnin let out a slow breath.

"What the heck was that?" Claire asked. Ada creeped her out, and besides, Ada *really* didn't like her. Claire was, in some sense, a rival for Myrnin's attention, and Ada . . .

Ada was kind of in love with him.

Myrnin looked down at the necklace and the portrait lying flat in his palm. For a moment, he didn't say anything, and Claire honestly thought he wouldn't bother. Then, without looking up, he said, "I did care for her, you know." She thought he was saying it to himself more than to her. "Ada wanted me to turn her, and I did. She was with me for almost a hundred years before . . ."

Before he snapped one day, Claire thought. And Ada died before he could stop himself. Myrnin had told her the first day she'd met him that he was dangerous to be around, and that he'd gone through a lot of assistants.

Ada had been the first one he'd killed.

"It wasn't your fault," Claire heard herself saying. "You were sick."

Myrnin's shoulders moved just a little, up and down— a shrug, a very small one. "It's an explanation, not an excuse," he said, and looked up at her. She was a little startled by what she saw—he almost looked, well, human.

And then it was gone. He straightened, slid the necklace into the pocket of his vest, and nodded toward the box. "Continue," he said. "There may yet be something more useful than sentimental nonsense in there."

Ouch. She didn't even like Ada, and that still stung. She hoped the computer—the computer that held Ada's still-sort-of-living brain—wasn't listening.

Fat chance.

The afternoon passed. Claire learned to scan the sheets of paper instead of read them; mostly, they were just letters, an archive of Myrnin's friendship with people long gone, or vampires still around. A lot were from Amelie, over the years—interesting, but it was all still history, and history equaled *boring*.

It wasn't until she was almost to the bottom of the second box that she found something she didn't recognize. She picked up the odd-shaped thing—sculpture?—and sat it on her palm. It was metal, but it was surprisingly light. Kind of a faintly rusty sheen, but it definitely wasn't iron. It was etched with symbols, some of which she recognized as alchemical. "What's this?"

Before the words were out of her mouth, her palm was empty, Myrnin was across the room, and he was turning the weird little object over and over in his hands, fingers gliding over every angle and trembling on the outlined symbols. "Yes," he whispered, and then louder, "Yes!" He bounced in place, for all the world like Eve with her Blanche DuBois note, and stopped to wave the thing at Claire. "You see?"

"Sure," she said. "What is it?"

His lips parted, and for a second she thought he was going to tell her, but then some crafty little light came into his eyes, and he closed his hand around the sharp outlines of the thing. "Nothing," he purred. "Pray continue. I'll be—over here." He moved to an area of the lab where he had a reading corner with a big leather armchair and a stained-glass lamp. He carefully moved the chair so its back was toward her, and plunked himself down with his bunny-slippered feet up on a hassock to examine his find.

"Freak," she sighed.

"I heard that!"

"Good." Claire sawed through the ropes on the next-to-last box.

It exploded.

2

When Claire opened her eyes again, she saw three faces looming over her. One was Myrnin's, and he looked concerned. One was the shining blond head of her housemate Michael Glass—Michael had her hand in his, which was nice, because he was sweet, and he had beautiful hands, too. The last face took her a moment, and then recognition clicked into place. "Oh," Claire murmured. "Hello, Dr. Theo."

"Hello, Claire," said Theo Goldman, and put a finger to his lips. He was a kind-looking older man, a bit frayed around the edges, and he had an antique black stethoscope in his ears. He was listening to her heart. "Ah. Very good. Your heart is still beating, I'm sure you'll be very pleased to hear."

"Yay," Claire said, and tried to sit up. That was a bad idea, and Michael had to support her when she lost her balance. The headache hit a moment later, massive as a hurricane inside her skull. "Ow?"

"You struck your head when you fell," Theo said. "I don't believe there's any permanent damage, but you should see your physician and have the tests done. I should hate to think I missed anything."

Claire pulled in a deep breath. "Maybe I should see Dr. Mills. Just in case—hey, wait. Why did I fall?"

They all exchanged looks. "You don't remember?" Michael asked.

"Why? Is that bad? Is that brain damage?"

"No," Theo said firmly, "it is quite natural to have some loss of memory around such an event."

"What kind of event?" There it was again, that silence, and Claire raised her personal terror alert from yellow to orange. "Anybody?"

Myrnin said, "It was a bomb."

She blinked, not entirely sure she'd heard him right. "A *bomb*. Are you sure you understand what that is? Because—" She gestured vaguely at herself, then around at the room, which looked pretty much untouched. All glassware intact. "Because generally bombs go boom."

"It was a light bomb," Myrnin said. "Touch your face."

Now that she thought about it, her face *did* feel a bit hot. She put her fingers on her cheeks. *Burning* hot. "What happened to me?" She couldn't keep the fear out of her voice.

Theo and Michael both tried to talk at once, but Michael won. "It's like a sunburn," he said. "Your face is a little pink, that's all."

Michael wasn't a very good liar. "Great. I'm red as a cherry, right?"

"Not at all," Myrnin said cheerfully. "You're definitely not as red as a cherry. Or an apple. Yet. That will take some time."

Claire tried to focus back on what was—hopefully—more important. "A light bomb?"

Myrnin looked suddenly a great deal more serious. "It's an inconvenience for a human," he said. "It would have been extremely damaging to me, or to any vampire, had I been the one to open the box."

"So who sent you a bomb?"

He shrugged. "Eh, it was so long ago. Might have been Klaus. But I might have actually sent it to myself. I'm not always that rational, you know. Mind you, I wouldn't open the last box if I were you."

Claire sent him a long, wordless look, then accepted the hand Michael extended to help her to her feet. She felt dizzy and—yes—sunburned, and a whole lot filthy. "Great. You might have booby-trapped your own boxes. Why would you do a thing like that?"

"Excellent question." Myrnin left her and went to the table, where he lifted from the open box a complicated-looking tangle of metal and wires—the kind of bomb an insane Victorian inventor might have made—and set it very carefully to one side. "I can only think that I meant it to protect what else was in the container."

He stood there staring into the box, not moving, and Claire finally rolled her eyes and said, "Well?"

"What?"

"What's in the box, Myrnin?"

In answer, he tipped it over in her direction. A cloud of dust fogged the air, and when it cleared, Claire saw that there was nothing in the box.

Nothing at all.

"I'm going home," she sighed. "This job *sucks.*"

Michael gave her a ride back to the Glass House, which was what she meant when she said *home*, although technically she didn't live there. Technically, her parents had a room for her in their house, and her stuff was there. Mostly. Well, partly. And, according to the agreement she'd reached with them, she slept there most every night—for a few hours, anyway.

It was all part of her parents' grand scheme to keep her and Shane—well, maybe *apart* was too harsh. *Casual.* They didn't want their little girl shacking up with the town bad boy, even though Shane was *not* the town bad boy, and he and Claire were in love.

In love. That still gave her a delicious little tingle every time she thought about it.

"Parents," Claire said aloud. Michael sent her a look. "And?"

"They bring the crazy," she said. "Is Shane home?"

"Not yet. I dropped Eve off at her first rehearsal." He smiled slowly. "Was she that excited when she got the letter?"

"Define excited. You mean, did she look like a cartoon character on crack? Yes. I never knew she was all into acting and stuff."

"She loves it. She's always acting out scenes from movies and TV shows in her room. When we were in high school, she used to organize these little plays in study hall, give us all parts she'd written out on little pieces of paper, and the teacher never knew what the hell was going on. Insane, but fun." Michael braked his car; Claire couldn't see beyond the tinted windows, but she assumed there was some kind of red light. Good thing Michael had special vampire vision, or they'd be exchanging insurance with some other driver right about now. "So this is a big deal for her."

"Yeah, I got that. Speaking of big deals, I heard that you're playing at the TPU theater tomorrow."

The tips of his ears got a little pink, which (even in a vampire) was adorable. "Yeah, apparently they heard about the last three sets at Common Grounds." Those had been pretty spectacular events, Claire had to admit—people jammed in shoulder to shoulder, including an impressive number of vampires all playing nice, at least for the evening. "Not a big deal."

"I heard the tickets were sold out," Claire said smugly. "So there. It *is* a big deal, dude. Deal with it."

There was a complicated expression on Michael's face—pride, nerves, outright fear. He shook his head and sighed. "You ever feel like your life is kind of out of control?"

"I just went to work for a vampire, was scared by a spider, and got knocked down by a tanning bomb. And that's just my day, not my week."

"Okay, yeah. Point." Michael turned the wheel and hit the brakes again. "You're home, Pinky."

"Don't even *think* about calling me that."

Except, when she got upstairs and in front of a mirror, she realized that Michael wouldn't be the only one calling her that, or worse. Her face was *shiny* pink. As if she'd been dipped in blush and then wrapped in plastic. Ugh. When she pressed her fingers against her skin, she left dramatic white spots that slowly filled in again. "I'm going to *kill* him," she muttered, and slammed the bathroom door, locked it, and flipped on the shower as she glared at her hot pink reflection. "Lock him in a tanning bed. Drive him out in the desert with the top down. Myrnin, you are toast. Burned toast."

It was worse when she had her clothes off; her naturally pale skin was a violent, gut-wrenching contrast to the sunburn on her face. She hadn't realized it before, but she had burns on the tops of her hands and arms, too—anywhere that had been exposed to the blast of light.

Radiation. UV radiation. It didn't really hurt yet, but Claire knew it would, and soon. She showered fast, already uncomfortable with the sting of water on shocked flesh, and then searched her closet in vain for something that wouldn't clash with her new, hot pink color scheme.

Oh, Monica was going to love this like a new puppy.

Finally, she put on her bra and panties and flopped back on the bed, staring at the ceiling. She knew she should dry her hair, but she was in too bad of a mood to care. Shiny, pretty hair wasn't going to help at all. And tangled, ratty hair would at least fit her current mood.

After spending a solid fifteen minutes of glum brooding—which was pretty much her limit—Claire grabbed her headphones and loaded up the latest lecture from Myrnin on string theory. Well, she assumed it was string theory, although Myrnin had a tendency to confuse science with mythology and alchemy and magic and who knew what. Pieces of it still made more sense than anything she'd heard from a tenured professor—and pieces of it were complete gibberish.

The trick was figuring out which were which.

She didn't even know that anyone was in the room until the bed tilted to one side. Claire opened her eyes on near-complete darkness—when had that happened?—and instinctively grabbed for the covers, then remembered she was on top of them, and nearly naked, and panic went nuclear. She yanked off her headphones and slithered off her side of the bed, away from whatever weight had settled on the other side. . . .

The bedside light snapped on, revealing Eve sitting there in all her Gothy glory. Purple was still the color of the day, but she'd gone informal—purple tights, some baggy black shorts, a purple tee with Gothic lettering all over it.

Eve tilted her head to one side, staring at Claire. "Wow," she said. "Respect, girl. That is one *hell* of a sunburn. I haven't seen one that bad since my cousin fell asleep in a deck chair on the Fourth of July at nine a.m. and nobody woke her up until four."

Claire, still trying to control her racing heartbeat, gulped down breaths and grabbed her bathrobe from the chair in the corner of the room. As she yanked it on, it dragged over the backs of her hands and arms, and she almost yelped, again, from the pain. Her face felt as if it were on fire. Literally, with flames. "It's not a sunburn," she said. "It was some kind of UV bomb. It was meant for Myrnin."

"Ouch. Right, so we should get you some of that sunburn cream crap in the gallon size. Note taken."

Claire belted her robe. "Did you just come to see the freak show?"

"Well . . . entertaining as it is, no. I came to tell you that dinner was ready, but you were all grooved out on tunes."

Claire considered telling her that she'd been listening to lectures, but decided that in Eve's world, that was too much information. "Sorry," she said.

"Hey, I wouldn't have dared come in except that Shane's downstairs setting the table." Eve winked. "And if I'd sent him, well. Dinner would get cold, right?"

Oh God. *Shane.* Shane was going to see her like this, looking like some exile from Planet Magenta. "I—I don't think I feel well enough to eat," she lied, even as her stomach rumbled at the thought of food. "Maybe you could bring me—"

"It's only going to get worse," Eve broke in with ruthless cheerfulness. "Oh yeah. Big-time worse. First, the red face, then the blisters, then the peeling skin. Trust me, unless you're going to hide for the next week, minimum, you might as well just get on downstairs. We're having tacos."

"Tacos?" Claire repeated wistfully.

"I even made that funky rice stuff you like. Well. I boiled the water and put the funky rice stuff in it, anyway. That's cooking, right?"

"Close enough." Claire sighed. Across the room, a mirror reflected someone standing in her clothes that she refused to believe was really her. "Okay. I'll be right down."

"Better be." Eve kissed her fingers at Claire and scooted out the door, slamming it behind her.

Claire was still trying to decide whether her pink shirt made her look marginally better or marginally worse, when she felt an ice-cold sensation travel through her like a wave. No drafts, nothing like that—this was internal. It was a warning, straight from the semi-self-aware house.

Something was wrong *in the house.*

Claire grabbed her emergency home defense kit on the way out of her room—a bag of everything from pepper spray to silver-plated stakes—and raced down the hall, then down the stairs, and arrived with a jolt to find everybody else, including Michael, calmly sitting down to dinner.

"What?" Eve asked. Michael rose to his feet, evidently reading the look on Claire's face, if nothing else.

Shane blurted out, "What the hell happened to you?" Under normal circumstances this might have made her feel really bad, but she was off that right now.

"Something's wrong," she said. "Didn't anybody else feel that?"

They exchanged looks. "Feel what?" Michael asked.

"The—cold. It was like a wave . . . of cold?" Her words slowed down, because she wasn't getting any reaction from them. "You didn't feel it. How is that possible? Michael?" Because it was Michael's house, and technically, she didn't even live here anymore. Exactly. The house shouldn't have communicated anything to her before it talked to him.

"I don't know," he said. "Does it feel the same now?"

"Yes." Claire still felt cold, cold enough that she had chills running through her body. She was surprised her breath didn't smoke in the air. "Worse," she managed to say, and Shane got over his shock about her burn and came to take her hands. She winced as the tender skin complained, but she was grateful for the warmth, too.

"You're freezing," he said, and grabbed a fleece blanket from the back of the couch, which he wrapped around her. "Damn, Claire. Maybe it's the sunburn—"

"Not a—sunburn," she said through chattering teeth as he led her to the table and sat her down. "It's the house. It's got to be the house!"

"I—don't think it is," Michael said, and slowly sank back into his chair. "I'd know, Claire; there's no way I wouldn't. This is something else."

She shook her head and hugged the blanket closer,

miserable both ways—her face burning hot, her body shaking with cold.

"Try to eat something," Eve said, and loaded tacos on her plate. "How about something hot to drink?"

Claire nodded. The chill seemed to be sinking in deeper, drilling toward her bones. She had no idea what would happen when it got there, but it didn't seem good. Not good at all.

She kept the blanket tight with her right hand and reached out for a taco with the left, hoping her shaking hand wouldn't scatter the contents all over the table . . . and Shane grabbed her arm. "Look," he said, before she could protest. "Look at the bracelet."

It was Amelie's bracelet, the one she wore clasped around her left wrist, the one she couldn't remove, that reminded people who it was Claire worked for (and reminded Claire, every second).

It was supposed to be gold, but its center was now pale white, as if it had turned to crystal.

Or ice.

It was smoking in the air, so cold it was giving off its own mist.

"We need to get it off," Shane said, and turned her wrist over, looking for a clasp. Claire tried to tell him there wasn't one, but he wasn't listening. "Michael, it's cold, man. It's really cold. Something's really wrong."

They were all out of their chairs now, gathered around her. Michael touched the bracelet, drew back, and locked gazes with Shane. "It doesn't come off," Michael said.

"I don't give a crap if it's not *supposed* to come off!" Shane snapped. "Help me!"

"It won't do any good. It's a Founder's bracelet." Michael grabbed Shane's arm when Shane tried to yank on the bracelet. "Dude, *listen*! You can't get it off! All we can do is get to Amelie. She can take it off."

"Amelie," Claire repeated, and tried to control her violent shaking so she could get the words out. The whole world seemed to be turning to ice, cold and toxic. "Something—wrong—with—Amelie—"

Shane glared at Michael. "Let go." When Michael did, he kept on glaring. "Shouldn't you know if something was wrong with Amelie, you being her demonic spawn and everything?"

"It's not like that," Michael said, although anger was starting to build in his blue eyes and in the set of his face. "I'm not her *spawn.*"

"Not arguing the demonic part? Whatever you call it. She made you a vampire. Can't you tell if she's in trouble?"

"You're confusing vampires with Spider-Man," Michael shot back, but he'd already left the fight and was pulling out his cell phone. A one-button press, and he was talking, but not to Shane. "Oliver. Are you with Amelie? No? Where is she?"

Whatever the answer, he snapped the phone shut without answering, locked eyes with Shane, and said, "Let's go."

"W-w-wait," Claire managed to say, and grabbed for Shane's arm. "Wh-wh-where—"

"My question, too. Where are you going? Because I'm going with," Eve said, and jumped up to grab her patent leather skull purse.

"No, you're not. Someone needs to stay with Claire."

"Then *she's* going with. Womenfolk don't stay behind anymore, Mikey; it's so last century," Eve said, and Claire nodded. She thought she did, anyway; it was hard to tell, with all the shaking. "Right. Up you go, kiddo."

3

The ride in Michael's car felt like a nightmare. Eve had brought loads of blankets, and Claire was almost smothering under them, but she was still cold, and getting colder, as if her thermostat had gone drastically wrong. Her skin was turning white, her fingernails and lips blue.

She was starting to look ... dead.

Even if she'd been trying to look where they were going, it wouldn't have done any good; Michael's car was vampire-standard, with ultratint on the windows. Human eyes couldn't get anything but murky hints of lights through it, so she just kept her attention on taking another breath, and another.

"Hey, Michael?" she heard Eve say. "Like, soon, okay?"

"I'm already breaking the speed limit."

"Go faster."

A surge of acceleration pressed Claire back in her seat. Shane was holding her, but she couldn't feel it. She'd stopped shivering now, which felt better, but she was also very, very tired, barely able to stay awake. At least the shaking had been something she could hold on to, but now there was nothing but cold, and silence. Everything seemed to be moving away from her, leaving her behind.

"Hey!" She felt something, a flash of heat against her skin, and opened her eyes to see Shane's face inches away. He looked scared. His hands were on her cheeks, trying to force heat into her. "Claire! Don't close your eyes. Stay with me. Okay?"

"Okay," she whispered. "Tired."

"I see that. But don't you go away from me, you hear me? Don't you even think about it." He stroked her skin, her hair, with hands that shook almost as much as she had before. "Claire?"

"Here."

"I love you." He said it quietly, almost a whisper, a secret between the two of them, and she felt a burst of what was almost warmth travel through her chest. "You hear me?"

She managed a nod, and thought she smiled.

Michael brought the car to a quick, sliding stop, and was out of the car before Claire could register that they'd arrived at their destination. "Hey!" Eve protested, and scrambled out after him. Shane opened the back and lifted Claire out in his arms—or rather, lifted the bundle of laundry that Claire felt like, wrapped in half a dozen blankets.

Moonlight fell blue-white over grass, trees, and headstones.

They were at Morganville's official cemetery—Restland.

"Crap," Shane breathed. "Not my idea of a great night out, you know? Claire? Still with us?"

"Yes," she said. She actually felt a little better, and didn't know why. Not *good*, of course. But not going away anymore.

Ahead, she could see that Michael and Eve were making their way together through the maze of leaning tombstones, crosses, and marble statues. A big white mausoleum dominated the hill at the top, but they weren't going that way—they veered off to the right.

Claire thought she knew where they were heading.

"Sam," she whispered. Shane pulled in a breath, let it out, and headed in that direction, too.

It had been months since Sam Glass, Michael's grandfather, had died . . . given his life to save them all, really, but most especially Amelie. He was, as far as Claire knew, the only vampire buried here in the cemetery; he'd had a real service, real mourners, and he was maybe the only vampire Morganville had ever had who was universally liked and respected by both sides.

But he'd been loved, too—by Amelie. By vampire standards, Amelie and Sam's had been a whirlwind relationship; he'd been born in Morganville, hadn't even been a hundred years old when he'd died, but from what Claire had seen, it had been an old-style, intense love affair, and one they'd tried to deny themselves more than once.

They found Amelie kneeling at his grave.

From a distance, she looked like one of the marble angels—pale, dressed in white, unmoving. But her long, pale blond hair was down, falling in waves around her face and down her back, and the icy wind lifted and fluttered it like a flag.

As cold as Claire felt, Amelie looked far colder. There was no grief in her expression. There was nothing— just . . . nothing. She didn't seem to see them as the four stopped near her; she didn't move, or speak, or react in any way.

"Hey," Shane said. "Stop it, whatever you're doing. You're hurting Claire."

"Am I?" Amelie's voice came slowly, and it seemed somehow distant, too, as if she were miles away but speaking through the body in front of them. "Your pardon."

She didn't move. She didn't say anything else. Shane and Michael exchanged looks, and Michael clearly got the message that if he didn't do something, Shane would, and it wouldn't be pretty.

Michael reached out for Amelie, to help her up. And she turned on him, suddenly and completely alive and viciously enraged, eyes flaring bloodred in her stark white face, fangs snapping down in place in sharp, lethal angles. "Do not touch me, boy!"

He stepped off, holding up both hands in surrender. Amelie glared at him—at all of them—for another few seconds, and then returned her stare to the grave in front of her. The red swirled away, leaving her eyes pale gray and once again, distant.

Amelie's surge of rage had burned through Claire like summer, driving off the chill for a moment. She squirmed in Shane's arms, and he let her down. Claire shed blankets, except for the last one, and crouched down across from Amelie, facing her over the grave.

Amelie looked right through her, even when Claire lifted her wrist and showed her the bracelet. The gold was frosting over again, already, and Claire felt the insidious chill coming back.

"You're a coward," Claire said.

Amelie's eyes snapped into focus on her. No other reaction, but that alone was enough to make Claire want to shut up and take it all back.

She didn't. Instead, she took a deep breath and forged on. "You think Sam wants you to sit here and wish yourself to death? I mean, I get that you're hurting. But it's just so high school."

Amelie frowned, very faintly—just a tiny wrinkle of her brow. "What happened to your face?"

Oh. The burns. "Forget about me. What's going on with *you*? It feels—so cold."

While she was talking, she realized there was something strange about Amelie's hands. She was wearing gloves ... dark ones. No, that wasn't it. There were spots of white skin showing through the ...

The blood. Her hands were covered with *blood*. And there were slashes on her wrists, deep ones. *Those should have healed*, Claire thought as her skin tightened all over her body, and she shivered in panic-shock. She had no idea why Amelie's wounds stayed open, and kept on bleeding; vampires just didn't do that.

But Amelie had found a way. And that meant she was trying to kill herself, for real. This wasn't some melodramatic cry for help. She hadn't expected help, or looked for it.

That was why she'd been angry.

Claire felt a burst of absolute terror. *What do I do? What do I say?* She looked up at Michael, but he was standing behind and away from Amelie—he couldn't see what she saw.

Eve, though, did. And unlike Claire, she didn't hesitate. She flopped down on her knees on the cold grass next to Amelie, grabbed the vampire's left arm, and turned it so her wrist faced upward. There was something sticking out of the cut, and Claire might have gone a little faint when she realized that Amelie had stuck a *silver coin* into the wound to keep it from healing.

Eve pulled it out. Amelie shuddered, and in seconds, the cut sealed itself, and the blood stopped flowing.

"Idiot child!" she snarled, and shoved Eve back as she reached for the other arm. "You don't know what you're doing!"

"Saving your life? No, I pretty much get the concept. Now *behave*. Bite me and I swear I'll stake you."

Amelie's eyes swirled red, then went back to their normal, not-quite-human gray. "You have no stake."

"Wow, you're literal. Maybe I don't have one now, but just *wait*. You bite me, and it is *on*, bitch. . . . I don't mean you're a bitch; it's just an expression. You know?" Eve's chatter was only meant to distract. While she was talking, she took Amelie's right arm and pulled the silver coin out of that cut, too.

The flow of blood from Amelie's hands into the dirt of the grave slowed to a drip, then stopped.

And Claire felt the chill inside her own body fade, too, as Amelie healed. Finally, she could feel her life again—the heat in her body, the beating of her heart. She wondered if that was how Amelie felt all the time— that icy winter silence inside.

If it was, she understood why Amelie was here.

The night rattled through the branches of the trees and swirled Amelie's pale hair around her face, hiding her expression. Claire watched the wounds on the vampire's arms fade from red slashes to pale lines, then to nothing.

"What the hell were you doing?" Michael asked.

Amelie shrugged. "It's an old custom," she said. "Offering blood to the lost. It takes will and ingenuity to do it properly."

"Don't forget stupidity," Eve said. "That kind of thing would kill most people, never mind most vampires."

Amelie slowly nodded. "It might have."

Michael, who'd been more appalled than any of them, from the look on his face, finally found something to say. "Why?" he asked. "Why would you do this? Because of Sam?"

That actually got a smile, or at least a suggestion of one, on her pale lips. "Your grandfather would be very angry with me if he thought he was the cause. He'd think me a helpless romantic."

Eve snorted. "There's romantic, then there's dramatic, and then there's moronic. Guess which this would be."

Amelie's smile faded, and some of the spark came back into her eyes. She lifted her chin, staring down her nose at Eve. "And you do not wake up daily and paint on your clown makeup, knowing it sets you apart from your fellows? What's the phrase your generation uses? *It takes one to know one?*"

"I'm pretty sure that phrase was hot about fourteen generations back, but yeah, I get your point. And I may be into drama, but hey, at least I'm not a cutter."

"A what?"

"A cutter." Eve pointed to Amelie's bloody wrists. "You know, bad poetry, emo music, I have to hurt myself to feel, because the world's so awful?"

"That isn't why—" Amelie fell silent a moment, then slowly nodded. "Perhaps. Perhaps that is how I feel, yes."

"Well, too damn bad," Eve said, and there was some freaky chill in her voice that made Claire blink. "You want to waste away by your lover's grave, go for it. I'm Goth; I get it. But don't you dare drag Claire along with you, or I'll chase you down in hell and stake you *there*."

Even Shane was staring at Eve now as if he'd never seen her before. Claire opened her mouth to say something, and couldn't for the life of her figure out what it would be. The silence went on, and on, and finally Amelie turned her head toward Claire and said, "The bracelet. It warned you of my—situation."

"*Warned* her? It almost killed her," Shane said. "You were taking her with you. But you knew that, right?"

Amelie shook her head. "I did not." She sighed, and she looked very young, and very human. And, Claire thought, very tired. "I had forgotten that such a thing could happen, though now I think on it, it is very possible. I must apologize to you, Claire. You are feeling better now?"

Claire was still cold, but figured that it had more to do with the icy wind and the cold ground than any magic. She nodded and tried not to show any shivers. "I'm fine. But you lost a lot of blood."

Amelie shrugged, just a tiny roll of her shoulders, as if it didn't matter. "I will recover." She didn't sound overly thrilled about it. "Leave me now. I have amends to make to Samuel."

"You can bleed all over his grave some other time," Eve said. "Come on, lady. Up. Let's get you home."

She reached out, and once again, Amelie let herself

be touched. Odd, Claire thought; Michael was the vampire, but Amelie trusted Eve more right now. Michael was feeling that, too; there was a complicated look on his face, mostly worry.

"No biting," Eve said, as she helped Amelie to her feet. The vampire gave her a withering look. "Hey, all my teachers said that repetition was the only way to learn. You got a car or something?"

"No."

"Um . . . what about your people? Lurking in the shadows, preferably with a limo?"

Amelie raised a single white eyebrow. "If I had brought an entourage, surely they might have objected to my purpose here."

"The dramatic death scene? Yeah, guess so. Okay, then, we'll give you a ride. Blood bank first, right?"

"Unless you are offering a donation."

"Ugh. No. And don't even *look* at Claire, either."

"Me neither," Shane put in. "Homie don't play that."

"I wonder, sometimes, if your generation speaks English at all," Amelie said. "But yes, if you would drive me to the blood bank, you may leave me there safely enough. My *people*"—she gave it just enough of an ironic edge to let them know she found it as funny to say as they did—"will find me there."

They were walking away from Sam's grave, moving slowly and in a tight group, when a shadow stepped out from behind the big marble mausoleum at the top of the hill. It was a vampire, but not the kind Claire was used to seeing around Morganville; this one looked like he lived rough, and without access to showers or personal-grooming equipment.

He also didn't look quite *sane.*

"Amelie," the man said—at least Claire thought it a man, but it was tough to be sure with the tangle of hair that hadn't been combed since the last century, and the shapeless mass of dirty clothes, topped by a filthy raincoat. "Come to visit your peasants and distribute charity, like olden times?" He had a thick accent, English maybe—but rough, too, not like Oliver's refined voice. "Oh, please, mistress, alms for the poor?" And he laughed. It was a dry, hollow sound, and it grew . . . until it came from all around them, from out of the darkness.

There were more of them out there.

Michael turned, staring into the night; maybe he could see something, but to Claire it was all just shadows and tombstones, and that *laughter.* Shane put his arm around her.

Amelie shook off the support of Eve's arm and stepped out from their little group. "Morley," she said. "I see you crawled out of your sewer."

"And you've come down from your ivory tower, my lady," he said. "And here we are, meeting in the midden where humans discard their trash. And you brought *lunch.* How kind."

Ghostly chuckles came from the dark. Michael turned, tracking something Claire couldn't see; his eyes were turning red, and she could see him shifting away from the Michael she knew into something else, something scarier—the Michael she *didn't* know. Eve sensed it, too, and stepped back, closer to Shane. She looked calm, but her hands were balled into fists at her sides.

"Do something," she said to Amelie. "Get us out of here."

"And how do you imagine I will do that?"

"Think of something!"

"You really are a very trying child," Amelie said, but her eyes stayed fixed on Morley, the scarecrow next to the marble tomb. "I don't know why I bother."

"I don't know why you do, either," Morley said. "Confidentially, your dear old da had the right idea. Kill them all, or pen them up for their blood; this living as equals is nonsense, and you know it. They'll never be our equals, will they?"

"Right back atcha," Eve said, and shot him the finger. Shane quickly grabbed her arm and forced it down. "What, you're Mr. Discretion now? Is it Opposite Day?"

"Just shut up," Shane whispered. "In case you haven't noticed, we're outnumbered."

"And? When are we not?"

Claire shrugged when Shane looked at her. "She does have a point. We usually are."

"You're not helping. Michael?" Shane asked. "Whatcha got, man?"

"Trouble," Michael said. His voice sounded different, too—deeper than Claire was used to hearing it. Darker. "There are at least eight of them, all vampires. Stay with the girls."

"I *know* you didn't mean that how it came out. And you need me. Amelie's weak, and you're way outgunned, bro."

"Am I?" Michael flashed them a disconcerting smile that showed fang. "Just stay with the girls, Shane."

"I'd say you suck, but why state the obvious?" Shane's words were banter, but his tone was dead serious, tense, and worried. "Go careful, man. Real careful."

Amelie said, "We're not fighting."

At the top of the hill, with the big white mausoleum glowing like bone behind him, Morley cocked his head and crossed his arms. "No?"

"No," she said. "You are going to walk away, and take your friends with you."

"And why would I do that, when you have such delicious company with you? My people are hungry, Amelie. The occasional rat and drunken stranger really don't make a well-balanced diet."

"You and your pack of jackals can come to the blood bank like any other vampire," she said, just as if she were in charge of the situation, even though Claire could see she was weak and exhausted. "All that's stopping you is your own stubbornness."

"I won't bend my neck to the likes of you. I have my pride."

"Then enjoy your rats," Amelie said, and cast a commanding look at the rest of them. "We're going."

Morley laughed. "You really think so?"

"Oh yes." Amelie smiled, and it felt like the temperature around them dropped by several degrees. "I really *do*. Because you may like your games and your displays, Morley, but you are hardly so stupid to think that crossing me comes without a price."

This time, it wasn't laughter coming from all around them; it was a low rumble of sound, picked up and carried all around the circle.

Growling.

"You're threatening us," the ragged vampire said, and leaned against the tomb behind him. "You, who reeks of your own blood and weakness. Who stands with a newborn vampire as your only ally, and three juicy snacks to defend. Truly? You've always been bold, my highborn lady, but there is a boundary between bold and foolhardy, and I think that if you look, you'll find it's just behind you."

Amelie said nothing. She just stood there, silent and icy calm, and Morley finally straightened up.

"I'm not your vassal," he said. "Turn over the prey, and I'll let you and the boy walk away."

Claire guessed, with a sick sensation, that *the prey* meant her, Eve, and Shane. Shane didn't like it, either; she felt him tense at her side.

"Why would you think I'd do such a thing?" Amelie asked. She sounded only vaguely interested in the whole problem.

"You're a chess master. You understand the sacrifice of pawns." Morley smiled, revealing brown, crooked fangs that didn't look any less lethal for never having seen a toothbrush. "It's tactics, not strategy."

"When I want to be lectured on strategy, I'll consult someone who actually won battles," Amelie said. "Not one who ran away from them."

"Snap," Eve said.

"You know what they're talking about?" Shane asked.

"Don't need to know to get that one. She smacked him so hard his momma felt it."

Morley felt it, too; he took a step toward them, and this time when he bared his teeth, it wasn't a smile. "Last chance," he said. "Walk away, Amelie."

"I can open a portal," Claire whispered, trying to make it quiet enough that Morley, twenty feet away, couldn't hear. Amelie shot her a look, one of *those* looks.

"If I simply leave in that fashion, even with all of you, he can claim to have driven me away in defeat," she said. "It isn't enough to simply escape."

"Exactly," Morley said, and clapped. The sound was shocking and loud as it echoed off the tombstones. A flock of birds took off from the trees, twittering in alarm. "You must show me the error of my ways. And that, my dear liege lady, will be difficult. You're all hat and no cattle, as they like to say in this part of the world. Unless you count the three with you as cattle, of course. In which case you are short a hat."

"I'm bored with this. Attack, or do nothing as you always do," Amelie said. "We are leaving, regardless." She turned to the rest of them and said, in exactly the same cool, calm voice, "Ignore him. Morley is a posturing coward, a degenerate, a liar. He skulks here because he is afraid that standing with the rest of us will only show him for the sad, lacking beggar that he—"

"Kill them all!" Morley shouted, and blurred into motion, heading for Amelie.

Michael hit him head-on, and the two of them tumbled

over headstones. Claire whirled as shadows appeared out of the darkness, moving too fast to see clearly. Her pulse jumped wildly, and she tried to get ready to fight.

And then Amelie said, "Oliver, please demonstrate to Morley why he has been so badly mistaken."

One of the shadows came forward into the moonlight, and it wasn't a stranger at all. Oliver, Amelie's second-in-command in Morganville, was in his kindly shopkeeper disguise—the tie-dyed shirt with the Common Grounds logo on the front, and a pair of blue jeans—and with his graying hair clubbed back in a ponytail, he looked like a typical coffeehouse radical.

Except for his expression, which looked like he was *not* pleased to be here at Amelie's beck and call, and even less pleased to be dealing with Morley. The shapes coming out of the darkness behind him weren't Morley's people after all, but Oliver's . . . neatly groomed, polished vampires with an edge of chill and distance that made Claire shiver. They were polite, but they were killers.

"Michael," Oliver said. "Let that fool go." Michael seemed just as surprised as Morley—or as Claire felt—but he let go of the other vampire and backed off. Morley lunged to his feet, then paused as he took in the sight of Oliver and all his backup. "Your *followers*—if one can dignify a starving pack of dogs by such a name—have been persuaded to leave. You're alone, Morley."

"Checkmate," Amelie said softly. "Strategy, not tactics. I trust you see the point."

Morley did. He hesitated a moment, then darted between the cover of tombstones and shadows, and then he was just . . . gone.

Crisis over.

"Well," Eve said. "That was disappointing. Usually in the movies there's kickboxing."

Oliver turned his head slightly, looking at Amelie in a fast, comprehensive glance that fixed on the blood on her hands. His mouth tightened in what looked like disgust. "Are you finished here?" he asked.

"I believe so," Amelie said.

"Then may I offer you an escort home?"

Her smile turned cynical. "Are you worried for me, my friend? How kind."

"Not at all. I am so gratified that I could be of use to defend your honor."

"Michael defended me," Amelie said. "You showed up."

Claire thought, *Snap, again.* She could see Eve thinking the same thing. Neither of them was quite brave enough to say it, though.

Oliver shrugged. "Strategy, and tactics. I do know the difference. And I *have* won battles, unlike Morley."

"Which is why I rely on you, Oliver, for your counsel. I trust I can continue to count on you for that."

Their gazes locked, and Claire shivered a little. Morley was bluff; Oliver wasn't. He was the kind of guy who'd do what he said, if he thought he could get away with it. He also wanted Morganville. Maybe not quite enough to kill Amelie to get it, but the line was pretty thin.

In fact, Claire could see the line right now, in the faint and fading scars on Amelie's wrists.

"Michael and his friends were kind enough to offer me an escort to the blood bank," Amelie said. "I will go with them. Perhaps you can summon my car to meet me there."

Oliver's smile was sharp as a paper cut. "As ever, I exist to serve."

"I sincerely doubt that."

Michael fell in next to Amelie, and the five of them moved down the rambling path toward where they'd left the car. When Claire looked back, there was no sign of Oliver and his people, or of Morley. There was just the silent cemetery, and the gleaming mausoleum at the top of the hill.

"Anybody else think that was weird?" Shane asked as they got into the car. Eve sent him an exasperated glance; the three of them were, of course, in the backseat. Amelie had the front, with Michael.

"Ya think? In general, or in particular?"

"Weird that we got through the entire thing, and I didn't have to hit anybody."

There was a moment of silence. Michael said, as he started the car, "You're right, Shane. That *is* strange."

When Michael parked at the blood bank, Amelie's security detail was already in place, with the limousine parked at the curb. Claire half expected to see those little devices the Secret Service wore curved around their pale ears, but she supposed the vampires didn't really need technology to hear one another. They did wear snappy black suits and sunglasses, though, and the second Michael's car came to a stop, one of them was opening the passenger-side door and offering Amelie a hand. She took it without a bit of awkwardness, graceful as water, and looked back before the door closed to say, "I thank you. All of you."

That was it. From Amelie, though, that was kind of a lot.

"Shotgun," Eve and Shane said at the same time, and promptly launched into rock-paper-scissors to settle things. Shane won, then got an odd look on his face.

"You take it," he said to Eve, who was still holding her scissors position, which had lost to his rock.

"Seriously?" Her eyes widened. "You're giving up shotgun? I mean, you did win."

"I know," he said. "I'd rather stay back here."

Meaning, with Claire. Eve didn't waste any time; she bailed and slipped into the front passenger seat, wiggling in satisfaction. Michael smiled at her, and she took his hand.

Shane put his arm around Claire, and she rested her head on his chest. Warm, finally. Warm, safe, and loved. "Man, dinner must be cold," he said. "Sorry. I know how much you like tacos."

"Cold tacos are good, too."

"Sick." He meant that in a good way. "So, after the tacos, you want to watch a movie or something?"

Claire made a vague sound of agreement, closed her eyes, and without any conscious decision to do it, fell asleep in his arms. She remembered waking up, vaguely, to Shane saying, "Better take her home," and then another very fuzzy memory of his lips pressed against hers. . . .

Then, nothing.

Morning dawned, and she woke up in her twin bed, at her parents' house. The first few seconds she felt nothing but a vague sense of disappointment that she'd wasted the opportunity to stay with Shane, but then all that was wiped out by the incredible *heat* she felt on her face. It was as if she'd fallen asleep under a sunlamp, except the room was pleasantly dim.

Claire slid out of bed, stumbled over the pile of clothes on the floor—she didn't remember taking them off, but she was wearing a mom-approved cotton nightgown, which meant *Shane* hadn't taken them off—and made her way into the bathroom.

The blinding lights came on, and they were cruel. Claire whimpered as she stared at the red blotch of her face, with white patches that must have been forming blisters underneath the first layers of skin. She pressed on her face, tentatively; it hurt—a lot. "*Really* going to kill you, Myrnin," she said. "And laugh, too."

The shower was horrible; hot water turned nuclear when it hit the burns, and she got through it mainly by gritting her teeth and chanting a variety of gruesome and creative ways she could kill her boss. Afterward she felt a little better, but she thought she looked worse. Not a great exchange, really.

She ran into her mother in the hallway, as Mom climbed the last few steps with a neatly folded stack of sheets and towels in her arms. "Oh, you're up, sweetie," Mom said, and flashed her a distracted smile. "Want me to change your—oh lord, what happened to your face?"

Mom fumbled the laundry, and Claire caught the toppling stack. "It's not that bad," she lied. "I, ah, fell asleep. In the sun."

"Honey, that's dangerous! Skin cancer!"

"Yeah, I know. Sorry. It was an accident. These go in the linen closet?"

"Oh—wait, let me take those. I have a system." The threat to take her mother's neatly folded laundry and mess it up had the desired effect; Mom left the subject of Claire's sunburn and focused on the task at hand. "Breakfast is ready downstairs, honey. Oh, dear, your face—can I get you some lotion?"

"No, I've got it already. Thanks." Claire went back to her room, finished dressing, and opened up her backpack. Truthfully, the backpack itself had seen better days; the nylon was ripped and frayed in places, there were stains that Claire was queasily sure were blood over part of the back, and the straps were starting to work their way loose, too. Probably that was because of the amount she crammed into it. She wiggled the books until she was able to pull out her *Advanced Particle Physics* and the sadly lame *Fundamentals of Matrix Computations*, which was just about the worst text ever on the subject. Behind that was the giant, backbreaking book of English lit, and all her color-coded notebooks. Behind *that* was the other stuff. *Alchemy and the Hermetic Arts*, which wasn't so much a textbook as an analysis of why the whole field was crap. Myrnin hadn't recommended it; Claire had ordered it off the Internet from a Web site run by a guy who was creepily paranoid. Of course, if he knew what she knew, he'd probably run screaming, so maybe paranoia was the right attitude.

At the back, in a special Velcro pocket, were her *special* supplies—the vampire-related ones: a couple of heavy, silver-plated stakes that she hoped never to have to use; a couple of injectable pens that she and Myrnin had rigged up with the serum Dr. Mills had developed, just in case there were still a few vampires around who hadn't gotten the shot and might be—to put it kindly—unstable. And she wasn't sure Morley from the cemetery didn't qualify, but she was glad she hadn't gotten close enough to use the pen, either.

Folded and shoved all the way to the back was the piece of paper Myrnin had given her with a sequence scribbled on it in symbols. As she did daily, Claire memorized it. She'd test herself later, drawing out the symbols and comparing them against the original. Myrnin had said the reset sequence was only to be used in emergencies, but she had the feeling that if it really got to that point, the last thing she'd have time for would be to try to figure out his sloppy drawing.

She repacked her bag, making sure she could easily slide the books in and out this time, and hefted it experimentally. The strap creaked, and she heard another thread snap. *Really need a new one.* She wondered where Eve picked up her cute patent leather ones, embossed either with the pink kitty or cute skulls; probably not in town, Claire guessed. Morganville wasn't exactly Fashion Central.

Breakfast was a family thing in the Danvers house, and Claire actually kind of looked forward to it. She didn't often make it back for lunch or dinner, but every morning she sat with her mom and dad. Mom asked her about classes; Dad asked her about her job. Claire didn't know how other families in Morganville worked, but hers seemed pretty ... normal. At least in the abstract. The specifics were bound to be freaky.

Breakfast over (and, as always, delicious), Claire headed out for school. Morganville was a small-enough town that walking was easy, if you liked that sort of thing, and Claire did—usually. Today, with her gross-looking face throbbing with the heat of the sun, she wished she'd taken up her dad's offer of buying her a car, even if it had come with the attached strings of also seeing a lot less of her boyfriend. She hadn't told Shane that he meant more to her than having a car. That seemed like commitment any guy would find scary.

Claire stopped in at the first open store—Pablo's Market, near the university district—and found a black cloth cap with a brim that shaded her face. That helped, and it made her feel a bit less obviously disfigured ... until she heard a horn honk behind her, and looked over her shoulder to see a red convertible gliding up next to her on the street.

Claire turned face-forward and kept walking. Faster.

"What is it?" she heard a voice ask from the backseat of the car. Gina or Jennifer; Claire could never tell their voices apart. "It *looks* kind of human."

"I don't know. Zombie? We've had zombies here, right?" Gina (or Jennifer)'s vocal twin said. "Could be a zombie. Hey, how do you kill a zombie?"

"Cut its head off," a third voice said. There was no doubt about whom that voice belonged to, no doubt at all: Monica. It was cool, confident, and commanding. "Let's find the brain-freak and ask her—she'd know. Hey, zombie chick. Have you seen Claire Danvers, Girl Brain?"

Claire flipped her off and kept walking. Monica—black-haired again, no doubt looking shiny and pretty—was just a vague shadow in her peripheral vision, and Claire wanted to keep it that way.

And she knew, fatalistically, that it was never going to happen.

In fact, Monica didn't like being flipped off. She accelerated the sports car, whipped it around the corner, and came to a hard stop to block Claire's progress across the street. Monica and Gina snapped at each other, probably arguing about the specifics of how to kick Claire's ass without breaking a nail or scuffing a shoe.

Claire gave it up and crossed the street.

Monica threw the car into reverse, and blocked her there, too.

They played the game two more times, back and forth, before Claire finally just stopped and stood there, staring at Monica.

Who laughed. "Oh my God, it *is* the brain-freak. You know *freak* is only an expression, right? You didn't actually have to become a circus attraction just for me."

"It's the new thing. High-speed tanning. I'm on the way to an awesome summer glow; you should try it," Claire said. Jennifer actually laughed. She looked immediately guilty. "I'm going to be late for class."

"Good. That'll move the bell curve back toward the middle."

"Only if you actually attended to drag it down."

"Ooooh, zing," Monica said. "I'm crushed, because brains are my only asset. No, wait—that would be you, right?"

Claire sighed. "What do you want?" Because it was kind of obvious they wanted something—and probably something other than just the daily harassment. Monica had worked at cutting her off, after all, and Monica just didn't do work.

"I need a tutor," Monica said. "I don't get this economics bullshit. There are fractions and stuff."

Economics, in Claire's opinion, was voodoo science, but she shrugged. Math was math. "Okay. Tomorrow. Fifty bucks, and before we get into it, I won't take a test for you, steal the answers, or come up with some high-tech way for you to cheat."

Monica raised her perfect eyebrows. "You *do* know me."

"Yes or no."

"Fine."

"Common Grounds, three o'clock. You buy the mocha."

"Greedy little bitch," Monica said. Business deal concluded, she flipped Claire off with a perfectly manicured finger, smiled, and said, "You look like shit. Love the hat—where'd you get it, Cousin Cletus on the short bus?"

Their laughter lingered, along with the exhaust, as the three girls sped off on their usual mission of chaos and destruction.

Claire took a deep breath, pulled the hat down lower over her face, and went across the street to enter the gates of Texas Prairie University.

Claire loved classes. Oh, not the actual lectures, really—professors were, as a rule, not that exciting in person. But the *knowledge*. That was right there for the taking, as much as you could grab and hold on to—more than you ever wanted, in some classes.

Like English Lit, which she still didn't know why she had to take, and which was her last class of the day. It wasn't as if the Brontë sisters were going to make a difference in her daily life, right? Not like math, which was underneath everything from cooking to construction to going to the moon. No, science was definitely cooler.

At least until today, when her attention was temporarily pulled in by the class assignment.

Those who read the symbol do so at their peril. It is the spectator, and not life, that art really mirrors. Diversity of opinion about a work of art shows that the work is new, complex, and vital. When critics disagree, the artist is in accord with himself. We can forgive a man for making a useful thing as long as he does not admire it. The only excuse for making a useless thing is that one admires it intensely.

All art is quite useless.

It was the strangest thing to read those words of Oscar Wilde at the beginning of *The Picture of Dorian Gray*, and think of Myrnin saying them, because it was eerily like the kind of explanation he'd give. It gave Claire a strange little lurch, wondering if Myrnin had ever met Oscar Wilde, who had been quite a partyer, apparently. She'd never really considered the lives of vampires much, but now reality set in, and it was strange.

For Myrnin—and Oliver, and Amelie, and most of the vampires she'd ever met—history wasn't just stuff written in a book, or sometimes captured in an old, stiff photo. For them, history happened day after day after day. Oscar Wilde had just happened a whole lot of days ago.

She bet Myrnin had met him. Probably borrowed his hat or something.

That thought distracted her so much, she didn't hear her phone ring at first; she'd set it to ultrasonic, so the professor rambled on down on the stage of the stadium-seating room without noticing a thing. Those around her did, though, and she smiled an apology, switched it to silent, and checked the name on the tiny screen. It was Eve. Claire texted her back—*IC* for in class. It was their standard code. Eve texted *CG ASAP OMG*. Meaning, get to Common Grounds as soon as she could.

911?

No.

Shane?

No.

Tell!

No!

Claire smiled and folded up the phone, and refocused on the professor, who hadn't noticed a thing. The last ten minutes of class seemed to crawl by, but she did try to pay close attention. If she was going to seriously ask Myrnin about Oscar Wilde, it might help to actually know something about the dude. Something other than he was snarky, and more or less gay.

After class, Claire jogged through the campus quad, across the grass, and out to the gates. It was still midafternoon, so there was loads of time left before sunset. That was a good thing, because it was kind of nice to be out in the fresh air before it got, as Eve liked to title it, THTL—too hot to live, which lasted from about June through October. It didn't take long to make the trip to Common Grounds. Claire kept her head down, mostly using the cap shading her face to keep passersby from staring at her in horror.

She got to Common Grounds, and for the first time it occurred to her that the place might very well be totally packed, and she might really get stared at, for real. *Wonderful.* Well, nothing she could do about that.

Claire took a deep breath, pulled the door open, and stepped inside. The interior was dim after the brilliant sunlight, and she blinked away glare and looked around the room. It was crowded, all right—maybe forty people clustered around small café tables, drinking their mochas and lattes and espresso shots. Students, at this hour. The mix of caffeine enthusiasts changed after dark.

Everybody stared as she passed. Claire tried to pretend it was because of how fabulously cute she was, but that was a leap of faith she really couldn't make, and now her sunburn was worse because she was blushing on top of it, and also, *ow.*

Eve was all the way toward the back, jammed into a corner and defending an empty chair across the table with sharp glares and careful deployment of harsh words. She looked relieved as Claire dropped into the seat, leaned her heavy backpack against the table leg, and sighed, "I *really* need coffee."

Eve stared at her face for a few long seconds, then said, "And I can see why. Yo! Mocha!"

She snapped her fingers.

She snapped her fingers at *Oliver*, who was behind the counter pulling espresso shots. He looked up at her with blank contempt. "Yo," he repeated with poisonous sarcasm. "I am not your waitress."

"Really? Because we tip, if that helps. And you'd look really good in a frilly apron."

Oliver slammed back the pass-through hinged section of the bar and came out to stand over their table, giving them the full benefit of his presence. And that, to put it mildly, was intimidating. "What do you want, Eve?"

"Well, I'd like the blue-plate special of you thrown out of Morganville, with a side order of dead, but I'll settle for a mocha for my friend." Eve tapped purple metallic fingernails against the china of her coffee cup, and didn't look away from Oliver's glare. "What you going to do, Oliver? Ban me for life from your crappy shop?"

"I'm considering it." Some of the aggression faded out of him, replaced by curiosity. "Why are you challenging me, Eve?"

"Why shouldn't I? We're not exactly besties," Eve said. "And besides, you're a jerk."

He smiled, but it wasn't a nice sort of smile. "And how have I offended you recently?"

"You were totally going to screw us over last night, weren't you?"

Oliver's smile faded. "I came when Amelie called. As I always do."

"Until you don't, right? Sooner or later, she's going to ring the little bell and faithful servant Ollie isn't going to show up to save her ass. That's the plan. Death by slacking, and you don't even get your hands dirty."

"And how is that any business of yours, in any case?" Oliver's eyes were dark, very dark, and full of secrets that Claire wasn't sure she wanted to know.

"It's not. I just don't like you." Eve tapped her talons again. "Mocha?"

He glanced at Claire's blistered face and said, without too much sympathy, "That's quite disfiguring."

"I know."

"A week should see it right." Which was, weirdly, kind of comforting in its dismissal of her problems. "Very well, mocha." But he didn't leave. Eve widened her eyes and looked irritated.

"What?"

"It's customary to pay for things you buy."

"Oh, come *on*. . . ."

"Four fifty."

Claire dug a five-dollar bill from the pocket of her jeans and handed it over. Oliver left.

"Why are you doing that?" she asked Eve, a little anxiously. Because hey, it was cool and everything, to get in Oliver's face, but it was also not exactly safe.

"Because they cast him as Mitch, which means I have to pretend to actually like the dude. Ugh."

"Oh, the play. Right. I, uh, looked it up. Looks interesting." Claire said that kind of halfheartedly, because it didn't, at least to her. It sounded like a lot of middle-aged people having melodrama.

"It *is* interesting," Eve said, and brightened up immediately. "Blanche is sort of really the symbol of the way women oppress themselves; she just can't live without a man. Come to think of it, based on that, I guess Oliver's casting was genius."

"So . . . you're playing a woman who can't live without a man?"

"It's a stretch, but the director wanted to do this postmodern kind of take on it, so he went with Goth girls for Blanche and Stella."

"Goth girls, plural," Claire repeated. "I kind of thought you were the only one in town."

"Not quite."

"Eve? You 911ed me?"

"Oh—uh, yeah, I did. I wanted you to meet—oh, there she is! Kim!"

Claire looked around. A girl had just come in the door of the coffee shop, not quite as Goth as Eve, but quite a bit farther down the curve than anybody else in the room. She had long black hair, dyed jet-black, with bubble-gum pink stripes. Her makeup was mostly eyeliner. She wore less-outrageous stuff, but what she did wear seemed kind of grim—black cargo pants, plain black shirt, black leather wristband, which had (of course) a vampire symbol on it.

Kim had signed up with a vampire named Valerie, apparently. Claire didn't know much about her, but she supposed that was a good thing. If nobody was talking about her, Valerie was probably playing by the rules. Mostly.

"Hey, Eve," Kim said, and slid into the third chair at the small table. "Who's the burn victim?"

Claire felt herself stiffen, she just couldn't stop herself. "I'm Claire," she said, and forced a smile. "Hi."

"Hey," Kim said, and dropped Claire like a bad boyfriend to focus on Eve. "Oh my God, did you hear they cast Stanley?"

"No! Who?" Eve leaned forward, wide-eyed. "God, tell me it's not that kid from high school."

"No. Guess again."

"Um . . . no clue."

"Radovic."

"Get out!" Eve jiggled in her chair, grabbed Kim's hands, and then they both let out a wild, high-pitched scream of excitement.

Claire blinked as a mocha was thumped down in front of her. She looked up at Oliver, who was studying her with cool, distant eyes. He raised his eyebrows, didn't speak, and went back to his job.

"Who's Radovic?" Claire asked, since he seemed to be the most exciting thing since indoor plumbing. She couldn't remember which character Stanley was, but she thought he was the wife-beating rapist—not somebody she felt inclined to squeal over.

"He runs the motorcycle shop," Eve said. "Big biker dude, shaved head, muscles TDF."

"TDF?" Claire cocked her head. "Oh. To die for." She lowered her voice. "So, is he . . . you know?" She mimed fangs. Both of the Goth girls laughed.

"Hell no," Kim said. "Rad? He's just cool, that's all. In that dangerous kind of way. I think he's way more scary than any of *them* I ever met." By which she meant vampires.

"I guess we don't meet the same ones," Claire said. "Because mine? Plenty scary." And . . . she knew that all of a sudden, she was trying to one-up Kim, and she didn't like that about herself. She also didn't like Eve and Kim being besties all of a sudden while she was sitting like a poor, pathetic lump on the sidelines with her disfigured face, with Oliver bringing her sympathy mocha.

That was just *sad*.

Kim barely glanced at her. "Yeah?" She sounded totally uninterested. "Hey, E, can I catch a ride to rehearsal tonight? Would you mind?"

"Nope. Hey, can I come in and see what you're working on?" Eve threw Claire a quick smile. "Kim's kind of an avant-garde artist. She's really cool; I love her stuff." There was a real glow in Eve's eyes, an excitement that made Claire feel cold and a little pissed off. *I'm your friend*, she wanted to say. *I'm cool, too, right?* So she wasn't some weird artist type who made art out of used toilet paper rolls and chicken bones—so what? What made that cool, anyway?

Eve didn't hear all the mental arguments. Kim said something about the script, and they both got out their copies and flipped pages, talking about theme and motif and things Claire honestly couldn't care less about, because she was now officially in a miserable mood.

She gulped the mocha as fast as humanly possible, given that Oliver had heated it up to the surface temperature of lava. She felt truly betrayed, not just because Eve had dragged her into the middle of Common Grounds with her face looking like undercooked hamburger, but because she was sitting there chattering away with *Kim*, ignoring Claire's presence entirely now.

As Claire got up, though, Eve blinked and looked at her. "You're leaving?"

"Yeah." Claire couldn't bring herself to sound too apologetic. "I need to get home."

"Oh. I'm sorry, I just thought—I thought you'd like to meet Kim, that's all. Because she's cool."

"It's nice to meet you," Kim said. She didn't sound all that sincere about it, but more like she wished Claire would hurry up and hit the bricks so she could get back to her BFF-fest with Eve. "Hey, you guys live in that house with Michael Glass and Shane Collins, right? What a couple of hotties!"

Claire didn't like that Kim had even *noticed* Shane, much less knew his last name. Eve didn't seem to mind at all. She just nodded, eyes wide. "They are, right? Man candy. We know!"

Claire grabbed her backpack. "I really have to go."

"Claire—you okay?"

"I'm fine," she said. Kim was kind of smirking at her behind her drink, and Claire had a wild impulse to dump that coffee all over her.

But she didn't.

"Bye?" Eve said, and made it a kind of pathetic question. Claire didn't answer. She just pushed past Kim's chair, not being too careful about it, and headed for the door.

Behind her, she heard Kim's clear, carrying voice say, "Wow, what crawled up her ass and didn't die?"

Claire threw a venomous look back over her shoulder, and saw Oliver watching her with a very slight frown grooving his forehead. Eve looked stricken, clearly surprised at Claire's departure. Kim . . . Kim wasn't even watching her. She just lifted one shoulder in an I-can't-be-bothered shrug.

Then Claire was outside, taking deep breaths of the dry air and lifting her face to the sudden, swirling push of the wind. Sand hissed over the sidewalk, blown in from the desert.

Claire, miserably aware that she was in a horrible mood, walked home with the feeling that everyone, absolutely everyone, was watching her.

4

Michael was playing guitar in the living room of the house when Claire stomped down the hall, dumped her backpack without much care for the electronic feelings of the laptop inside, and threw herself full length down on the sofa. Michael stopped in mid-chord, and she sensed he was staring at her, but she didn't look. Eventually, he started up again. The music spilled over her, beautiful and complicated, and as Claire lay there and just concentrated on breathing, she felt some of the awful tension inside her start to ease up. Still a horrible day, but she could never feel too angry when Michael was playing.

"So," he said, not looking up from the frets as he tried out a complicated new flood of sound, "I'm thinking of going electric. What do you think?"

"Eve dumped me. I've been best-friend dumped."

Michael's playing stuttered, then smoothed out again. "Huh. I'm guessing that's a no?"

"There's this girl, Kim? You know who she is?" Michael nodded, but didn't say anything. Claire felt her hands curl into fists, and deliberately, carefully straightened them out. "So this Kim, she's like perfect and all. Ooooh, she's an *artist*. And all of a sudden she and Eve have everything in common and I'm just—the stranger who doesn't get the jokes."

"I've met Kim," Michael said. His voice was neutral, and he kept his gaze on his guitar. "She's like a black hole; she just pulls people right out of their orbits. Eve's still your friend. She's just crushing on Kim because Kim never wanted to hang with her before."

"So what's the story of the fantastic Kim, anyway?"

He shrugged, and shot her a quick, unreadable look. "She went to OLOM, so I didn't know her all that well."

"OLOM?" Claire repeated.

"I forget you didn't grow up here. Our Lady of Mystery. Catholic school across town run by the scariest nuns you've ever seen. Anyway, Kim bailed on school when she was fourteen, I think. She's our resident funky-artist type, I guess—more likely to flip you off than shake your hand."

"I'll bet she sucks."

It looked like Michael was trying hard to hide a smile. "Art's always subjective. She may suck to you."

"She doesn't to you?" Claire felt a little sinking sensation. Oh, great, of course Michael would like Kim, too. Shane probably not only liked her, but had dated her, and was secretly still in love with her. Claire Danvers, New Girl, was probably the only person in Morganville who didn't think Kim was all that, supersized.

Michael stilled the strings on his guitar with the flat of his palm and sat back, finally looking right at her. "You should get to know her," he said. "She's—interesting. Just don't get too close."

"She treated me like crap."

"She does that," he agreed. "Did you know she survived a vampire attack when she was homeless and sixteen?"

Claire swallowed whatever she'd been about to say, which would have been snarky and sarcastic. Instead, she said, "Survived how?"

"Killed the vamp trying to drain her. She could have

been executed—town rules. Instead, she was acquitted. No jail time. Brandon wasn't happy about it—he was Amelie's second-in-command at the time—but he had to swallow it. So really, there are only two humans in Morganville who've ever killed a vampire and gotten away with it."

"Kim and who else?"

Michael raised his eyebrows. "You didn't know?"

"Know what?"

"Richard Morrell," he said.

"Seriously?" Because Richard Morrell was now the mayor of Morganville, one of the three most important people in town, and it boggled Claire's mind to think that the vamps had allowed him to just . . . walk away from that. "When?"

Michael didn't have time to answer, because his cell phone started playing "Born to Be Wild," and he pulled it to check the screen. "Got to get ready," he said. "Sorry. Story time later. Hey, trust me, Kim's a force of nature, but like a storm, she moves on. Eve will be fascinated for a while, but Kim will find somebody else soon enough. It's how she rolls."

Claire had the really strong impression that he wasn't telling her everything. Or anything, really. But he didn't give her time to go into it, either, just storing his guitar in the case and heading upstairs.

"Get ready," she repeated, still simmering. "Yeah, everybody's got somewhere to be but me. *You should get to know Kim; she's interesting.*" Claire put a load of mockery into her Michael impression. "Yeah right."

The back door opened and closed, floorboards creaked in the kitchen, and Claire smelled the delicious wood-smoke aroma of barbecue. She couldn't help but smile, because hey—barbecue.

And, of course, the one bringing it.

"Hey," Shane said, and leaned over the couch to stare down at her. His hair was getting longer, and even more slacker-messy, as if he'd gone after the most annoying bits with a pair of scissors. Or garden trimmers. It should have looked horrible, but on him, somehow . . . it looked hot.

Not that she was in any way prejudiced.

"Hey," she replied, and held up her hand for him to smack. Instead, he took it and kissed it lightly.

"Why the mopey face? Did I forget to say something?"

"From you, *hey* is good enough." She sighed. Complaining about Kim hadn't been the great release she'd thought it would be; Michael had been on the fence, at best, and she had no reason to think Shane would be any different. "I'm just in a terrible mood."

"This I've got to see." Shane leaned over and stared into her eyes. "Wow. Yeah, that's terrifying. I can see that you're one second from snapping, Hannibal Lecter."

She sighed. "Nobody's scared of me."

"Nope. Nobody. That's a good thing, Claire."

"Says the guy who scares everybody."

Shane considered that and smiled slowly. She loved the way one side of his smile pulled higher than the other, and the little dimple that formed there. "I don't scare you."

"Well. Only a little, maybe."

"I'll have to work on getting rid of that little bit," he said. "Speaking of scary, how's your freaky boss?"

"Don't know, didn't go, don't care," she said. "My face hurts."

"So you're moping because your face hurts?"

"I'm ugly and nobody loves me."

"Wrong," he said, "and *really* wrong." He kissed her fingers again, and this time, his lips stayed warm on her skin for a long time. "Michael's getting ready?"

Claire let out an annoyed breath. "Yeah. Everybody's got somewhere to go but me, and—what?" Because she was getting an odd look.

"The theater at TPU? He's playing tonight? Packed house? Remember?"

Oh *crap*. No, she'd forgotten all about it, and now she felt—if possible—even worse. "I'm an idiot," she said. "Oh man. I've been whining like a two-year-old about Kim. I forgot he was trying to get himself together for the show."

"Kim?" Shane's attention snapped into bright focus. "Kim. Goth Kim?"

"Yeah, what's her last name, anyway? Weird Kim. That one."

"Where'd you meet Kim?"

"Eve. I guess they're in the play together?"

"Oh, crap," Shane said. His expression changed, went guarded. "So you talked to her."

"I wasn't worth talking to."

Was she wrong, or was that a little flicker of relief? "Probably a good thing. She's kind of a flake."

"Kind of?" Claire's eyes narrowed. "Did you date her?"

His eyes went wide, and there was a fatal second of silence before he said, "Not—exactly. No. I—no."

"Did you hook up?"

He started to answer, then shook his head. "I've got no good options here," he said. "Whatever I say, you're going to believe I did, right? But even if I did, it was a long time ago, and anyway, I'm with you now. All right?"

"All right," she said. She felt as if pieces of herself were breaking off, and somehow, it was all Kim's fault. *I'm an adult*, she told herself. *Adults don't get stressed out about ex-girlfriends or ex-hookups or whatever.* Except she wanted to go find Kim and punch her out, which was not good, because she was pretty sure Kim would punch back, and harder. "Sure. It's all good."

Shane didn't believe that for a second, but she saw him decide to fake it. "Right," he said. "So. Barbecue. You in?"

"I can't believe you eat barbecue after you serve it all day long. Doesn't that get old?"

"It's *barbecue*," he said. "What's your point? Come on, mopey. Come eat."

He half dragged her off the couch, tickled her into giggles, and chased her into the kitchen.

He was right. Barbecue really was kind of a magic cure for the mopeys.

Claire dressed up for Michael's show at TPU, but given the state of her sunburn, she wasn't sure it was worth the effort—at least, until she got downstairs. Shane and Michael were standing together, talking, and *wow.* Claire lingered on the stairs, admiring.

"What?" Shane asked, catching her.

"Nothing. You guys look great."

Michael shrugged, as if it were no big thing. So did Shane, even though he'd taken the time to put on his good black shirt and black leather jacket, and even sort of comb his hair.

Michael, though—rock star. Not in the glam hair-band sense, no, but he just looked ... important. Claire wondered if Eve had picked his clothes for him; if she had, she really loved him, because they were completely perfect. Speaking of which—"Where's Eve?"

"Running late," Michael said. "She's meeting us there."

Eve passed up barbecue? That was odd. Claire came down the rest of the steps and did a little inspection twirl for Shane. "Okay?"

"Spectacular," he said, and kissed her—carefully, because of the sunburn. "You know I love that skirt."

She blushed under the burn. "Yes. I know." It was a short, pleated skirt. Plaid. The shoes she had on with it were the ones that Eve had bought for her last Halloween—funky, but cool and kind of sexy. Claire still felt a little uncomfortable with her body in general, but there was something about the signals Shane was giving her that made her feel less awkward. More—confident.

"You guys going with me?" Michael asked, juggling his car keys. "If so, the bus is leaving."

They were, of course; with Eve MIA, they had no other car, and walking in the dark was still not the best idea in the world, even in the new, calmer Morganville. It wasn't a long trip, and Michael drummed his fingers on the steering wheel as if he were practicing fingerings for his guitar; nobody said much. Claire leaned against Shane in the back, her head on his shoulder, and his presence went a long way toward making her forget about how bad her day had been.

At least, until she remembered that he'd once sat like this with Kim, back in undefined olden times. "Hey," she said. "About Kim—"

"Oh man, I knew it. You're not letting it go, are you?"

"I just want to know—did you guys date, or—"

"No," Shane said, and looked away. He'd have been staring out the window, except that the dark tinting prevented him from actually seeing anything out there. "Okay, I took her bowling once. She was pretty good at it. Does that count as a date?"

"It does if you hooked up after."

He hesitated, and finally sighed. "Yes," he said. "Guilty. Dated. Hooked up. She moved on to the next guy. Anything else?"

Claire was totally unprepared for how awful that made her feel. "Did you—did you really like her?"

"Do we need to have this talk now, with witnesses?"

Michael held up his hand. "I want it on the record that I'm not paying attention."

"And . . . yet."

"Dude, you got yourself into this; don't blame me."

Michael sounded definitely amused, which didn't make Claire feel any better.

"I'm sorry," Claire said miserably. "I guess—we can talk about it later. It doesn't matter, anyway." Except it did. A lot.

Shane turned back to look into her eyes. His pupils were huge in the faint glow of the dashboard. "I was looking for a girl," he said. "Kim wasn't it. You are, so stop worrying about that. But to answer the question, yeah, I liked her. *Really* liked her? Probably not. I wasn't exactly brokenhearted when she moved on. More like relieved."

Claire blinked. "Oh." She didn't know what to do with that. It made her feel better, and also, a little confused and childish and ashamed. Being jealous of a girl he'd been happy to let go? It seemed wrong, somehow.

"Hey," he said, and carefully traced the line of her cheek, avoiding the burned spots. "I like that you care. I do."

She pulled in a deep breath. "I just don't want to share you," she said. "Not ever. Even before I met you. I know that doesn't make sense, but—"

"It does," he said, and kissed her. "It really does."

Michael was smiling, she could see it in the rearview mirror. He caught her watching him, and shook his head.

"What?" she challenged.

"It's a good thing I've got to live with the two of you," he said, "or I'd be putting this on YouTube later. And mocking you."

"Ass."

"Don't forget *bloodsucking* ass."

"Also, *undead* bloodsucking ass," Shane said. "That's kind of critical, too."

Michael stopped the car. "We're here." He grabbed his guitar case and got out, looked in on them, and flashed them a knowing grin. "Lock it when you leave. Oh, and remember—vampires can see through the tinting. I'm just saying."

"Ugh," Claire sighed. "And there goes the mood."

Michael disappeared into the artists' entrance, walking as if he owned the stage already; Claire and Shane walked, hand in hand, through the parking garage toward the front. There were a lot of other people parking, talking, walking in groups toward the entrance to the theater. Like most of TPU's buildings, it wasn't exactly pretty—a product of the blocky 1970s, glass and concrete, solid and plain and functional, at least on the outside.

The lobby was warmer, with dark red carpet and side drapes that looked only about ten years out of fashion. Claire saw people staring at her and wished she'd worn her cap, but since she hadn't, she held her chin up and clasped Shane's hand more tightly as he checked their tickets and led her up to the balcony. On the way, Claire spotted a lot of familiar faces—Father Joe, from the church, standing out in his black shirt, white collar, and red hair. People she recognized from classes, who probably had no idea they were coming to hear a vampire play guitar. Oh, and a ton of vamps, blending in except for the glitter in their eyes and the slightly hungry way they scanned the crowd. Some of them even dressed pretty well.

She didn't see Amelie anywhere, or Myrnin, or Oliver, and they were all pretty notable by their absence. She *did* see the unpleasant Mr. Pennywell, though, looking smug and remote and sexless in his plain black jacket and pants. He was sitting at a small table near the stairs, watching everyone pass. She had the strong feeling he was like those people who stood in front of the lobster tank to choose what was going on their plate.

Ugh.

"Everything okay?" Shane asked her, and she realized that he wasn't talking about the vampires or anything else like that. He quickly amended, "You know, between us?"

"Oh. Uh—yeah. I guess so." She must not have seemed too confident, because he stopped climbing the stairs, looked around, and headed her toward a small group of chairs off to the side at the landing. Nobody near them. It was a darker corner, kind of intimate in the glow of the light on the wall. People moved past in a stream, but nobody seemed to look.

"I need to be sure," he said. "Because I don't want you to think Kim is competition. She's not. Until today, I hadn't thought about her twice."

But, by implication, he was thinking about her now—comparing her to Claire. And Claire couldn't be totally sure she was winning, either. "It's just that everybody thinks she's so *interesting*. And I'm just—you know."

"A supersmart apprentice to a bipolar vampire, not to mention just about the only person in town Amelie listens to these days? Yeah. You're dead boring." Shane's warm hands cupped her face and tilted her chin up so he could meet her eyes in the dim light. "There. That's better."

"Why?" The word trembled on her lips, a restrained wail of bitterness. "So you can see how ugly I look, compared to Kim?"

"You got some layers of skin burned off," he said. "Big freaking deal. In a week you'll have a killer tan, and everybody will be wondering where you got the spray-on stuff. It doesn't matter. Not even a little. Get me?"

She didn't want to cry, and for a wonder, she didn't. She gulped in one hitching breath, held it, and let it slowly out, and that was it.

Then she smiled. "I get you."

"All right then. Because I love you. Remember?"

Warmth zipped through her nerves and took up a hot

glowing spot somewhere just below the pit of her stomach. "I remember," she said. "I love you, too."

He kissed the tip of her nose. "Jealous. I kind of like it."

Hand in hand, they headed for the concert hall.

Mr. Pennywell blocked their path.

There was something really, unpleasantly *wrong* about Pennywell, in ways Claire couldn't put her finger on; the vampire looked awkwardly built, female in one light, male in another, but that wasn't the thing that made him frightening.

It was the complete, soulless absence of feeling in his expression and eyes. Even when he smiled, nothing happened in the top half of his face. It was just muscles, not emotion.

"Move," Shane said, and Claire felt his hold on her hand unconsciously tighten. "Dude, you are *not* crazy enough to go after us in the middle of neutral ground, in front of witnesses. Right?"

"That would entirely depend on what I planned to accomplish," Pennywell said. "But I am not here to threaten you. I am here to summon you."

"To our seats? Thanks. Don't need an usher."

Pennywell stayed right in their path. The crowd was thinning out around them. The last thing Claire wanted was to be alone out here with him, everyone else inside and cheering and clapping and covering up her all-too-likely screams. She traded a look with Shane.

"Oliver would like a word," Pennywell said, and made a graceful gesture to his left. "If you please."

"Now?"

"He is not taking appointments. Yes. Now."

There didn't seem to be many options available, but Claire could see that Shane was tempted to tell Pennywell to beat it. That would be bad. Pennywell wasn't someone who took rejection well.

It didn't come to that, and for the worst possible reason.

"Shane? Shane *Collins*? Are you kidding me?" A girl's voice came from over Pennywell's shoulder, and was followed by the girl sliding around the vampire and throwing herself all over Shane. He dropped Claire's hand in surprise, and to catch the girl before they both toppled over.

It took a second to put the dyed-black-and-pink hair and voice together, but Claire knew even before her brain supplied the name.

Kim. Oh, perfect.

And Kim was *kissing Shane.*

It wasn't like he was kissing her back . . . more like he was trying to push her off his lips. But still. Her lips. Touching Shane's.

Even Pennywell looked thrown.

"Hey!" Claire protested, not sure what she ought to do, but she wanted very badly to grab a handful of that black hair and yank, hard. She didn't need to. Shane picked Kim up, bodily, and set her at arm's length—and held her there.

"Kim," he said. "Uh—hi."

"How's it going, Collins? Wow, it's been a while, huh? Sorry about the family stuff, that sucks, man. Oh, did you hear I've got a loft now? I'm selling on the Internet. Very cool." Kim's wide eyes were fixed on Shane's face, and there was a sickeningly delighted expression on her face. "I just can't believe it's you, Shane. Wow. So great to see you."

"Yeah," he said, and looked at Claire, just a quick (and panicked) glance. "This is Claire. My girlfriend." He stressed the word. It didn't seem to register, or if it did, Kim shrugged it off. She barely glanced at Claire at all.

"Cool," she said. "Hey, you're the one from the coffee shop. Eve's friend. Small world, right?"

"Claustrophobic," Claire said. "What are you doing here?" She knew she sounded angry; she just couldn't help it. Pennywell looked from her to Kim, clearly trying to decide whom he should kill first. From his expression, he was leaning toward Kim, which didn't distress Claire much at all.

"I came to hear Michael Glass," Kim said. "I mean, Eve told me all about it. Michael's always been the coolest guy in town—present company excepted." She *winked* at Shane. *Winked.* Claire wanted to vomit. "I just wanted to show my support."

"I'm not interested in you," Pennywell said to her. "Go away."

Kim blinked and turned to look at the vampire for the first time. Then she reacted as if she hadn't even known he was there. *Seriously? She got a part in the play?* Because that was the worst reaction Claire had ever seen, outside of really old silent movies. "Oh my God! What the hell are *you*? I mean, yes, obviously—" She held up two fingers in what Claire thought was a peace sign before realizing it was probably a *V*—for vampire. "But damn, you're freaky."

Pennywell had no idea what to do, from the frown that grooved that smooth, high forehead. He cocked his head and looked at Kim without saying a word, just studying her.

Then he said, "You are the historian."

Kim smiled. "Bingo, dude. I'm the historian. And you're kinda new, am I right? I have *got* to get you on camera. Make an appointment, okay? Here. Here's my number." She dug in the small black bag strapped to her wrist, came out with some kind of business card, and handed it to him. Pennywell took it—mostly in self-defense—and tucked it in his coat pocket. "Word of advice? Nehru jackets went out with the groovy sixties. Go for Brooks Brothers. You do not want to be preserved for posterity in a bad look, right? Also, maybe some work with the hair, butch you up some. Think about it."

While she was talking, Shane took Claire's elbow and quietly hustled her around Pennywell, whose eyes remained fixed on Kim as she chattered. By the time the vampire realized what was happening and thrust Kim aside, Shane and Claire were slipping through the door into the hall, out of his reach.

Hopefully.

"Did she do that on purpose?" Claire asked.

"Don't know," Shane said. "But I wasn't about to waste the chance. Call Oliver. Find out if he was really wanting to see us."

Claire nodded. The crowd in the hall was still buzzing around, and the noise level was high. Nobody would notice her on the phone; there had to be a hundred or more of them glowing like jewels in the tiers of seats as people caught up with their friends, gossiped, made dates.

Claire speed dialed a vampire and got voice mail. Oliver didn't bother to identify himself, but just told the caller to leave a message, which she did, and then she put her phone on vibrate.

Shane kept looking at the closed doors they'd come through. Claire suppressed the urge to grit her teeth. "You're worried about her?" she asked, and tried to keep her voice neutral.

"We left her alone with Pennywell," he said. "Dammit. I thought she was following us."

Well, Kim hadn't followed them. Claire tried to be more worried, but the best she could really summon up was a dim sense of annoyance. And that really wasn't like her; she was always trying to find excuses for the worst people, and somehow, she just couldn't get on Kim's side, no matter what.

But she knew the right thing to do. "We should go look for her."

"No," Shane said. "You stay here. I'm just going to see if she's out there. I just want to be sure she's all right."

Because you don't at all care, Claire thought, but had enough sense to keep it to herself. She just nodded. Shane let go of her hand and moved to the doors, which he eased open and looked out. After a moment of hesitation, he let it close and came back. "Not there," he said.

"Which one?"

"Both." Shane sounded tense, and she couldn't blame him. He tended to take a lot on himself, and if something ended up going badly with Kim, he'd see it as his failure, which was nonsense, but it was how Shane rolled. "I need to—"

"Need to what?"

Kim again, coming up from right behind Claire. Claire squeezed her eyes shut and almost screamed in frustration—not relief—but she managed to control herself, turn, and say, very calmly, "Need to be sure you were okay. Which you are. Obviously."

Kim looked at her for a moment; then a knowing smile slowly spread over her lips. "Obviously," she almost purred. She transferred the look to Shane. And the smile. "You were worried about me? That's sweet, but gender-bender vamp back there wasn't about to hurt me."

"Why not?" Claire asked.

Kim shrugged. "Eh, you know. Damn, I really haven't seen you in forever, Collins. What you been up to?"

"Not much," he said, and reached out for Claire's hand again. "We've got seats down there. Sorry. Thanks for the intervention out there."

"Sure," Kim said. "Catch you later, then."

Their seats were close to the front, and by the time they'd reached them, the lights were going down. Claire looked back, but couldn't see Kim anywhere in the shadows.

"I think I might really hate that girl," she said.

Shane kissed her fingers lightly. "Don't be jealous. I'm not into her. Now or later."

Claire wished she could believe that, but there was still some small, difficult part of herself that was too aware of her own flaws.

Then the spotlights came up, the house lights went down, and Michael walked onto the stage, to a sudden rush of applause, and he wasn't the Michael Claire knew—he wasn't the one who hung out in the living room and played video games and noodled around on his guitar and picked terrible Westerns for movie night.

This was someone else.

Someone almost frightening, the way he grabbed and held the spotlight. He'd looked good earlier, but now Claire saw him the way that Michael Glass had always been meant to be seen . . . center stage. The light turned his hair brilliant gold, made his pale skin glow like moonstone, turned him into something exotic and fabulous and untouchable—and, at the same time, something you wanted to touch. Badly.

Someone pushed into the chair next to Claire. Eve. She'd put on her best, mostly backless black velvet gown, fixed her hair into a chic, gleaming black cap, and when she crossed her legs, the slit in her dress revealed an acre of leg and stiletto heels.

She was out of breath.

"Oh God, I thought I'd never make it," she whispered to Claire, and snapped open a black silk fan, which she fluttered to cool herself off. "That's my boyfriend, you know."

"I know," Claire said. She'd been prepared to not talk to Eve, but in two sentences, she found herself smiling. There was something so *happy* in sharing her joy. "He's okay, I guess."

Eve smacked her with the folded-up fan. "Bite your tongue. My boyfriend is a rock *god*, baby."

And this, with the first few notes of his song, Michael Glass proved vividly to the entire hall.

The concert was great. The after-party was overwhelming, mostly because Claire hadn't really known there would be one, and she wasn't up for being stared at by a few hundred strangers who were all pressing around, trying to get to Michael and wondering why she was so special that she got to be behind the autograph table, instead of in front of it. Michael had barely had time to say hi since he'd come out the stage door into the lobby; he'd been mobbed, and not even Eve, standing there looking gorgeous and movie-star sleek, could get private time with him while the fans circled. There was no sign of Kim. The vampires didn't bother to mix with the crowd, but as each of them left the building, they stopped to look at Michael, and nod. Claire supposed that was their version of a standing ovation.

As the number of autograph seekers finally died down, there were only a few people left. One was Pennywell, leaning against a marble pillar a hundred feet away, looking bored but eternal, as if he could wait another ten thousand years if necessary without a change of underwear. One was Kim, who was locked in animated conversation with a couple of TPU guys who looked, to Claire's eyes, like liberal arts students. She kept casting glances at their little group, and Claire figured that any minute she'd kick her holding-pattern boys to the curb and make straight for Shane.

The last person, though, was a human—an older guy dressed in a black tailored leather jacket and jeans— kind of like business tough, if there was such a thing. He had great hair, and one of those nice, even, white smiles people had on TV shows—and a tan.

"Michael, great show," the man said, and leaned over to shake Michael's hand. "Seriously, that was out of the park. My name is Harry Sloan, my daughter, Hillary, goes to school here. She wanted me to come and check you out, and I have to say, I was very impressed."

"Thanks," Michael said. He looked a little tired, no longer the mighty god of guitar that he'd been onstage, and Claire thought he just wanted to get this done and get home. "I appreciate that, Mr. Sloan."

Mr. Sloan produced a business card, which he slid across the table toward Michael's hand. "Yeah, here's the thing. I think you've got real potential, Michael. I work for a major recording company, and I want to take a demo CD back with me."

There was a moment where they all stared at him, and then Michael said, blankly, "Demo CD?"

"You don't have one?"

"No. I've been—" Michael didn't know how to finish that sentence. "Busy." Busy getting killed, then being made into a ghost, then turning into a vampire. Fighting wars. Et cetera.

"You really have to get in the studio, man, right now. I'll set it up—there's a good place in Dallas. I'll book the time for you if you tell me dates. But I want to take your stuff into our next discovery meeting. I think we can really do some business. Think about it, will you? First thing is to get that demo CD done. Call me."

He held out his hand again, and Michael shook it. He looked pale, and a little vacant, Claire thought. Mr. Sloan flashed them all that Hollywood smile again, slid on a very expensive pair of sunglasses, and left.

"He can't be," Eve said. "It's a joke, right? Monica's idea of a joke or something."

Michael held up the business card. Eve examined it, blinked, and passed it to Shane, who passed it on to Claire.

"Vice president," Claire read. "Oh. Wow."

"It's not a joke," Michael said. "There was an article about this guy in *Rolling Stone* about six weeks ago."

Michael slowly got to his feet, and it really hit home. "He wants to sign me. As a musician."

Shane held up his hand, palm out, and Michael slapped it, then grabbed Eve and spun her around in a rush of velvet and squeals. He went still, buried his face in the soft shine of her hair, and just held her. "All my life," he said. "I've been waiting for this all my life."

"I know," Eve said, and kissed him. "I'm so proud of you."

Across the gap of a hundred feet of outdated carpet, Mr. Pennywell started clapping. It had the crisp, startling sound of gunshots. The two boys Kim was chatting with discovered they had places to be, and hit the doors to flee into the night; Kim, just as Claire had feared, walked back over toward them. Pennywell finished clapping and said, "You do realize, of course, that they'll never allow you to leave?"

Michael raised his head, and it felt to Claire like the rest of them faded out of the world. It was just Michael and Pennywell.

"They?" Michael said. "You mean Oliver and Amelie."

"They want all vampires here, under their control. Under their *care*." Pennywell's sneer was like a slap across the face. "Two frightened little pups trying to control a pack of wolves. Are you a pack animal, Michael? I myself am not."

"What do you want?" Michael asked.

"Of you? Nothing. You are only a dog running to heel." His empty gaze moved away from Michael and fixed with a snap onto Claire. "I want *her*." Shane, Michael, and Eve closed ranks in front of her before Claire could draw a breath. Pennywell clicked his tongue. "No, no, no, children. This is a waste of blood. I will kill you all—yes, even you, fledgling—and take what I want in any case. You, girl—do you want to see your friends dead on this rather unpleasant carpet?"

"Fat chance," Shane said. "We already fought your

punk ass once, remember? Go ask Bishop how that went for him if you're scared to think about it."

Pennywell sent him a scorching look of contempt. "You were not alone, boy. You had allies. Here, you have—" He turned a slow circle, and focused on Kim. "Her. Perhaps not your most persuasive argument." His tone went eerily quiet, and very serious as he moved his gaze back toward Claire. "I have been alive seven hundred years, and I have been a killer since I was old enough to hold a sword. I have hunted witches and heretics down across Europe. I have destroyed stronger than you, in harder times. Do not mistake me when I tell you that I will not give you another chance."

Claire swallowed and stepped out from behind Shane. He tried to grab her arm, but she twisted away, never taking her eyes off Pennywell. "Don't hurt them," she said. "What do you want?"

"I want you to come with me," he said, "and I am entirely out of patience. *Now.*"

Claire held out her hands, palm out, to her friends—Michael, in his rock-star clothes, looking pale and focused and dangerous; Eve, dressed in a fall of black velvet, looking like a silent film star, right down to the look of fear on her face.

Shane was practically begging her not to go. His need to protect her pulled at her like gravity.

She said, "He won't hurt me. I'll call as soon as I can. You guys go home. Please."

"Claire—"

"Shane, *go.*"

To her utter dismay, she saw Kim move over to her friends and stand next to Shane. Kim put a hand on his arm, and he looked down at her. "Let her go," she told him. "She'll be fine."

Claire knew that this was *not* the right time to be wanting to scream, *Take your hands off my boyfriend, bitch,* but it was all she could do to hold the words inside. Pennywell's hand closed around her wrist, cold and strong as a handcuff, and as he began to pull her away, Claire met Shane's eyes one last time.

"I'll be back," she said. "Don't do anything crazy."

He probably thought she meant fighting vampires.

What she really meant, deep down, was *Don't fall in love with Kim.*

5

Pennywell marched her outside of the concert hall, into the chilly night. There was a smell of rain in the air, and thunder rumbling far off in the distance. Lightning shattered across the sky, briefly turning Pennywell almost luminous, and as Claire blinked away the glare, she saw that he was pulling her in the direction of an idling limousine parked at the curb.

"In," he barked, and shoved her at the open back door. She stumbled, caught herself, and crawled in. It was dark, of course. And it smelled like cigar smoke. Pennywell clambered in behind her, agile as a spider, and slammed the door behind him. The big car accelerated away from the curb.

"Where are we going?" Claire asked.

"Nowhere," said a voice out of the dark—Oliver's voice. The lights in the back slowly came up, revealing him sitting on the bench seat opposite her. Next to him was the source of the smoke, who smirked at her as he took a long pull on his cigar. Myrnin had put on a wine red jacket for the evening, something with elaborate embroidery on it. He looked almost normal, actually. He was even wearing the right shoes.

There was nothing normal about his smile, though.

"Cohiba?" he asked, and took an unlit cigar out of his

pocket to offer it to her. She shook her head, violently. "Pity. You know, daring women used to smoke."

"Cancer isn't sexy."

He raised his shoulders in a lazy shrug. "You all die of something," he said. "And we all pay for our pleasures, one way or another."

"Myrnin, what the *hell* is going on? You send this freak to abduct me...."

"Actually," Oliver said, "I sent Pennywell. It seemed to me he would be the one of us you and your friends would be least likely to argue with."

Pennywell laughed. "There you are wrong."

"I never said it would be easy." Oliver slammed the door on that conversation, and focused back on Claire. He leaned forward, elbows on his knees, and she tried not to be intimidated. "Myrnin and I wish to ask you about Amelie."

"Amelie." Claire stared back at him blankly, and then she felt the first tinglings of alarm. "What about her?"

"That display of foolishness last night. How did you know what she was doing? I didn't."

"I think it's the bracelet. I don't know. Maybe—" *Maybe it's Ada*, she thought, but didn't say. Myrnin stared at her thoughtfully through half-lidded eyes and blew smoke in a cloud at the roof. "Maybe she wanted me to know. Deep down. Maybe she wanted someone to stop her."

"Was she surprised to see you?" Myrnin asked. Claire slowly nodded. "Then she didn't summon you, consciously or unconsciously. Interesting."

"Theories?" Oliver asked.

"Not at present." Myrnin shrugged; then he spoiled his cool by catching sight of something outside of the limousine windows and brightening like a three-year-old with a new toy. "Oh, an all-night drive-through! I could murder a cheeseburger. Don't you just love this century?"

"Focus, you fool," Oliver growled. "What is Amelie up to? Is she fit to remain in control?"

"What makes you think she is in control?" Myrnin asked absently, then shot Claire a frown. "What happened to your face?"

"You," she snapped. "Remember?"

"I certainly did not order you to stand out in the sun. What possible good would that do?"

"Box? UV bomb? Ringing any bells?"

"Oh." Myrnin considered this carefully, then sighed. "Yes. Quite my fault. So sorry. What were we talking about?"

"Amelie," Oliver said, almost growling. *"Is she fit to lead?"*

Myrnin stubbed out his cigar in the wineglass. "Careful, my old friend," he said. "You come very close to saying something you would regret. I'm not your creature."

"No," Oliver agreed. "You're her creature to the bone. You built her this madhouse of a town. I would assume you could destroy it, if you chose."

Myrnin's attention seemed to be focused on crushing the cigar into submission. "Your point?"

"Amelie said herself that Morganville was built as an experiment, to see if it was possible for vampires and humans to live openly, and in peace. Well, I think that after all this time, we know the answer to that question. The only way to control humans is through fear, intimidation, and appeals to their greed. This exercise hasn't made us stronger; it's made us weaker."

"We were dying already," Myrnin said. "Out in the world."

Pennywell, who hadn't spoken since entering the limo, let out a derisive laugh. "Some of us," he said. "And some of us were killing."

"Any fool can kill. It takes genius to create."

"Hey!" Claire broke in. "Why me? Why grab me?"

"We're still debating that," Myrnin said.

Oliver looked frustrated enough to claw steel. "No, we are *not* debating it. The girl clearly has a connection to Amelie. It's the one way we can guarantee she will come to us."

"Don't be stupid. Amelie may have a connection to her, but Claire is eminently replaceable," Myrnin said. "No offense, my dear, but you're human. Humans are, by definition, replaceable."

"So are vampires," Pennywell said. "Including you, you bedlamite wretch."

"I was never in Bedlam," Myrnin said. "Although I hear you picked off inmates there when the rats ran scarce."

That must have been a serious vampire insult or something, because Pennywell launched himself across the space to latch his hands around Myrnin's throat.

Myrnin didn't even bother to react. He *yawned.* "Oliver," he said, "control your beast before I am forced to."

Pennywell snarled. His fangs snapped down.

Myrnin's eyes sparked red, and he grabbed Pennywell's wrist in his hand and twisted.

Bones snapped. Pennywell howled, clearly shocked at Myrnin's strength. From the look on his face, Oliver hadn't exactly expected it, either. Myrnin shoved Pennywell back to his place, pointed a finger at him, and smiled. "Next time, I will take your fangs," he said. "Then you'll be a toothless tiger. I don't think you'd enjoy it. Play nicely, witchfinder."

"Boys," Oliver said coolly, "the question at hand is an important one: Do we allow Amelie to continue to run Morganville? Or do we use the girl to take it from her control, once and for all?"

Myrnin sighed. "You do understand that Amelie is aware of your intentions? That she's planned for your eventual rebellion? Because it was plain as the moon that you'd betray her, sooner or later."

"I'd hate to disappoint," Oliver said. "And she has become weak. The weak can't lead."

"I've known Amelie a very long time, and I would never describe her as *weak*." Myrnin lit up another cigar, with much puffing and use of a lighter with a hot blue flame. Claire almost choked on the smoke. Her eyes burned and teared, and she had to wipe them clear. "Wounded, perhaps. Less certain of herself than before. But not weak, which you will discover if you think to push her."

Oliver frowned at him. "I thought you were with me in this."

"Did I say that? Well, I'm not very reliable, as you know." Myrnin closed his eyes in delight as he drew in the smoke from the cigar. "You very nearly succeeded in bribing me with these excellent Cubans. I haven't had the like since Victoria was still Queen of England. But in the end, I must remain loyal to my lady. And I really can't allow you to torment my apprentice. After all, that's my job."

"I thought that might be the case," Oliver said.

He pulled a stake from inside his coat and slammed it into Myrnin's chest.

Claire screamed and lunged for Oliver, or at least she started to—the limousine violently swerved, sending them all flying, and Claire ended up on the carpeted floor with Myrnin's deadweight on top of her. Something hit them, hard, and Claire felt the car lift, twist in the air, and slam down on its top, sending her and Myrnin in a tangle to the roof of the limo.

Oliver and Pennywell had somehow stayed in their seats—holding themselves in by main force, apparently. Claire fought free of Myrnin's body, panting and disoriented. She wasn't hurt, or at least she didn't feel hurt, but everything seemed a little odd. Too bright. Too sharp. Pennywell's eyes were bright red, and his fangs were out.

Oliver was looking at her like lunch, too.

The side window had broken out when the car rolled. Claire grabbed Myrnin's shoulders, crawled backward through the wrecked window, and dragged him along with her. As soon as she had his chest clear of the limo, she wrapped both hands around the stake and yanked it free with a wrench.

"Ahhhhhh!" Myrnin screamed, and came bolt upright, both hands slapping at his chest. "My *God,* I hate that!"

Pennywell dropped down onto his legs like some pale jumping spider. Myrnin slammed a boot into his face and crawled free of the wreckage, grabbing Claire as he rose to his feet. There was blood staining his shirt, and some on his face where he'd been cut by flying glass, but he looked fine, really.

Angry as hell, though.

Pennywell crawled out of the limo. His expression was no longer empty; it was full of hate. "Heretic," he hissed. "*Witch.* I'll see you burn, you and your familiar." He cast a venomous look at Claire, too, and she swallowed hard.

"What's a familiar?" she asked Myrnin.

"A demonic spirit who aids a witch," he said. "Usually in the form of a black cat, but I suppose you'd do. Although in my experience you are not nearly demonic enough."

"Thanks."

"Don't mention it." Myrnin raised his eyebrows and thrust his chin at Pennywell. "Well? Are you waiting for your lynch mob to bring your spine?"

Claire had a very nasty flash of intuition. "Where's Oliver?"

And then a cold hand closed around her neck, choking off her breath and igniting blind panic inside. She was pulled away, completely off balance and out of control, and saw Myrnin spinning toward her but not quickly enough; she was moving away from him, off into the dark. . . .

It all freeze-framed for her: Myrnin, bloody and wide-eyed, reaching out for her. Pennywell smirking from where he stood near the wreckage of the limo. The smoking sedan that had sent the limo rolling—hood crumpled like used tinfoil.

That was a vampire car.

And the driver's side door was open.

Claire choked, gasped for breath, and tore at the hand holding her throat closed. No good. Her fingernails didn't concern him any more than her heels when she kicked backward.

"Hush," Oliver chided her, and squeezed harder. "I'd like to say this will hurt me more than you, but that wouldn't be strictly true—"

He broke off with a stunned gasp, and his hand slid away from Claire's throat. She stumbled forward two steps, both hands holding her aching neck, and then looked back.

Oliver was staring down at his chest, where the point of a stake had emerged from his rib cage.

"Damn," he said, and pitched down to his knees, fighting it all the way.

Michael was behind him.

Michael had just *staked Oliver.*

He dashed around the older vampire and grabbed Claire. "You okay?"

She couldn't get words out through her bruised throat, but she nodded, eyes wide. In seconds Myrnin was there, too, picking her up and dumping her unceremoniously into Michael's arms. "Take her," he said. "Oliver is not going to be pleased, boy. Better go."

"I had to," Michael said. "I had to stake him. He was going to kill her."

"In point of fact, he wasn't; he was going to hurt her so badly that Amelie would feel it, that's all. But that's not what I meant. You crashed a car into the limousine. Oliver *loves* his limousine."

Michael opened his mouth, then closed it without thinking of anything to say to that.

Myrnin, watching Pennywell, said, "Michael, take the girl and go. I have things to do here. Do leave the stake where it is—I can't have Oliver interfering just yet. The witchfinder and I have old debts to settle." When Michael hesitated, Myrnin's dark eyes flashed toward him in command. *"Take her."*

Michael nodded, and Claire lost all sense of where she was, except that she was held firmly in his arms, and moving fast. Lights flashed by, moving too quickly for her to focus on. The burning in her throat died down from a bonfire to a slow broil, and she tried clearing it. It felt like gargling with glass, but she got a weak sound out.

Michael slowed to a normal human-speed run, then a walk, and Claire saw that they were back at the TPU theater. Eve, Shane, and Kim were standing in front of Eve's car. Two of them looked shocked; Kim just looked like none of it was much concern of hers.

"Claire!" Shane got there first, taking her out of Michael's arms and easing her to her feet. When she faltered, he held on to her, anxiously looking her over. "What the hell happened, Michael?"

"Crash," Claire whispered. "Car crash. Hi."

"Hi," Shane said. "What do you mean, car crash? Jesus, Michael, you crashed your car?"

"Into the limo," Claire said. It seemed important to get it right, for some reason. "Saved me."

Sort of, anyway. She really wasn't sure what would have happened to her if Oliver had managed to take Myrnin out and had time to do whatever unpleasant thing he'd had planned, or if Pennywell had gotten hold of her. There were so many nasty possibilities.

"We need to get out of here," Michael said. "Right now. Eve?"

She pulled her car keys out of her tiny black purse, hiked up her velvet skirt, and climbed behind the wheel of her big boxy sedan. Kim smoothly claimed the front passenger seat, leaving Claire in the back, sandwiched between Shane and Michael—which was not at all a bad place to be. She was shaking, she realized. She supposed that was shock or something. Shane held her left hand, and Michael her right, and she closed her eyes as Eve peeled rubber out of the parking lot, heading home.

6

"Mom?" Claire looked at the clock, bit her lip, and prepared for the worst. "Hey. Sorry to be calling so late. We just got out of the concert—you know Michael was playing tonight, right? So I'm at the Glass House. I'm going to stay over tonight; I'll see you in the morning, okay? Bye. Love you."

She hung up and gave a long sigh, leaning back against Shane's chest. "Thank God for voice mail," she said. "I don't think I could have done that if she'd picked up."

He kissed her neck gently. "I don't care what your parents say; I'm not letting you out of my sight. Not tonight."

They were home, safe in the warmth of the Glass House. Michael had gone upstairs to change, but Eve was still there, slinking around in her glam-rags. Also, ugh, *Kim* was still with them.

But somehow it felt like the two of them were all alone.

Shane wrapped his arms around her, and she relaxed, all her fear bleeding away. Her small hand wrapped around his forearm, she felt so safe as she sensed his muscles moving underneath his velvety skin.

Even if she wasn't really safe, ever.

"I need to thank Michael," she said, and stopped to

clear her throat. It didn't make it feel much better. "He didn't have to come after me."

"I'd have killed his ass if he didn't," Shane said, and there was a grimness behind it that made her wince. "He wouldn't let me come with him."

"You could have gotten hurt in the crash."

"He wasn't worried about *you.*"

"He was. I was about to be dinner."

Shane sighed and dropped his forehead onto her shoulder. "And he'd have a point."

"He saved my life."

"I get that. Could we stop talking about Michael for a second?" He sounded actually pained.

"You are *not* jealous."

Shane held up two fingers pinched almost together. "That much, maybe. And only because he's got that rock-star thing going on. You girls get into that."

"Shut up!"

"Seriously, you throw panties and stuff. I've heard."

She turned in the circle of his arms to face him, staring up into his face. No words. He was drawn down to her like gravity, lips warm against hers, lazy at first, then getting hotter, breath coming faster. Her brain exploded in a thousand thoughts and memories . . . the soft skin at the back of his neck, the way he said her name in that sweet, hushed whisper, the sheer heat of him against her.

"Hey." Eve's voice, mostly amused, made Claire jump. "I know, mad love, et cetera, but could you please not make out in the living room? I really want to be able to tell your parents I've never seen anything going on when they bring the Inquisition over for lunch."

Shane kissed her one more time, lightly and softly, and fluffed her hair back from her face. "To be continued," he said.

"I hate cliff-hangers."

"Blame Eve."

Claire stepped back from him, and the world came back to life around her—funny how it all seemed to disappear when she was with him. Eve was sitting on the couch, flipping channels on the TV. Kim was cross-legged on the floor reading the backs of game cases.

"Hey," Kim said. "Who plays the zombie game?"

"Ugh," Eve said. "No."

"I have, a little," Claire admitted.

"So that's a no, a maybe—come on, somebody must be game master around here?"

Shane finally held up his hand. Kim smiled.

"Rock on, Collins," she said. "Let's see what you've got."

Claire's lips still tingled from the kisses, and her whole body from anticipation, but the gleam in Kim's eyes made her tense up. She could tell Shane was reluctant, but also, Shane wasn't really in the habit of passing up a challenge, either.

Except that this time, he did. "Can't," he said. "Got to check on Michael."

"I already did," Eve said, "which you'd have known if you weren't on Planet Wonderful, the two of you. And he's fine. He's on the phone with Amelie. I wouldn't go there."

"Oh." Shane's excuse had just vanished, and Claire could tell he wasn't quite up to outright telling Kim no. He went to the couch; Eve scooted over and handed him a game controller. Kim snagged the other one from the side table. "Lock and load, I guess."

Claire left him to go upstairs. The bathroom was free, and she used the facilities, cleaned up, mourned the state of her face and the fast-emerging bruises around her neck, then went to her bedroom and found a pair of comfortable jeans and a top. A cute top. And she made sure it showcased the cross Shane had bought her. She also put on a little lip gloss. Just a little.

She could hear the shouts and smack talk from downstairs when she opened her bedroom door; Kim and Shane were all about the competition, which did not make her feel less left out. "Come on, suck it up," she told herself in a harsh, hoarse whisper, plastered a smile on, and started down the hall.

The hidden door opposite Eve's bedroom opened with a soft click, and in the dim reflected light, Claire saw the flicker of a black-and-white image of a woman in full Victorian-style skirts. It looked like a specter, which anywhere but in Morganville would have made Claire scream and make a run for the local ghostbusters.

But this *was* Morganville, and Claire knew Ada all too well. "What?" she demanded. Ada—or Ada's image projection, anyway—made a hushing motion of a finger to her lips. She turned, the way a two-dimensional cardboard cutout turns, disappearing in the middle and then expanding again to a back view, and glided up the stairs beyond the hidden door without touching the wood.

"Seriously?" Claire sighed. "Wonderful. Just great."

She followed Ada up. Behind her, the door shut with the same hushed click. Upstairs the lights blazed on, a kaleidoscope of color through Tiffany glass lamps, and Claire saw Ada's image—face forward again—standing against the wall near the old red velvet sofa. "Okay, I'm here," she said. "What do you want?"

Ada made the shushing motion again, which was deeply annoying. Ada was a computer—a smart one, and arguably kind of human, but still . . . She was acting all secretive and clever, and Claire really didn't like the rather cruel smile on those smooth dark gray lips.

Ada touched the wall, and it shimmered, taking on the darkness of one of the portals that Ada controlled through town . . . a kind of magic tunnel, although Claire hated to call it magic. It was physics, that was all. Scary advanced physics. That meant it was the ultimate fast lane, but dangerous. . . . Claire frowned at the opening, trying to feel where the destination might be on the other end. Nothing. And it looked way too dark to be safe.

"No," she said. "I don't think so. Sorry."

Why she was apologizing to a crazy computer lady, she didn't know. Ada wasn't her friend. Ada didn't even like her very much, although—by Myrnin's orders—Ada kind of had to obey her.

Ada lost her smile. She shrugged, turned, and glided through the portal.

She vanished into the dark. After a few seconds, a slender gray hand came out of the shadows and made a *Come on* impatient gesture.

"No," Claire said again, and this time, sat down on the couch. "No way. I've had way too much today. You have your little weird crisis on your own, Ada."

Her cell phone rang, and the sound of the song echoing through the hidden room made Claire jump and dig the phone out of her pocket. The screen read *Shane Calling*. She flipped it open.

"Shane?"

Static, and then came Ada's weird machine-flat voice. "Myrnin needs you. Now. Come!" She sounded angry, and cold, but she usually did unless she was simpering at Myrnin. Claire slapped the phone shut, blew hair off her forehead, and stared at the darkness. It *could* be Myrnin's lab. She just couldn't tell. Myrnin had a vampire's habit of forgetting to turn on lights, which sucked.

"I really need to start carrying flashlights," she muttered, and then had an inspiration. There was a Tiffany-style pole lamp in the corner by the sofa; Claire lifted off the heavy glass shade, set it aside, and rolled the base to the limit of its electrical cord, then lowered it across the threshold of the portal, into the darkness on the other side.

She saw Ada standing there, hands clasped in front of

her, cold and expressionless, surrounded by at least *ten* albino-pale vampires, who cried out and flinched back at the touch of the light. They had oversized fangs and sharp talons, and they weren't like the regular vamps. . . . These were tunnel rats, the ones who stalked the dark places, keeping out of the light and existing just to kill. Failures, Myrnin had called them.

Ada had meant for her to walk right into the middle of them.

Claire yelled in shock, and slammed the portal closed in her mind, then put her hand on the blank wall of the room as it took on weight and reality again. There was a way to lock it—maybe—and she searched for the right frequency to trigger the security. It was like a deadbolt, and it would hold against Ada or anyone else who wanted to come through.

She hoped.

Closing the portal had chopped the pole lamp in half, and she dropped the base part as it sputtered and sparked, then kicked the plug out of the wall. Claire stood there staring at the wall, and the mutilated lamp, for a long moment with her hands curled into fists, then took out her phone and dialed Myrnin's lab.

"How kind of you to check up on me," he said. "I'm fine, as it happens."

"We've got a problem."

"Really? The stake in my chest didn't indicate that at all. I must send Oliver a bill for a new shirt."

"Ada just tried to kill me."

Myrnin was silent for a moment. Claire could almost see him, hunched over the old-fashioned wired phone that looked like it had come from a Victorian junk shop. "I see," he said, in an entirely different tone. "Are you certain?"

"She told me you needed to see me, and opened a portal into a nest of hungry vamps. So, yes. I'm pretty sure."

"Oh my. I will have a talk with her. I'm sure it was a misunderstanding."

"Myrnin—" Claire squeezed her eyes closed, counted to five, and started over. "She's not listening to you anymore. Don't you get that? She's doing her own thing, and her own thing means getting rid of the competition."

"Competition for what?"

"For you," Claire said. "Not that I am. But she thinks I am. Because you haven't killed me."

She was babbling, because saying this was making her feel a little sick and giddy. She wasn't in love with Myrnin, but she did love him, a little. He was crazy; he was dangerous; he was a vampire—and yet, he was somehow not any of those things, in his better moments.

"Claire." He sounded wounded. "I do *not* find you attractive, except for your mind. I hope you know that. I would never take such advantage of you." He paused, and thought about it for a second. "Except if I was hungry, of course. But probably not. Most likely."

"Yeah, that's comforting. The point is, Ada thinks you care for me, and she wants me out of the way so you'll care more for her. Right?"

"Right. I'll go have a talk with her."

"You need to pull her plug, Myrnin."

"Over that? Pshaw. It's merely a flaw in her programming. I'll take good care of it." He paused, then said, "Of course, in the meantime, I wouldn't follow her anywhere if I were you."

"No kidding. Thanks."

"Oh, don't mention it, my dear. Enjoy your evening. Oh, and tell Michael that I enjoyed his concert."

"You were there?"

She heard the smile in Myrnin's voice. "We were all there, Claire. All the vampires. We do so enjoy our entertainments."

That was ever so slightly creepy, and Claire hung up without saying good-bye.

* * *

Downstairs, the video game raged on; Kim was as good a player as Shane, apparently, which didn't surprise Claire but depressed her kind of a lot. Shane didn't even notice her reappearance; he was wiggling around on the couch, putting body language into his shooting as his game character ducked zombie attacks and kicked, punched, and shot his way out of trouble.

Kim's character was a slinky-looking girl with black hair in a ponytail, and half a costume. She fought in high heels.

Great.

Claire sat down on the stairs, watching through the railing, and hugged her knees to her chest. Eve was gone, probably to change clothes, so it was just Shane and Kim.

They looked oblivious to everything but the drama on the screen.

She was developing some kind of sixth sense where Michael was concerned; he didn't make any noise coming down the steps, but she knew he was coming, and turned her head to see that he'd switched out his rock-star gear for a faded, old gray T-shirt and, like her, jeans. He took a look at what was happening in the living room, then crouched down next to her. "Hey," he said. "You all right?"

"I wouldn't have been if you hadn't crashed into us," Claire said. "Thank you."

He looked ashamed. "Yeah, well, that wasn't quite the plan. I was just trying to make him stop. I didn't think he'd actually *hit* me."

She almost laughed, because he sounded so sad about it. She took his cool hand and squeezed. He squeezed back. "It was still a good plan."

"Except for the part where I nearly killed you, destroyed Amelie's limo, and my own car? Yeah. It rocked the house."

"Are they going to get you a new one? A car, I mean?"

"Amelie said they would."

"I shut all the portals to the house," Claire said. "Ada's acting weird."

"I thought that was normal."

"Weirder."

"Ah. Okay." Michael looked past the railings, at Kim and Shane. "Are you freaking out about Kim?" Claire made the same little-bit mime with her finger and thumb that Shane had earlier. "Yeah, well don't. Kim's not his type."

"I'm not sure *I'm* his type." Okay, that sounded really, really whiny. Claire bit her lip. "She's just so—much."

"Yep. She is that." He rose to his feet and padded down the last few steps silently, came up behind Kim, and leaned over her to say, "I vant to drink your blood" in a heavy, fake Dracula accent. She shrieked, flailed, and a zombie ate her brains on-screen.

"You *bastard*!" Kim yelled, dropped the controller, and smacked him hard on the chest. "I can't believe you just totally sabotaged me!"

"Can't let him lose," Michael said, as Shane hit the high score and the victory music sounded. "Gotta live with the dude."

They high-fived.

"You're seriously going to take that as a win," Kim said. "When he totally cheated for you."

"Yes," Shane said. "I seriously am." He canceled the game, put the controller down, and rose to stretch and yawn. "Damn. It's late. Don't you have someplace to go or something?"

Kim looked actually hurt for a second, and Claire felt a twinge of—something. Maybe pity. She hoped not.

"Sure," she said. "Johnny Depp's waiting for me back home. Guess I'd better blaze. Hey, where's Eve?"

"What, you're going?" Eve called from the top of the stairs, and jumped down past Claire in her eagerness to get to the bottom. "You can't! Kim, we need to run lines and stuff!"

"No, Shane's right. It's really late. How about tomorrow? I can meet you at Common Grounds—how about three? You're working until about then, right?"

"Yeah," Eve said. She still sounded disappointed. "Sure, that's okay. Hey—you want to go out tomorrow night? Maybe catch a movie? Um—Claire, you want to go, too?"

Great. She was officially an also-invited. "No thanks," she said. "I've got plans."

"Seriously? What?"

Claire looked at Shane, and he took one for the team. "Dinner with me," he said. "It's kind of an anniversary."

"Awwww, really? That's so sweet!" Eve leveled a finger at him. "Do *not* take her to the chili dog place."

"A real restaurant. With tablecloths. Hey, I'm not a complete idiot."

Kim stared at Shane, and in that moment, Claire realized this wasn't just an act. . . . Kim really *did* like Shane—a lot.

She recognized pain when she saw it.

"So," Eve said, and turned to Kim. "Movies, right? Something scary?"

Kim got herself together before Eve could see the same thing Claire had noticed. "Sure," she said. "Whatev. You pick. No girly movies."

Eve looked deeply offended. "Me? Girly movies? Bite your tongue off. No, seriously. Right now."

Kim laughed, and Eve walked her to the door. Claire said to Shane, "Anniversary?"

He raised his eyebrows. "Depends on how you count things," he said. "Yeah. It's got to be *some* kind of anniversary. Probably of one of us not getting killed."

Michael said, "Speak for yourself, man." He picked

up the controller and restarted the game. "I can't believe you almost let her win."

"Man, I almost let *you* win sometimes," Shane said, and dropped into his spot on the other end of the couch. "Game on."

7

The next day, Claire sat through classes without any real sense of accomplishment, took a quiz—which she aced—and dropped in on Myrnin's lab around noon. It looked neat and clean again, which was two miracles in a row as far as she was concerned. She went to the bookshelves and started looking over journals, trying to find the most recent ones, although those would be the most difficult to figure out, given that most of his notes would have been taken when he was sick, and mostly crazy.

But she was curious.

She was struggling through last summer's book when Myrnin popped in through the portal, wearing a big floppy black hat and a kind of crazy/stylish pimp coat that covered him from neck to ankles, black leather gloves, and a black and silver walking stick with a dragon's head on it.

And on his lapel was a button that said, IF YOU CAN READ THIS, THANK A TEACHER.

It was typical Myrnin, really. She was surprised the bunny slippers were absent.

"I didn't know you were coming today," he said, and draped his hat, coat, and cane on a nearby coat rack. "And I assume it isn't just a random occurrence, like gravity."

"Gravity isn't random."

"So *you* say." He came to the opposite side of the table

and looked at the book, then turned his head weirdly sideways to read the title. "Ah. Some of my best work. If only I could figure out what it actually meant."

"I was trying to figure out if you ever met a girl named Kim. Kim—" What the hell was her last name? Had anybody even told her? "Kim, something. Kind of Goth?"

"Oh, her," Myrnin said. He didn't sound too impressed, which made Claire just a little happy. "Yes, Kimberlie's known to us. She asked permission to film some of us, for the archives—a sort of permanent record of our histories. As you know, we do value that sort of thing. Many have agreed. She's been named our video historian, I believe."

"You haven't done it, though?"

"I write my own history. I see no reason to entrust it to a human with a video camera. Paper and ink, girl. Paper and ink will always survive, when electronic storage becomes random impulses lost to the ages."

"But the vampires do know her."

"Yes. She's a bit of a pet for the older ones. Besides me, of course. I don't like pets. They bite—ah! I almost forgot! Time to feed Bob." And Myrnin bustled off to another part of the lab, where presumably he'd stashed Bob the spider.

Or possibly Bob the auto mechanic—Claire wouldn't put anything past him. He seemed slightly manic today, from the glitter in his eyes. It made her nervous.

She was about to close the book, when she saw, in his spiky black handwriting, something about her:

New girl. Claire something. Small and fragile. No doubt they believe that will make me protective of her. It only makes me think how easy it is to destroy her. . . .

She shuddered, and decided she didn't really want to read the rest.

She left Myrnin making little weird kissy faces to Bob the spider as he shook a container of flies into Bob's plastic case, and went to the archives.

Since the first time she'd seen the Vampire Archives—which had been on the run, in a time of war, and it had been a place they'd hit up for weapons—she'd been fascinated by the idea. The vampires were packrats, no doubt about it; they loved *things*—historical things. Also—apparently—junk, because there were entire vaults of stuff that nobody had gotten around to categorizing yet, and probably never would. But the upper floors were amazing. The library was meticulous, and there was an entire section that contained every known book, magazine, and pamphlet with anything about vampires in it, cross-referenced by accuracy. *Dracula* scored only about a six, apparently.

Apart from that, the vampires had donated, bought, or stolen six floors of historical texts, in a wide variety of languages. There were even ancient scrolls that looked too delicate to properly handle, and a few wax tablets that Amelie had told her dated from Roman times.

The audiovisual area was new, but it contained everything from samples of the flickers made for penny arcades in the early 1900s to silent film, sound film, color film, all the way up to DVDs. Again, most of it was concerned somehow with vampires, but not everything. There seemed to be an awful lot of costume drama. And, for some reason, musicals.

Claire found the digital video interviews on the computer kiosk, listed by the vampire's name and date of—birth? Making? What did they call it? Anyway, the date they got fanged.

The newest one was Michael Glass.

Claire brought up the player and blinked as Michael fidgeted in front of the camera. He wasn't comfortable. This wasn't being onstage for him, obviously. He messed with the clip-on microphone until Kim's off-screen voice told him to cut it out, and then he sat, looking like he wished he'd never agreed to any of this, until the questions started. The first ones were obvious—name, current age, age at death, original birthplace.

Then Kim asked, "How did you become a vampire?"

Michael thought about his answer for a few seconds before he said, "Total stupidity."

"Yeah? Tell me."

"I grew up in Morganville. I knew the rules. I knew how dangerous things were, but when you grow up with Protection, I think you get careless. I'd just turned eighteen. My parents had already left town, my mom was sick and needed cancer treatments, so I was on my own. I wanted to sell the house and get on with my life."

"How's that going for you?"

Michael didn't smile. "Not like I'd hoped. I got careless. I met a guy who wanted to buy the house, somebody new in town. It never occurred to me he was a vampire. He—didn't come across that way. But the second he crossed the threshold, I knew. I just knew."

He shook his head. Kim cleared her throat. "Can I ask who . . . ?"

"Oliver," Michael said. "He killed me his first day in town."

"Wow. That sucks completely. But you didn't become a vampire then, right?"

"No. I died. Sort of. I remember dying, and then . . . then it was the next night, and I couldn't remember anything in between. I was fine. No holes in the neck, nothing. I figured maybe I'd dreamed it, but then—then I tried to leave the house."

"What happened?"

"I started to drift away. Like smoke. I got back inside before it was too late, but I realized after a few more tries that I couldn't leave. Didn't matter which door, or how I did it. I just—stopped being me." Michael's eyes looked haunted now, and Claire saw a shiver run through him. "That was bad enough, but then morning came."

"And what happened?"

"I died," Michael said. "All over again. And it hurt."

Claire turned it off. There was something wrong about hearing this, seeing him let down his guard so completely. Michael had always tried to make it all okay, somehow. She hadn't known how much it had freaked him out. And, she found, she didn't really want to know how it had felt when he'd been made a real vampire by Amelie, in order to be able to live outside of the house.

She knew too much already.

There were about twenty other video interviews in the folder, but there was one that made Claire hesitate, then double-click the icon.

The camera zoomed in, steadied focus, and then the lights came up. "Please give us your name, the date you became a vampire, your birthplace, and your death age." It was Kim's voice, but this time she sounded nervous, not at all the smart-ass Claire knew. "Please."

Oliver leaned back in his chair, looking like he'd smelled something nasty, and said, "Oliver. I will keep my family name to myself, if you please. I was made vampire in 1658. I was born in Huntingdon, Cambridgeshire, East Anglia, England, in 1599. So as you see, I was not a young man when I was turned."

"Was it your choice?"

Oliver stared at Kim, off camera, for so long that even Claire felt nervous. Then he said, "Yes. I was dying. It was my one chance to retain the power I'd attained. The thieving trick of it was that once I'd made my devil's bargain, I couldn't hold the power I sought to keep. So I gained new life, and lost my old one."

"Who made you?"

"Bishop."

"Ah—do you want to say anything about Bishop—"

"No." Oliver suddenly stood up, fire in his eyes, and

stripped the microphone off in a hail of static. "I'll do no more of this prying. Past is past. Let it die."

Kim, very quietly, said, "But you killed him. Didn't you? You and Amelie?"

Oliver's eyes turned red. "You know nothing about it, little girl with your foolish toys. And pray to God you never will."

Oliver knocked the camera over, and Kim yelped, and that was it.

Fade to black.

"Enjoying yourself?" Oliver's voice said, and for a second Claire thought it was on the computer screen, then realized that it came from *behind* her. She turned her head, slowly, to find him standing near the door of the small room, leaning against the wall. He was wearing a T-shirt with the Common Grounds logo on it, and cargo pants, and he didn't look like a five-hundred-year-old vampire. He even had a peace-sign earring in one ear.

"I—wanted to know about the historical interview project, that's all. Sorry." Claire shut down the kiosk and stood up. "Are you going to try to kill me again?"

"Why? Do you want to be prepared?" He cocked his head at her.

"I'd like to see it coming."

That got her a thin smile. "Not all of us have that luxury. But no. I have been schooled by my mistress. I won't raise a finger to you, little Claire. Not even if you ask me to."

Claire edged slowly toward the door. He smiled wider, and his gaze followed her all the way . . . but he let her go.

When she looked back, he was at the kiosk, clicking the mouse. She heard his interview start, and heard his nonrecorded voice murmur a curse. The recording cut off.

Then the entire kiosk was ripped out and smashed on

the floor with enough force to shatter a window three feet ahead of her.

Somebody wasn't happy with how he looked on camera.

Claire broke into a run, dodged around another row of books, turned left at the German books to make for the exit—

And tripped over Kim, who was sitting on the floor of the library, staring down at the screen of her cell phone as if it held the secrets of the universe.

"Hey!" Kim protested, and Claire pitched headlong to the carpet. She caught herself on the way down, kicked free of Kim's legs, and crawled backward. "You okay?"

"Fine," Claire said, and got up to dust herself off. "What the hell are you doing?"

"Research," Kim said.

"In *German*?"

"I didn't say I was looking at the books, dummy. But I *could* read German. It's possible."

"Do you?"

Kim grinned. "Just curse words. And where's the bathroom, in case I get stuck in Berlin. Hey, what was the crash?"

"Oh. Oliver. He just found the interview you did with him."

Kim's grin left the building. "He killed my computer, right? He just went all Hulk Smash on it."

"He wasn't happy."

"No," Oliver said, and rounded the corner of the aisle. There were flickers of red in his eyes, and his bone-pale hands were curled into fists. "No, Oliver isn't happy at all. You told me you'd destroyed the interview."

"I lied," Kim said. "Dude, I don't work for you. I was given a job to do by the council, with a grant and everything. I'm doing it. And now you owe me for a new computer. I'm thinking maybe a laptop."

She looked way too calm. Oliver noticed it, too. "That wasn't the only copy."

"Digital age. It's a sad, sad world, and it's just full of downloadable copies."

"You're going to bring them all to me."

"Duh, no," Kim said, and closed up her phone. "I'm pretty sure I'm not. And I'm pretty sure you're going to have to just get over it, because this is Amelie's pet project. We didn't even get that far, anyway. It's not like you told me you collect Precious Moments figures or something embarrassing. Get over it." She checked the big, clunky watch on her wrist, and rolled to her feet. "Whoops, time to go. I have rehearsal in half an hour. And hey, so do you, Mitch. No hard feelings, okay?"

Oliver said nothing. Kim shrugged and headed for the exit.

"I don't like her," Claire offered.

"At last, we have something in common," Oliver said. "But she is right about one thing: I have to get to rehearsal."

That sounded very—normal. More normal than most things Oliver said. Claire felt some of her tension slip away. "So how's that going? The play thing?"

"I have no idea. I haven't done a play in a hundred years, and the idea of Eve and Kim being our leading ladies doesn't fill me with confidence." That just *dripped* with sarcasm, and Claire winced a little.

"A hundred years. What was the last thing you performed?"

"*Hamlet.*"

Of course.

How rehearsal went Claire didn't know; she headed for Common Grounds, where she was set to meet up with (ugh) Monica. At least it was profitable.

"Money up front," she said, as she slid into the seat across from the mayor's favorite—and only—sister.

Monica had done something cute with her hair, and it framed her face in feathered curves. For once, she was alone; no sign of Gina and Jennifer, not even as coffee fetchers.

Monica sent Claire a dirty look, but she reached into her designer backpack, got out her designer wallet, and counted out fifty dollars that she shoved across the table. "Better be worth it," she said. "I really hate this class."

"Then drop it."

"Can't. It's a core class for my major."

"Which is?"

"Business."

It figured. "So where do you want to start? What's giving you the most trouble?"

"The teacher, since he keeps giving these stupid pop quizzes and I keep flunking them." Monica dug in her backpack and tossed over three stapled tests, which were marked up in green—the teacher must have read somewhere that red made students nervous or something, but Claire thought that with this many marks, the color of the pen was the least of Monica's problems.

"Wow," she said, and flipped the pages. "So you really don't get economics at all."

"I didn't pay fifty dollars for the pleasure of hearing you state the obvious," Monica pointed out. "So yeah. Don't get it, don't really want to, but I need it. So give me my fifty bucks' worth of a passing grade already."

"Well—economics is really game theory, only with money."

Monica just stared at her.

"That was going to be the simple version."

"Give me my money back."

Actually, Claire needed it—well, she needed to have had Monica pay it to her, really—so she came up with a few kind of cool explanations, showed Monica the way to memorize the formulas and when to use them . . . and before it was done, there were at least ten other students leaning in to listen and take notes at various points. That was cool, except that Monica kept demanding five bucks from each one of them, which meant that she got a free lesson.

Still, not a bad afternoon's work. Claire finished feeling a little happier; teaching—even teaching Monica—always made her feel better.

She felt *much* better when she saw that Shane had come to walk her home.

"Hey," he said as she fell in beside him. "Good day?"

She considered exactly how to answer that, and finally said, "Not bad." Nobody had gotten killed so far. In Morganville, that was probably a good day. "Monica paid me fifty for a private lesson." Shane held up his hand, and she jumped up to smack it without breaking stride. "And yours?"

"There was meat. I sliced it with a big, sharp knife. Very manly."

"I'm impressed."

"Of course you are. So, it's our anniversary—"

"It's not!"

"Well, I told Kim it was, and then I promised to take you out to a nice restaurant."

"With tablecloths," Claire agreed. "I distinctly remember tablecloths."

"The point is, I'm taking you out. Okay?"

"I don't think so. My face is just starting to heal. I've got bruises all over my throat. The last thing I want to do is go to a nice restaurant and have everybody stare at us and wonder if you're abusing me. I wouldn't enjoy my food at all."

"You think too much."

She took his hand. "Probably."

"Okay then. How about a sandwich offered up on a nice, clean napkin, in my room?"

"You're such a romantic."

"It's in my *room*."

They were about two blocks along from Common Grounds—about halfway home—when the streetlights began to go out, one after another, starting behind them and zooming past as each clicked off. It wasn't quite full dark yet, but it was getting there fast as the last hints of red sunset faded from the horizon.

"Claire?" Shane looked around, and so did she, feeling her instincts start to howl a warning.

"Something's wrong," she said. "Something's here."

A bloody form lurched out of the darkness toward them, and Shane shoved Claire behind him. It was a vampire—red eyes, fangs down, blood splashed on the pale face and hands.

Claire knew him, she realized after a second of pure adrenaline and shock. He was wearing the same ragged, greasy clothes from the last time she'd seen him: Morley, the graveyard vampire who'd tried to ambush Amelie.

He saw Claire and gasped out, "Fair lady, tell your mistress—tell her—"

He lunged for Claire, off balance, and Shane stiff-armed him away. Morley went sprawling on the pavement, and rolled up into a ball.

Afraid.

"It's okay," Claire said, and put a hand on Shane's arm. She carefully crouched down near Morley's blood-stained body. "Mr. Morley? What happened?"

"Ruffians," he whispered. "Tormentors. Hellhounds." Something made him flinch, and he listened for a second, then rolled painfully to his feet. Claire jumped backward, just in case, but Morley didn't even look at her. "They're coming. *Run.*"

Something was coming, all right. Morley stumbled away, moving at a fraction of normal vampire speed, and Claire heard the distant sound of running feet, voices calling to one another, and excited whoops.

In a few more seconds, she saw them—six young men, most no older than Shane. Two wore TPU jackets. They were all drunk, mean, and looking for trouble, and they all were armed—baseball bats, tire irons, stakes. They slowed when they caught sight of Claire and Shane, and changed course to come toward them.

"Hey!" one of them yelled. "You seen an old dude running through here?"

"Why? What did he do, steal your purse?" Shane shot back. Claire dug her fingernails into his arm in warning, but he wasn't paying attention. "Jesus, you idiots, what do you think you're doing?"

"Cleaning up the streets," another one said, and twirled his bat as if he really knew how to use it. "Somebody's gotta. The cops don't do it."

"We heard that one killed a kid," said the first man—the least drunk, as far as Claire could tell, and, also, maybe the meanest. She didn't like the way he was watching Shane, and her. "Drained her dry, right on the playground. We don't let that pass, man. He has to pay."

"You have any proof?"

"Screw your proof. These monsters have been running around killing for a hundred years. We catch them, we teach them a lesson they don't forget." He laughed, dug in his pocket, and pulled out something. He tossed it on the ground in front of Shane's feet. Claire couldn't tell what the scattered pieces were at first, and then she knew.

Teeth: vampire fangs, pulled out at the root.

Shane said, "Knock yourself out, man. He went that way." He nodded in a direction Morley hadn't gone. "Keep up the good work."

"It's Collins, right? Your dad was one hell of a guy. He stood up for us."

Shane's father had been an abusive asshole who didn't care about anyone, as far as Claire had been able to tell; he certainly hadn't cared about Shane. The idea that Frank Collins was becoming the underground hero of Morganville made Claire want to puke.

"Thanks," Shane said. His voice was neutral, and very steady. "I'm taking my girl home."

"Her? She's one of them. One of the Renfields. Works for the vamps."

"No better than the vamps," another put in.

"I heard she worked for Bishop," said a third, who had a tire iron resting on his shoulder. "Carrying around his death warrants. Like one of those Nazi collaborators."

"You heard wrong," Shane said. "She's my girl. Now back off."

"Let's hear from her," said the leader of the pack, and locked stares with Claire. "So? You working for the vamps?"

Shane sent her a quick, warning glance. Claire took in a deep breath and said, "Absolutely."

"Ah hell," Shane breathed. "Okay, then. *Run.*"

They took off, catching the minimob by surprise; alcohol slowed them down, Claire thought, and an argument broke out behind them over whom they should be chasing, humans or vampires. Shane grabbed Claire's hand and pulled her along, running as if their lives depended on it. The streetlights were all out, and Claire had trouble seeing curbs and cracks in the pavement in the dim starlight.

They made it almost a block before she heard a howl behind them. The pack was following.

"Come on," Shane gasped, and pushed her faster. It was harder for Claire; she was a bookworm, not a runner, and besides, her legs were about six inches shorter than his. "Come on, Claire! Don't slow down!"

Her lungs were already on fire. *Need to exercise more*, she thought crazily. *Note to self: practice wind sprints.*

Something hit her in the back, and Claire lost her balance and hit the pavement hard. Shane yelled, stopped, and turned to cover her. In seconds, the pack of guys was on them, and Claire saw Shane taking a bat away from one guy and using it to smack the tire iron away from another attacker.

A shadow loomed over her, and she looked up to see a guy who looked about ten feet tall raise a baseball bat over his head, aiming straight for hers.

Claire grabbed him around the knees and yanked, hard. He yelled in surprise as his legs folded, and he fell backward. The bat hit the ground with a clatter, and Claire picked it up as she climbed to her feet. Shane was swinging with precision, taking out weapons and maybe breaking an arm here and there if he had to. All she had to do was stand there and look threatening.

It was over in a few seconds. Something turned for the pack, and they'd had enough. Claire stood there shaking, bat still cocked in the ready position, as the last guy scrambled up off the pavement and lurched away.

Shane dropped his bat and put both hands on her shoulders. "Claire? Look at me. Are you all right? Anybody hit you?"

"No." She felt shaky, and she had some skinned knees and palms from her fall, but that was all. "My God. They were going to kill us. *Humans* were going to kill us. Because of me."

"It wouldn't have mattered," Shane told her, and kissed her forehead with burning hot lips. "They were going to go after anybody they came across. The vampire thing is just an excuse. God, Claire. Good job."

"All I did was hold the bat."

"You held it like you meant it." He put his arm around her and picked up both bats, slinging them over his left shoulder. "Let's get home."

When they got home, after getting the third degree from Michael, then Eve, they had to answer to the Founder. Not by choice; Claire was all for making a quick phone call to the police and letting it go through channels, but Michael thought Amelie might want to ask more questions.

He must have been right, because as soon as he hung up the phone, a wave of sensation swept through the house—like a gust of wind, only psychic. Claire actually felt the locks she'd put on the portals snap, and the connection open.

Amelie was coming in person.

Michael realized it, too—he and Claire seemed to be more connected to the house than Shane and Eve, generally. "That was fast," he said. "I guess we'd better go up."

"Up where?" Shane asked, frowning.

"Amelie," Claire sighed. "I was hoping for a hot bath, too."

The four of them, in the spirit of solidarity, trudged upstairs to the hidden room. The Tiffany lamps—minus that one pole lamp casualty—were blazing, filling the walls with color and light, but somehow none of it fell on Amelie, who looked pale as bone and just as hard. She was wearing pure, cold white, and her lips seemed almost blue. Her eyes looked more silver than gray, but maybe that was because of the metallic shine of her shirt under the tailored jacket.

Claire wondered why she bothered with the meticulous dressing, when Amelie rarely seemed to leave her home these days; she supposed that growing up as royalty in the distant past had made looking perfect a habit she couldn't seem to shake.

Amelie received the news of the gangs beating up on her vampires without much shock, Claire thought; she sat there looking cool and calm, hands folded, and listened to Shane and Claire's experience without any flicker of expression. There was *something* in her face when Claire described the handful of pulled vampire fangs that she'd seen, but what it was, Claire couldn't guess. Disgust, maybe, or pain. "Is that all?" Amelie asked. She sounded way too distant. "What of Morley? Did you see where he went?"

"We don't know," Claire said. "He looked—hurt. A lot hurt, maybe."

"I was afraid of this," Amelie said, and got up to pace the floor.

"Afraid of what?" Michael asked. He was leaning against the wall with his arms folded, looking very serious. "Losing control?"

Amelie stopped to frown at the broken pole lamp, trailing pale fingers over the neat slice through the metal. "Afraid that humans might lose their fear of reprisals if I offered too much leniency," she said. "The rules of Morganville existed for a reason. They were meant to protect the strong few from the fragile many. Even a giant may be destroyed by the stings of insects, if there are enough of them."

"That's not what your rules did," Shane said. "They just made it easier for vampires to kill us without letting humans hit them back."

Amelie sent him a cool glance, but didn't otherwise react. "I've received reports of other incidents, less serious than this. It seems these gangs of thugs are growing bolder, and that must be stopped."

"They said something about Morley killing a kid," Shane said. "Anything to that?"

"I doubt it." Amelie met his eyes for a few seconds, then continued to pace. "I've had no reports of children being victimized. As you know, that is strictly against all our laws, human or vampire. I can't say it never happens, but it happens in human society, as well. Yes?"

"Maybe, but why did they take it out on Morley?"

She shrugged. "Morley is an easy target, like all the vampires who choose not to declare an allegiance. They are powerful in themselves, but vulnerable. Morley's lived rough and alone for some time. It's not surprising that humans are taking vengeance on those easiest to hunt. In other towns, they target the homeless, as well, do they not?"

"Aren't you going to do anything about it?" Claire asked.

"There are laws. I assume they will be enforced. Until these thugs are caught and punished, I will caution all vampires to be careful." Amelie smiled slowly. "And I will allow them latitude in matters of self-defense, of course. That should put a stop to things quickly."

Claire wasn't so sure of that. First, Morley and his vamps had gotten all pushy with Amelie, and then Oliver had seemed about to bolt from her camp and set up as a pretender to the throne. Now, there were humans roaming around looking for trouble, too. And Amelie just seemed . . . disconnected.

It seemed that, as much as they'd tried to pull Morganville together, it was unraveling all around them.

"I believe I have heard enough," Amelie said. "You may go. All of you."

She kept on pacing, as if she didn't intend to leave. Claire hung back, watching her, as the others descended the stairs, and finally said, "Are you okay?"

Amelie stopped, but didn't look at her. "Of course," she said. "I am—troubled, but otherwise fine. Why do you ask?"

Because you tried to kill yourself two nights ago? Claire didn't think it would be smart to bring that up. "Just—if you need anything . . ."

Amelie did look at her this time, and there was something warm and almost human in her expression. "Thank you." Amelie's personal winter closed in again, leaving her face still and cold. "There's nothing you can do, Claire. Nothing any of you can do. Now go."

That last thing wasn't a request, and Claire took it for dismissal. Shane was waiting at the bottom of the stairs, looking up with a worried not-quite-frown that smoothed away in relief when he saw her coming to join him. "Don't do that," he said.

"Do what?"

"There's something off about her right now. Don't you see that? Don't try to help. Just walk away."

Claire tapped the gold bracelet on her wrist. "Yeah, that'll work."

He pulled her out of the stairwell and shut the hidden door. Michael and Eve were already going downstairs, hand in hand. "It's getting late," he said. "You going or staying?"

"Does it have to be one or the other? Maybe I stay for an hour, then go?"

"Works for me," he said, and took her hand. "I've got a surprise for you."

The surprise was that he'd cleaned his room. Not just randomly picked up a few things, but really *cleaned* it—everything put away, bed made, everything. Unless . . . "What did you trade with Eve?"

He looked wounded and way too innocent. "What do you mean?"

"Oh, come *on.* You totally traded with Eve to clean your room for you."

He sighed. "She needed some cash for something, so yeah. But it's good, right? You're impressed I thought of it?"

Claire suppressed a laugh. "Yes, I'm impressed that a boy thought about spending money on a clean room."

"Worth it, as long as you're impressed." He flopped on the bed, leaving space for her, and she curled up next to him in the circle of his arm. Her head rested on his chest, and she listened to the strong, steady beat of his heart. *I wonder if Eve misses that,* Claire suddenly wondered. *I wonder if she forgets, and then . . .*

"Hey," Shane said, and tickled her. She squirmed. "No thinking. This is the no-thinking zone."

"I can't help it."

"Guess I'll have to distract you, then."

She was going to say, *Yes, please,* but he was already kissing her, and his big hands slid around her waist, and all she could think was *yes* as her blood surged faster, hotter, and stronger.

It was more like two hours before she could even stand to think about going home. The temptation to stay here, curled in Shane's arms forever, was almost overwhelming, but she knew she had to keep her promises.

Shane knew it, too, and as he gently combed the hair back from her face with his fingers, he sighed and kissed her forehead. "You've got to go," he said. "Otherwise, it's parents with pitchforks and torches."

"Sorry."

"Hey, me, too. I'll get the keys." He slid out of bed, and she watched the light gleam off his skin as he picked up his T-shirt and pulled it on. It was all she could do not to reach out and pull it off again. "And you really need to get dressed, because if you keep looking at me like that, we're not going anywhere."

Claire retrieved her pants and shirt and put them on, and caught sight of herself in the mirror—for once, in Shane's room, not obscured by random piles of stuff. She looked . . . different. Adult. Flushed and happy and alive, and not really geeky at all.

He makes me better, she thought, but she didn't say it, because she was afraid he'd think that was weird.

Shane borrowed Eve's car to run her back to her parents' house—her home?—and by midnight she was at her bedroom window watching the big, black sedan pull away from the curb and accelerate away into the night.

Mom knocked on the door. Claire could tell her parents apart by their knocks. "Come in!"

When her mom didn't say anything, Claire turned to look at her. She looked tired, and worried, and Claire wondered if she was getting enough sleep. Probably not.

"I just wanted to tell you that I left you a plate in the fridge if you're hungry," Mom said. "Did you have a good day?"

Claire had no idea how to answer that in a way that wouldn't sound completely insane, and finally settled for, "It was okay." She hoped the scarf she'd wrapped around her throat covered up the bruises, which were turning rich sunset colors.

Mom knew that was a nonanswer, but she just nodded. "As long as you're being safe." Which was less about the vampires than about Shane. Claire rolled her eyes.

"Mom."

"I'm serious."

"I *know*."

"Then stop looking like I'm being an idiot. I'm worried about you getting hurt. I don't doubt Shane means well, but you're just so—" Mom looked for another word, but settled for the obvious one. "So young."

"Not as young as I was when this conversation started."

"Claire."

"Sorry." She yawned. "Tired."

Mom hugged her, kissed her cheek, and said, "Then get some rest. I'll let you sleep in."

The next day Claire missed her first class, because Mom was true to her word and the alarm clock failed in its duty, or at least Claire turned it off before she really woke up. She finally got up around ten o'clock, feeling happy and humming with energy. It might have been the sleep, but Claire knew it wasn't.

She was running on pure Shane sunlight.

Walking to the campus was a delight—the sun was out, warming up the streets and waking a soft breeze that smelled like new grass. The trees were all full of new green leaves, and in the gardens flowers were blooming.

Claire was in such a good mood that when she saw

Kim, armed with a video camera, she didn't actually wince.

Much.

Kim wasn't paying attention to her, which wasn't much of a change; she was focused on a guy in a TPU jacket tossing a football, who laughed at her jokes as she filmed. Kim circled around him, waved, and kept filming as she approached a group of girls camped out on the lawn under a spreading live oak tree. More laughter, and smiles all around.

Am I really the only one who doesn't like her?

Apparently.

Kim noticed her about the same time that Claire's phone rang. She turned her back on Kim—and the camera—and answered without checking the screen, because she was rattled. "Hello?"

"You *bitch*." It was Monica's voice. "Where are you?"

"Excuse me?"

"Are you on campus?"

Claire blinked and stepped out of the way of a crowd of students heading out from the English Building. "Uh, no. And why exactly am I a bitch, again?"

"I got that wrong. You are a *lying* bitch. I can hear the bells!" Monica meant the school's carillon, the tower bells that chimed out a silvery melody at the hour change. For some weird reason, it was playing Christmas music. Maybe somebody had forgotten to change over—or just really liked "O Holy Night." "Where are you—never mind, I see you. Stay right there."

Monica hung up. Claire looked around and saw that Kim was filming her—and Monica was charging down the steps of the English Building, heading her way and trailed by an entourage like a comet's tail. It wasn't just Gina and Jennifer this time; she'd picked up two strange girls wearing designer spring dresses and cute shoes, and a couple of big football-type guys—bland and handsome and not too smart, just the way Monica liked them.

Claire considered running, but not if Kim was planning on gleefully filming the whole thing. She could live with the shame. She just didn't think she could live with the reruns on YouTube.

Monica had gone with a floral pattern minidress, and it looked great on her; she hadn't let her tan go during the winter, and her skin looked healthy and glowy and toned. She strode up to Claire and came to a halt a couple of feet away, surrounded by her fashion army.

It was like being menaced by a gang of Barbie and Ken dolls.

"You," Monica said, and leveled an accusatory, perfectly manicured finger at her. Claire focused on the hot pink nail, then past it to Monica's face.

"Yes?"

"Come here."

And before Claire could even think about protesting, Monica had her wrapped up in a hug.

A hug.

With Monica.

Claire got control of herself, at least enough to grab Monica by the arms and push her back to a safe distance. "What the hell?"

"Bitch, you are the *best*. Seriously, I cannot believe it!"

Monica was . . . excited. Happy. Not about to beat her up.

Wow. "Don't take this the wrong way, but what are you on?"

Monica laughed, reached into her messenger bag, and pulled out a stapled two-page paper. It was an economics test.

And it had, written in the corner in red, A.

"That's what I'm on," she said. "Do you know how long it's been since I got an A? Like, ever? My brother is going to fall over."

Claire handed the paper back. "Congratulations."

"Thanks." Monica's good mood faded, replaced by her more-normal bitch face. "I guess I got my money's worth, anyway."

For some reason, Claire thought about Shane paying Eve to clean his room. "There's a lot of that going around, trust me. Okay then. We're good?"

"For now," Monica said. "Stay available. I've got other classes I suck at."

Claire bit her tongue before she could say, *I don't doubt it*, and watched Monica and her swirl of hangers-on sweep away, laughing and talking as if they were in their own private shampoo commercial.

She'd almost forgotten about Kim, and when she caught sight of the cold gleam of the camera lens out of the corner of her eye she turned and said, "Cut it out, will you?"

"Not a chance," Kim said cheerfully, camera still running. "Not until I run out of tape."

"It's digital!"

"That's the point. Hey, so, tell me about you and Monica. Secret love affair? Mortal enemies? Are you each other's evil twins? Come on, you can tell me; I won't tell anybody!"

"Except everybody on Facebook?"

"Well, obviously, yeah. Come on, you're wasting my minutes. Talk!"

"I have two words for you," Claire said, "and the second one is *off*. Fill in the blank."

Kim lowered the camera and switched it off, shaking her dark hair out of her face. "Wow. Who got up on the grumpy side of breakfast?"

"I don't like being on camera."

"Nobody does. That's the whole point. I want to catch people as they really are. That guy, for instance, Mr. Football Dude? He's a douche. I got him to talk long enough that you could actually *see* he was a douche. It's fun. You should try it."

"No thanks." Claire didn't think the powers that be in Morganville would take especially well to guerrilla film-making, and she wondered if anybody had told Oliver. He didn't seem to like Kim's little projects much.

Maybe it was time for a mocha.

"Hey," Kim said, as Claire started to walk on. "About Shane."

That pulled her to a full stop. "What about him?"

"I just wanted to know—so, are you guys serious or something?"

"Yeah, we're serious." Claire said it flatly, trying not to imagine what Shane might say to the same question. He didn't like to commit. He *was* committed; he just didn't like to go on the record. "You been filming any-where else?"

"Sure, all over," Kim said. "Why, you want to see?"

"No. Just curious. What are you planning to do with it?"

"You've seen *Borat*? Yeah, kind of like that—sort of a mockumentary." Kim gave a one-shoulder shrug, fo-cused on whatever was playing on the tiny screen of her camcorder. "Only with vampires."

"You're filming the vampires."

"Well, not officially. It's a hobby."

It was a dangerous hobby, but Claire guessed Kim knew that. "Just don't film me, okay?"

"Seriously? I'll make you a star!"

"I don't want to be a star."

As she walked away, Kim said plaintively, "But *every-body* wants to be a star!"

8

The rest of the day passed quietly enough. Claire dropped in to see Eve at the coffee shop, but all Eve could talk about was the play, how cool it all was, how she was so going to rock as Blanche DuBois, and how she had this plan to wear a black skull-patterned slip instead of the white one that the costume people wanted . . . and when she wasn't enthusing about the play, she was all about Kim. Kim, Kim, Kim.

"Cool necklace," Claire said, out of desperation, and pointed at the one around Eve's neck. It *was* cool—kind of a tribal dragon thing, full of angles and sinister curves. Eve touched it with her fingertips and smiled.

"Yeah," she said. "Michael got it for me. Not bad, right?"

"Not bad at all. Hey, did you clean Shane's room?"

"Actually? I just vacuumed and dusted. He picked it up himself. Why, did he tell you it was all me? Boys lie."

"About cleaning?"

Eve ate a bite of blueberry muffin and swallowed some coffee. "Why not? They think cleaning makes them look non-manly. Eek, sorry Claire Bear, gotta motor. Boss-man, he no like breaks. See you later?"

"Sure." Claire slid out of her seat and picked up her book bag. "See you at home."

"Oh, you should totally swing by rehearsal! Three o'clock at the auditorium. You know where it is?"

Claire knew, although she'd never been there—it was kind of a town civic center, and it was off Founder's Square—aka, Vamptown. Like most humans in Morganville, she'd never been really interested in traveling there at night.

Three in the afternoon, though . . . that sounded reasonable. "I'll try," Claire said. "So—I know you were worried about Oliver. Is that going okay, having him in the play?"

"Oh, actually, yeah. He's not bad! I almost believe he isn't a controlling jerk. Most of the time." Eve looked over her shoulder, made a scared face when the boss beckoned her, and waved good-bye.

Claire decided she couldn't put it off any longer, and pulled out her cell phone. She'd written and uploaded a program that allowed her phone to track and display available portals; according to the theory she'd been reading up on in Myrnin's lab recently, it wasn't such a good thing for humans to force a portal open, the way vampires could without too much effort. Over time, things *happened*—to the human. And Claire decided she liked her normal arrangement of eyes, ears, and nose—she liked Picasso okay, but she didn't want to become one of his paintings.

So she looked for a portal that was open—open meant that it was at a low level of availability, not active. The one open at the university just now was in the Administration Building.

She headed over there, blending in with all the other students, and as usual, the part of the Administration Building where the portal was located was empty. The chain-smoking dragon lady secretary at the front desk nodded her in without argument; apparently there'd been some kind of memo since Claire had begun doing this kind of thing—a convenient development.

Moving through the portal was a little like taking a microsecond-long ice bath; it felt like every cell in her body received a shock, woke up, screamed, and then went immediately back to normal. Not exactly pleasant, but ... memorable. It didn't usually feel that way, and Claire felt some distinct uneasiness. If the portal system went out of balance ...

"Myrnin?" She stepped away from the portal door of the lab, shoving aside a box of books he'd left lying around, probably for her to shelve. No sign of him here just now. The lab still looked clean and moderately organized, which wasn't like Myrnin at the best of times; she wondered if he'd gotten some kind of maid service. Who cleaned mad scientist lairs, anyway? The same people who did villain lairs and bat caves?

No Myrnin, but he'd left her a note, written in his spiky antique hand, that asked her to—wait for it—sort the box of books he'd left to trip her up. And to feed Bob the spider. Ugh. Why was she even surprised? Claire began unpacking, sorting, and shelving the books, which was surprisingly fun, in the hopes that the universe would end before she had to actually feed a *spider*.

She was in the middle of doing that when Ada's two-dimensional ghost formed in front of her. Claire's heart rate doubled, and she wondered if she ought to just make a dash for the portal ... but Ada made no threatening moves. In fact, Ada was being polite—she rang Claire's cell phone. She didn't actually have to do that before using the speaker. It was her version of knocking.

Claire swallowed an acidic mouthful of fear, and peered at the fading spine of the heavy book in her hand. German. She wasn't sure what it said. "Do you know German?"

Ada raised her chin and gave her a haughty look, smoothing down the front of her gray scale gown. "Of course," she said. "It's hardly a vanishing tongue."

I have to feed spiders and *put up with a bitchy, homi-*

cidal computer. My job really does suck. Claire didn't say that out loud, and as far as she knew, Ada couldn't read minds. Yet. "Good. Can you tell me what this means?" She held out the book, spine toward Ada. The ghost leaned forward.

"*Alchemical Experiments of the Great Magister Kleiss,*" she read, and the tinny voice sounded a little sad as it vibrated from Claire's cell phone speaker. "Myrnin already has a copy. I remember buying it for him in a little market outside Frankfurt."

Claire put it aside. Ada seemed to be in an odd mood—fragile, confrontational, and oddly nostalgic. "You tried to kill me," Claire said. "You lied to me, and tried to get me to step through the portal to get eaten. Why?"

A very odd expression fluttered over Ada's smooth, not-quite-human face. If Claire hadn't known better, she'd think it was . . . uncertainty? "I did not," she said. "You are mistaken."

"It's not the kind of thing you get wrong," Claire said. "I've got a pole lamp that got cut in half when I had to slam the portal closed for proof. Remember now?"

Ada just—shut down. Not literally: her ghost still hung there in the air, bobbing ever so slightly as if gravity were just a bothersome suggestion, not the law. A flicker like static ran through her image, then another one.

Then she smiled. "You should see a doctor," she said. "I believe you're ill, human."

"You don't remember." Claire heard the flat disbelief in her voice, but what she really was feeling was . . . fear. Pure, cold fear. Ada could lie—she had before—but this didn't *feel* like deception.

It felt like something was very, very wrong. And if something was wrong with Ada, it was wrong with Morganville.

"There's nothing to remember," Ada said coolly. "Do

you wish more translation done, or may I get on with my duties now?"

"No, I'm good. Where's Myrnin?"

Ada paused in the act of turning her back—stopping edge-on, almost disappearing from Claire's perspective—and slowly rotated in place. Her dark eyes looked like burned holes in her pale face.

"That's none of your business," she said.

"What?"

"Myrnin is mine. And you can't have him. I'll kill you first!"

And then she just—vanished.

Claire gaped at the space where she'd been, half expecting her to show up again, but Ada stayed gone. Claire replaced the book she was holding back on the worktable, and walked around toward the rear of the lab. The thick Persian carpet had been rolled back there, and the trapdoor Myrnin had installed—a clever job of painting the door to match the stone floor—was closed. Claire gritted her teeth and clicked the release, which was a book on frogs in the nearby bookcase. The lock released with a snap, and Claire hauled the trap to the catch position.

Myrnin never kept any lights on down there, in the basement/cave where Ada really lived. Claire grabbed a flashlight, checked the batteries, and then looked down into the darkness. "Myrnin?" she asked. No reply. She heard water dripping in the distance. "Myrnin, where are you?"

Great. This made feeding Bob the spider look like a day at the park.

No way am I going down there alone, she thought, and flipped open her cell phone. Michael answered on the second ring. "Yo," he said. "I'm guessing you don't want to go to a movie, or anything fun like that."

"Why would you say that?"

"Because that would be Shane's job. When you call me, it's usually an emergency."

"Well—okay, fair point. But this isn't. Not an emergency, anyway. I just need—some hand-holding. Can you come to Myrnin's lab?"

Michael's voice turned a lot more serious. "Is this crazy maintenance, or is something really wrong?"

Claire sighed. "I don't know, actually. I just don't want to go down into the dark without a big, strong vampire."

"You mean you can't get down there without my help."

"Well, actually, I can't get *out* without your help, since Ada's not letting me do the portal thing near her. It's still a compliment, right?"

"Except the part where you drag me into potentially deadly trouble? Yes. Stay put. I'll be there in ten minutes."

"Be careful," she said. She had no idea why she did; it wasn't as if Michael had anything much to be scared of, especially in Morganville. But it was something her mother always said, and it made her feel better to express a little concern for her friends.

"No exploring on your own, Dora," he said.

She felt lonely and exposed, even here with all the lights burning brightly, once his voice was gone from the call. She considered calling Shane, but honestly, what good would it do? He'd come running, but he needed his job, and Michael was already on the way.

Ten minutes.

Claire decided to get the Bob thing over with. Bob's terrarium sat on Myrnin's rolltop desk, amid stacks of books and some pens—quills, fountains, and rollerballs. Bob looked bigger than she remembered. And blacker. And hairier. Claire shuddered, looking in at him; all eight of his beady eyes looked back. He stayed very still.

There was a small bottle on the table that contained insects—live ones. Claire made a retching sound and tried not to look too hard; she just opened the top of the terrarium and tipped the contents of the jar into the cage.

Bob leaped on her hand.

Claire shrieked, and the bottle went flying to shatter against the wall. Bob didn't budge when she violently shook her hand, trying to get rid of him; he clung to her like Velcro, and he felt *different*, somehow—heavier. Yes, he was larger. Claire batted at him with her right hand, and his fangs glittered as he lunged for her, skittering up her left arm.

She grabbed a book in her right hand.

Bob leaped from her arm, headed to her face.

She smacked him out of the air with the book, and he landed on his back, all eight legs wriggling in the air. Before she could slam the book down on top of him, Bob flipped himself over and skittered underneath the table.

It was *not* her imagination. Bob was getting bigger. In the space of just a few seconds, he'd gone from the size of a walnut to her palm, and now he was almost as big as the book she'd used to smash him out of the air.

"Ada!" she screamed. "Ada, I need you!"

Her cell phone came on, and gave an unearthly screeching noise . . . and then a soft, ghostly laugh.

Something knocked over a pile of papers at the edge of the table, and Claire saw a long black leg waving in the air. She backed away, fast.

When Bob climbed up on top of the table, he was the size of a small dog. His fangs were clearly visible, and if she'd thought he was ugly at small size, he was terrifying now.

"Hi—Bob—," Claire said. Her voice was shaking, and sounded very small. "Nice Bob. Heel?"

Bob bounced off the table, landed lightly on the floor, and skittered toward her, racing incredibly fast. Claire screamed and ran, knocking over anything she could behind her to slow him down. Not that it did, but when she looked back as she reached the stairs, Bob had stopped chasing her.

He was sitting on a table in the center of the lab, trembling. She could actually see him shaking, as if he were having some kind of a fit . . . and then he rolled over on his back, and his legs curled in, and . . .

And he was dead.

"Bother," Ada said. Claire jumped in reaction, bit back a curse, and saw Ada glide out of a solid wall to her left. Ada's image went right up to Bob's motionless body, leaning over him, and shook her head. "So disappointing. I truly thought he'd be able to sustain the change."

"Change?" Claire swallowed hard. "Ada, what are you doing? What did you do to Bob?"

"Unfortunately, I believe I exploded his organs. So fragile, living things. I forget sometimes."

"You did this. Made him grow."

"It was an experiment." Ada's image slowly revolved toward Claire, and her smile was small and cold and terrifying. "We're both scientists, are we not?"

"You call that *science*?"

"Don't you?" Her hands folded primly at her waist, Ada was the image of one of those schoolteachers from the old days. "All science requires sacrifice. And you didn't even like Bob."

Well, that was true. "Just because I don't like something doesn't mean I want to see it die horribly!"

"Really? I find that . . . not very interesting at all, actually. Sentimentality has no place in science."

Just like that, poof, Ada was pixels and vapor, gone. Claire ventured slowly forward, to where Bob the Giant Spider was curled up on the table. She half expected him to suddenly flip upright in true horror-movie style, but he stayed still.

Claire wasn't falling for it. No way. She backed up to

the steps that led out of the lab, and sat down on the cold stone, wrapping her arms around her for warmth.

Minutes ticked by.

The dead spider didn't move, which meant that either he wasn't faking it, or he was really, really good at it.

"Claire?"

She shrieked and jumped, and Michael, standing about a foot behind her, jumped backward, as well. Being a vampire, he somehow made it look cool. She, not so much. "God, don't *do* that! Warn me!"

"I did!" He sounded wounded. "I said your name."

"Say it from across the room next time."

But Michael wasn't looking at her anymore; he was staring past her, at the dead spider. "What the hell is *that*?"

"Bob," she said. "I'll tell you later. Come on."

"Where?"

"Ada's cave."

Which was why she'd called him, because, of course, there were no stairs. Vampires didn't need them. They could jump twelve feet onto solid stone and not even feel a twinge; Claire figured she was sure to have a broken bone, at the very least. She wasn't a superhero, a magical vampire slayer, or even a particularly coordinated athlete. Michael was her way in—and, hopefully, out.

Of course, having a friend with her going down into the dark, that was a plus, too.

Luckily, Michael didn't seem too bothered at being asked to stand in for a ladder; he looked down into the darkness for a few moments, craning to see every detail of what, to Claire, was pitch-blackness. "Looks clear," he said. "You're sure you want to do this?"

"She won't say where Myrnin is. Well, he's not up here, and the carpet was rolled back. He must have gone down there."

"And there's a reason why we can't just wait for him to come back?"

"Yeah. Ada's tried to kill me twice now, and who knows what she's tried to do to him. There's something wrong with her, Michael."

"Then maybe we should call somebody for help."

Claire laughed a little wildly. "Like who, Amelie? You saw her at the cemetery. You really think we should rely on her right now?"

Whether Claire had a point or not, Michael must have realized that debating wasn't getting anything done. He shrugged and said, "Fine. If you get me killed, I'm haunting you."

"Wouldn't be the first time."

He winked at her, and stepped off the edge, dropping soundlessly into the dark. Claire rushed forward, grabbing up the flashlight along the way, and shone its glow down into the trapdoor. A dozen feet below, Michael's pale face looked up. His blue eyes looked supernaturally bright as his pupils contracted in the glare.

"Right," he said. "Jump."

She'd been through this with Myrnin, but it still never felt exactly *comfortable*. Still, it was Michael, and if any vampire was trustworthy . . .

She shut her eyes, took a deep breath, and plummeted, straight into his cool, strong arms. Michael let her slide down, already looking past her into the dark. "There are things down here," he said.

"Vampires."

"Not—sure I'd call them vampires. *Things* is pretty accurate." Michael sounded a little nervous. "They're just—watching us."

"They're sort of guard dogs. Watch them right back, okay?"

"Doing that, yeah. Which way?"

"This way." It was easy to get turned around in the dark, but Claire had a pretty good memory, and there were enough strange shapes in the rocks of the walls that she'd picked some out as signposts. Her flashlight's beam bounced and glittered on granite edges, and pieces of broken glass scattered on the floor. There were some bones. She didn't think these were human, though that was probably wishful thinking.

"Whoa," Michael said, and held her shoulder as the room opened up. She knew what he was seeing—the big cavern where Ada was housed. He'd been here before, but not through the tunnel; it was kind of a shock, the way it opened up into this vast, echoing space.

"Lights," Claire said. "To the left, on the wall."

"I see them. Stay here."

She did, clutching the metal of the Maglite more tightly, until a sudden hum of power accompanied the dazzling arrival of lights overhead. Claire blinked away glare and saw that Ada—the computer, not the flat, generated image she liked to present—was in full-power mode, gears clanking like giant teeth, steam hissing from pipes, liquid bubbling here and there in huge glass retorts.

Myrnin was slumped against the giant keyboard, face-down.

"Oh no," Claire breathed, and raced to his side. Before she could touch him, Michael flashed to her and caught her hand.

"No," he said, and picked up a stray piece of metal from the floor, which he flicked at Myrnin's back, where it landed, electricity arcing, and sizzling. "I can smell the ozone. She's got him wired. If you touch him, it'll kill you."

9

"Is he dead?" Claire's heart was racing, and not just because she'd nearly gotten herself barbecued. . . . Myrnin was just getting better, just becoming himself again. For Ada to do this to him, now . . .

But Michael was shaking his head. "More like he's unconscious. I don't think he's hurt too badly. We just have to break the circuit."

Claire hunkered down, trying to get a look at Myrnin's face; his head was turned to the side, but his black hair had fallen over his eyes, so she couldn't see if they were open or closed. He wasn't moving. "We need something wood or rubber to push him off the metal," she said. "See if you can find something."

And with a snap, the lights went off. Claire's breath went out of her, and she felt her heart accelerate to about two hundred beats a minute when she heard Ada's cell-phone-speaker voice whisper, "I don't think you should do that."

"Michael?"

"Right here. The circuit's still on to the keyboard; I can feel it." His hand touched her shoulder, and even though she flinched, she felt reassured. "Here. Take this."

He handed her something. It took her a second to figure out what it was—a hunk of wood? It felt odd. . . . "Oh God," Claire blurted, "is that a *bone*?"

"Don't ask," Michael said. "It's sharp on one end. Organic, like wood, so it makes a good weapon against vampires. Just don't stab me, okay?"

She wasn't making any promises, really. "Help me with Myrnin." She carefully reversed the bone in her hands to the non-sharp end, and used the flashlight to check that Michael had something nonconductive, as well. He did, and it was more bone. It might have been a rib. She tried not to think about that too much. "You push from that side; I'll push from here. Push hard. We need to knock him completely away from the panel."

Claire's cell phone screamed so loudly that it seemed like the speaker was melting from the force of it; the sound dissolved into high-pitched static, and Claire took a deep breath and put the end of the bone against Myrnin's shoulder. He was wearing a black velvet jacket, and the bone looked very white against it, almost blue in the Maglite beam.

She saw Michael as a shadow in the backwash of the light. "Ready," Michael said.

"Go!"

They pushed. Michael, of course, had vampire strength, so it was over in a flash—Myrnin's body flying backward from the console, crashing on its back in the darkness. A glittering, frustrated arc of blue sparks from the keyboard snapped toward Claire and fell short.

Claire almost dropped the bone as she turned it in her hand so the sharp end was ready to use, then got on one knee next to Myrnin's motionless body. She carefully brushed hair away from his marble-pale face. His eyes were open, and fixed. They looked dry, but as she watched, moisture flooded over them, and he blinked, blinked again, gasped, and came bolt upright. His gaze fixed on Claire's face, and he grabbed her arm in a tight, grinding grip.

"Let go," she said. He didn't. "Myrnin!"

"Hush," he whispered. "I'm thinking."

"Yeah, great—can you do it without breaking my arm?"

"No." He didn't even try to explain that, but just got to his feet while still clamped on to her wrist like a person-sized handcuff. "That hurt."

"You need to shut her down; she just tried to kill you!"

Myrnin's eyes flashed a bloody red. *"You will not tell me what to do!"* He shoved her abruptly at Michael, and the glare was even angrier for him. "What are you doing here?"

"Talk later. Go now," Michael said, and grabbed Claire up in his arms before she could protest. "Those things are coming for us."

Myrnin looked around into darkness that hid whatever it was that scared Michael so much. Claire didn't think she wanted to know; she put her arms around his neck and hung on for dear life as she felt his muscles tense. Things moved past, and she noticed a sense of air pressing against her. *The tunnel*, she thought, because things felt closed in, sounds seemed muffled and strange. "Myrnin?" she called behind them, but got no reply. Then she felt Michael jump, and for a breathless second she was weightless, suspended in midair as the light seemed to rush over her.

Michael landed perfectly just beyond the trapdoor set into the lab's concrete and stone, and quickly spun around, backing away at the same time.

Myrnin seemed to almost levitate up out of the hole in the floor, graceful as a cat. As his coat swirled like black fog, he turned in midair, reached out, and slammed the trapdoor shut.

Then he landed on it, light and perfectly balanced, and leaned over to slam his palm down on a red panel on top. It lit up, and a metallic *clunk* echoed through the lab. Myrnin stepped off the door, stared at it for a second, and then carefully unrolled the carpet and smoothed it back over the entrance to Ada's cave.

Claire let go of Michael and slid to her feet. She was still gripping her sharp-pointed bone weapon, and she didn't really feel inclined to put it down. Not yet. "What just happened?"

"I set the lock," Myrnin said, and tapped a toe on the carpet, in case she'd missed the point. "It's quite clever, you know. Electromagnetic. Keyed to my own handprint."

"Yeah, that's great. Why were you down there in the first place? You know she's not—well."

Myrnin fussily adjusted the lapels of his velvet coat, frowned at his bright blue vest as if he didn't remember wearing it, and shrugged. "Something to do with adjusting her emotional responses. Unfortunately, she was ready for me, it seems. She's quite clever, you know." He seemed almost proud. "Now—was there something you wanted, Claire?"

"A thank-you might be nice."

He blinked. "Whatever for? Oh, that. The electricity was only to keep me immobilized. She'd have had to let me go, eventually."

"Not really. She could have just kept you like that until you starved, right?"

"I can't die. Not like that. I can be made very uncomfortable, and very hungry, and quite a bit mad, but not dead. She'd have to have one of her creatures—cut my head—off. . . ." Myrnin's voice trailed away, and he seemed very distant for a few seconds; then he said, "I see. Yes, you're quite correct. She would have options. But she wouldn't kill me."

"Why not?"

"I think we both know why, Claire."

"You mean, because she loves you? I'm not really seeing it right now."

"Ada needs me as much as I need her," Myrnin snapped, suddenly—and very un-Myrnin-like—offended. "You know nothing about her, or me, and I am ordering

you to stay out of my affairs where they concern Ada."
He suddenly staggered, and had to put out a hand to
steady himself against the nearest lab table. "And fetch
me some blood, Claire."

"Get it yourself." She couldn't believe she'd said it,
but he'd really stung her. "Also, your precious Ada killed
Bob by supersizing him and trying to get him to bite me.
So maybe *you* don't know anything about Ada."

"Get me blood, or I'll have to take what's available,"
Myrnin said softly. He didn't seem dramatic about it,
and it wasn't a threat. He raised his head and looked at
her, and she saw that shine there—lunatic and focused
and very, very scary. "I'm very hungry."

"Claire, go," Michael said, and moved to stand between her and Myrnin. "He's not faking it."

He really wasn't, because Myrnin lunged for her. He
was faster than she or Michael could have expected, and
Michael was off balance and nowhere near the right
place as Myrnin shoved him out of the way and sent him
crashing into the nearest stone wall. . . .

Then he grabbed Claire by her shoulder and a fistful
of hair. He wrenched her head painfully to the side, ex-
posing her neck, and she felt the cool puff of his breath
against her skin, and she knew she had only one move
left.

She touched the tip of the bone stake to his chest,
right over his heart, and said, "I swear to God I'll stake
you and cut your head off if you bite me." Her hands
were shaking, and so was her voice, but she meant it. She
couldn't live in fear of him; it hurt her to see him lose
control like this. There was something shining and good
in Myrnin, but there were times it just drowned in the
darkness. "If I let you do this, you'll never forgive yourself. Now let go, and get yourself a bag of blood."

She could actually feel his fangs pressing dimples
into her skin. And Myrnin himself was trembling now,
a very fine vibration that told her just how much he was

in trouble—well, that and the fact he was about to kill her.

She pressed harder with the stake, and felt the blue satin tapestry vest give way to the point.

She didn't see Michael move, but in only a few breathless seconds he was at her side, carefully putting in her free hand a squishy bag of blood. It was straight out of the refrigeration; he hadn't taken time to warm it, which was probably lifesaving.

"Let go," Claire said.

And Myrnin did, loosening his hands just enough to let her step back. His eyes were wild and desperate, and his fangs stayed down like glittering exclamation points.

Claire held out the blood bag.

After a second's hesitation, Myrnin grabbed it, brought it to his mouth, and bit down so hard, blood squirted over his face, the way a really juicy tomato would.

Claire shuddered. "I'll get you a towel."

She went to the small bathroom—so well hidden, it had taken her forever to find it—and turned on the rusty tap to moisten a towel marked PROPERTY OF MORGANVILLE; it was probably hospital supply, or from a prison. She splashed some water on her face, too, and looked at herself in the mirror for a few seconds. A stranger looked back at her—someone who didn't look that frightened. Someone who had just faced down a vampire intent on feeding.

Someone who could handle that kind of thing, and still be his friend.

The towel was soaked through. Claire squeezed to wring out the excess warm water, then went back to help her boss get cleaned up.

She knew he'd say how sorry he was, and he did—first thing, as she sponged the splatter off his face. *Tomato juice*, she told herself when what she was doing hit home.

It's just tomato juice. You've cleaned up after exploded catsup bottles; this is nothing.

"Claire," Myrnin whispered. She glanced into his face, then away as she tried to scrub the worst of the stain off his vest. He seemed tired, and he was sitting in his big leather wing chair. "It came on me so suddenly. I couldn't—you understand? I never meant it."

"Is this what happened to Ada when she was alive?" Claire asked. There was blood on his long white hands, too. She gave him the warm towel, and he wiped his fingers on it, then found a clean spot and scrubbed his face again, although she'd gotten the blood off already. He held the warm towel there, covering up whatever his expression was doing. When he lowered it, he was completely in control of himself. "Ada and I were complicated," he said. "This situation is nothing like that one. For one thing, Ada was then a vampire."

"Well, things have changed," Claire said. Myrnin meticulously folded the towel and handed it back to her. "You know she's going to kill you? You get it now?"

"I'm not yet prepared to make any such claim." He looked down at his vest and sighed. "Oh dear. That's never coming out."

"The stain?"

"The hole." He continued to stare at the hole her bone stake had made, and said, "You really would have killed me, wouldn't you?"

"I—wish I could tell you it was a bluff. But I would have. I can't bluff with you."

"You're correct. If you do, I'll know, and you'll be dead. I'm a predator. Weakness is . . . seductive." He cleared his throat. "Mutually assured destruction was good enough for the United States and the Soviet Union; I believe it will be good enough for us. I'd have preferred it not to come to that, but it's hardly your fault—" He broke off, because as he looked up, his gaze fell on the motionless corpse lying on the table in the middle of the lab. "Oh dear. What is that?"

"That would be Bob. Remember Bob? That's what Ada did to him."

"Impossible," Myrnin said, and rose out of his chair to stalk to the table and lean over alarmingly close, poking at the spider's body with curious fingers. "No, quite impossible."

"Excuse me? I was here! He grew, just like in a monster movie!"

"Oh, I can see that. Clearly, that isn't impossible. No, what I meant was your identification of him as Bob."

"What?"

"This isn't Bob," Myrnin said.

Claire rolled her eyes. "He came out of Bob's cage."

"Ah, that explains it. I found a companion for Bob. I thought it was likely they'd try to eat each other, but they seemed content enough. So this must have been Edgar. Or possibly Charlotte."

"Edgar," Claire repeated. "Or Charlotte. Right."

Myrnin left the dead spider and went to Bob's container. He rooted around in it for a few seconds, then triumphantly held out his palm toward Claire.

Bob—presumably—sat crouched there, looking as confused and frightened as a spider could.

"So it was only Edgar," Myrnin said. "Not the same thing at all."

"Was Edgar always the size of a *dog*?"

"Oh, of course not, he—oh, I see your point. Regardless of which spider it is, there are some mysteries to be solved." Myrnin carefully nudged Bob off his palm, back into the container, and then rubbed his hands together eagerly. "Yes, there's definitely work to be done. Ada must have made tremendous strides recently in her research, for her to be able to create this kind of effect. I must know how, and what went wrong."

"Myrnin. Ada made a spider grow into a monster and tried to *kill me with it*. This isn't about *how* she did it. It's *why*."

"Why is for other people. I am much more concerned with the method, and I'm surprised, Claire; I thought you would be the same. Well, not surprised, perhaps. Disappointed." He carefully uncurled one of the spider's long legs. Claire shuddered. "I'll need a corkboard. A large one. And some very large pins."

Claire and Michael exchanged a look. He'd been standing there, a fascinated but disgusted observer to all this, and now he just shook his head. "If all he wants is for you to fetch and carry, maybe you should just leave him to it."

"She's my *assistant*; it's her job to fetch and carry," Myrnin snapped, and then looked sorry. "But—perhaps you've done enough for one day."

Claire ticked them off on her fingers. "Survived spider attack. Rescued you. Got you blood. Cleaned up blood leftovers."

"I shall therefore fetch my own corkboard. Claire?"

She turned and looked at him as she and Michael headed for the exit. Myrnin looked back in control again, and except for the bloodstain on his vest, you'd never have known he'd been anything less.

"Thank you," he said softly. "I shall consider what you said. About Ada."

She nodded, and escaped.

Michael, as it turned out, was headed for the rehearsal of the play Eve was in, and Claire belatedly remembered that she'd been invited, too. His car was parked at the end of the alley, on the cul-de-sac, and he had an umbrella with him to block the sun. It looked kind of funny, but at least it was a giant golf umbrella, very manly. It had a duck carved into the handle.

Michael even opened the passenger door for her, like a

gentleman, but instead of getting in, she reached for the umbrella. "You're the one who combusts," she said. "You get in first." He gave her a funny look as she walked him to the driver's side, and shaded him as he sat. "What?"

"I was thinking how different you are," he said. "You really stood up to Myrnin in there. I'm not sure a lot of vampires could have done that. Including me."

"I'm not different. I'm the same Claire as ever." She grinned, though. "Okay, fewer bruises than when you first met me."

He smiled and closed the car door; she folded the umbrella and got in on the shotgun side. She was careful to open the door only enough to get in; the angle of the sun was cutting uncomfortably close to reaching Michael's side of the car. Inside, the tinting cut the light almost completely. It was like being in a cave, again, only she hoped this one didn't house giant mutated spiders and—what had Michael called them? *Things*.

"Some people come to Morganville and collapse," Michael said as he put the car in motion. "I've seen it a dozen times. But there are a few who come here and just—bloom. You're one of those."

Claire didn't feel especially bloomy. "So you're saying I thrive on chaos."

"No. I'm saying you thrive on challenge. But do me a favor, okay?"

"Considering you came running and jumped into a cave to help me out? Yes."

He shot her a smile so sweet it melted her heart. "Don't ever let him get that close to you again. I like Myrnin, but he can't be trusted. You know that."

"I know." She took his hand and squeezed it. "Thanks."

"No problem. You die, I have to call your parents and explain why. I really don't want to do that. I've already got the whole vampire thing against me."

That took up the entirety of the short drive to the rehearsal hall, which of course had underground park-

ing, being in the vampire part of town. It also had security, Claire was interested to note—a vampire on duty
in a blacked-out security booth whom she thought she
remembered as being from Amelie's personal security
detail. Hard to tell when they all wore dark suits and
looked like the Secret Service, only with fangs. Michael
showed ID and got a pass to put in his windshield, and
within five minutes, they were heading up a sweeping
flight of stairs into the Civic Center's main auditorium.

There they found the director having a total YouTube
moment.

"What do you mean, *not here*?" he bellowed, and
slammed a clipboard to the stage floor. He had an
accent—German, maybe—and he was a neat little man,
older, with thinning gray hair and a very sharp face.
"How can she not be here? Is she not in this play? Who
is responsible for the call sheet?"

One of the other people standing in a group around
the director onstage waved her hand. She had a clipboard, a microphone headset, and a tense, worried expression. Claire didn't recognize her. "Sir, I tried calling
her cell phone six times. It went to voice mail."

"You are the assistant director! Find her! I don't want
to hear about this voice mail nonsense!" He dismissed
her with a flip of his hand and glared at the rest of the
group. "Well? We must shift the schedule, then, until she
gets here, yes? Script!"

He held out his hand; some quick thinker slapped a
bundle of paper into his hand. He flipped pages. "No, no,
no—ah! Yes, we will do that. Is our Stanley here?"

A big, tattooed guy shouldered through the crowd.
"Here," he said. That, Claire guessed, was Rad, the one
Eve and Kim were going gaga over. He looked—big.
And tough. She didn't see the appeal; for one thing, he
wasn't anything like Shane, who was almost as big, and
probably just as tough. Shane wore it like part of his
body. This guy made a production out of it.

"Good, we'll do the bar scene. We have Mitch? Yes? And all the others?"

Claire stopped listening and glanced at Michael. "Where's Eve? They're missing a *her.*"

"I don't know." He looked at the crowd of people rushing around the stage, resetting the scenery, going over lines, arguing with one another. "I don't see her anywhere."

"You don't think—"

Michael was already walking down the aisle, heading for the stage.

"I guess you do think." Claire hurried after him.

Michael put himself directly in front of the frazzled-looking assistant director, who had a cell phone to one ear, and a finger jammed in the other. She turned a shoulder toward him, clearly indicating she was busy, but he grabbed it and swung her around to face him. Her eyes widened in shock. Michael took the phone from her hand and checked the number. "It's not Eve's," he told Claire, and she saw the intense relief that flooded over his face. "Sorry, Heather."

"It's okay, it's still voice mail." Heather, the assistant director, looked even more worried. She was biting her lip, gnawing on it actually, and darting her eyes toward the livid director, who was stomping around the stage throwing pages of the script to the floor. "Eve's in the dressing room. Man, I am so *fired.*"

Michael zipped off, ruffling their hair with the speed of his passage, leaving Claire standing with Heather. After a hesitation, she stuck out her hand. "Hi," she said. "Claire Danvers."

"Oh, that's you? Funny. I thought you'd be—"

"Taller?"

"Older."

"So who's missing?"

Heather held up a finger to silence her, tapped the device strapped to her belt, and spoke into her headset mike. "What's the problem? Well, tell him that the director wants it that way, so just do it, okay? I don't care if it looks good. And quit complaining." She clicked it to OFF and wiped sweat from her forehead. "I don't know what's worse, having a crew who's a bunch of newbies, or having a crew who's been doing this kind of thing since they still used gas in footlights."

Claire blinked. "You've got vampires on the crew."

"Of course. Also in the cast, and of course, Mein Herr, there." Heather jerked her chin at the director, who was lecturing some poor sap trying to position a potted plant. "He's kind of a perfectionist. He imported the costumes from vintage shops. You tell me, who worries about authentic fabrics when you've just cast two Goth girls as the leads?"

Heather wasn't so much talking to her as at her, Claire decided, so she just shrugged. "So, who's missing?"

"Oh. Our second female lead. Kimberlie Magness."

Kim. Claire felt a slow roll of irritation. "Does she usually show up on time?" Because that would be a surprise.

Heather raised her eyebrows. "In this production, *everybody* shows up on time. According to Mein Herr, to be early is to be on time, and to be on time is to be late. She's never been late."

Still. *Kim.* Probably nothing at all.

"Where is my Stella?" the director bellowed suddenly, and the sound bounced around the stage and also out of Heather's earpiece. She winced and turned down the volume. "Stella!" He drew it out, Brando-style.

And in the wings of the stage, Eve stepped out from behind the curtains, tightly holding Michael's hand. She was dressed in tight black jeans, a black baby-doll shirt with a pentagram on it, and lots of chains and spikes as accessories.

From the director's sudden silence, and Heather's intake of breath, Claire figured that wasn't what Eve was supposed to be wearing. "Oh no," Heather whispered. "This isn't happening."

"What?"

"He insists on rehearsal in costume. Something about getting inside the characters. She's supposed to be in her slip."

The director stomped to Eve, stopping inches away from her. He looked her up and down, and said coldly, "What do you think you are doing?"

"I have to go," she said. Her knuckles were white where she gripped Michael's hand, but she stared the director right in the eyes. "I'm sorry, but I have to."

"No one leaves my rehearsals except in a body bag," he said. "Is that how you'd prefer it?"

"Is that really how *you* want this to go?" Michael asked quietly. "Because somebody could leave in a body bag, but it won't be her."

The director showed teeth in a grimace—it actually looked painful for him to smile. "Are you threatening me, boy?"

"Yes," Michael said, completely still. "I know I'm new at this. I know I'm not a thousand years old with a pile of bodies behind me. But I'm telling you that she has to go, and you're going to let her."

"Or?"

Michael's eyes took on a shine—not red, but almost white. It was eerie. "Let's not find out. You can spare her for the day."

The director hissed, very softly, and held the stare for so long, Claire thought things were about to go very, very wrong . . . and then a mild-looking man in a retro bowling shirt stepped up and said, "Is there a problem? Because I am responsible for these two in Amelie's absence."

And Claire blinked, and realized it was Oliver. Not really Oliver, because he looked . . . different—not just the clothes, but his whole body language. She'd seen him do that before, but not quite this dramatically. His accent was different, too—more of a flat Midwest kind of sound, nothing exotic about it at all.

The director threw him a look, then blinked and seemed to reconsider his position. "I suppose not," he finally said. "I can't have this kind of disruption, you know. This is serious business."

"I know," Oliver said. "But a day won't matter. Let the girl go."

"We're going to find Kim," Eve said. "So really, we're still on company business, right?"

The director's face tensed again, on the verge of an outburst, but he swallowed his words and finally said, "You may tell Miss Magness that she may have *one* rehearsal as a grace period. If she is late one second to any other time I call, she will be *mine*." He didn't mean fired. He meant lunch.

Claire swallowed. Heather didn't seem surprised. She made a note on her clipboard, shook her head, and then cocked her head again as a burst of words came out of her headphone. "Dammit," she sighed. "Are you kidding me? Great. No, I don't care how you do it; just make it happen." She clicked off and looked at Claire. "Wish me luck."

"Um, luck?"

Heather mounted the stairs to the stage and approached the director to whisper something to him. He shouted in fury and stomped away, waving his arms.

Michael and Eve took the chance to escape down to where Claire waited.

Oliver followed them.

"Nice shirt," Claire said, straight-faced.

He glanced down at it, dismissed it, and said, "Now tell me what's going on. Immediately."

"Kim's missing," Eve said. "I tried to find her before the rehearsal; we were supposed to get together— anyway, she didn't show. I was really worried. I was almost late, and I couldn't find her. She's not answering her phone, either."

"Kim," Oliver said. "Valerie owns her contract. Her unreliability is very much Valerie's problem." He didn't sound overly bothered about it. Claire guessed Kim hadn't made friends there, either.

"We need you to call the police. Tell them to look for her."

"No."

"No?"

"Kim has a Protector, who is responsible for her," he repeated. "I will not order town resources to be spent chasing down someone who is, in all likelihood, a victim of her own folly in one way or another."

"Wait a minute. According to the Morganville rules, she's got rights," Claire said. "Whether she's got a vampire Protector or not, she's still a resident. You can't just abandon her!"

"In fact, I can," Oliver said. "I am neither required to help nor harm. Kim Magness is no concern of mine, or any other vampire except Valerie, whom I will inform in due course. If you wish to call Chief Moses and explain the situation, you are free to do so. She and the mayor have jurisdiction over the humans. But I sincerely doubt that a human well known to be unstable, who's been missing only a few hours, will be a top priority." He dismissed the whole thing, and walked away, back up the steps. By the time he'd reached the stage, he was back in his meek, mild persona.

That was just *weird.*

"Son of a bitch," Eve hissed through clenched teeth.

"Come on, we don't need him," Michael said. "Where first?"

Eve took a deep breath. "I guess her apartment." She cast an almost apologetic look at Claire. "I'm sorry. I know you guys don't exactly, ah, click, but—"

"I'll help," Claire said. Not because she cared so much

about Kim, but because she cared about Eve. Eve gave her a quick hug. "Want me to call Shane?"

"Would you?" Eve was making puppy-dog eyes now, really pitiful. "Any help we can get—I'm really worried, Claire. This isn't like Kim. It really isn't."

Claire nodded, took out her phone, and dialed Shane's number. He didn't seem to need a lot of encouragement to yell to his boss that he had to go, family emergency. Claire told him they'd swing by to pick him up.

By the time the call was over, they were heading down into the darkened parking garage again. "I can't believe I did that," Eve said. "I just totally blew my shot at the play, forever. He's going to replace me. I'll never get a part in anything, ever again. My life is over."

"Blame Kim," Claire said. "You're a good friend."

Eve looked miserable anyway. "Not good enough, or she'd be here, right?"

"So not your fault."

Eve raised her eyebrows. "What if it were me missing? Wouldn't you guys feel guilty, somehow?"

That shut Claire up, because she would, and she knew it. Even if she'd had nothing to do with it, she'd feel she should have done something.

She was still thinking that over when she felt the tingle of a portal opening nearby. Claire felt a spike of alarm drive deep, and grabbed her phone to look at the tracking app she'd loaded on it. *Yes.* An unplanned portal was getting forced open, right here, in the shadows about a dozen feet away.

"Get to the car!" she yelled, and sprinted for it. Eve didn't ask why, thankfully; she just tore off in pursuit, and Michael bounded ahead to jump in the driver's side.

A flood of spiders poured out, skittering across the concrete floor—bouncing, as if they were being poured out of a giant bucket.

Thousands of Bobs, only larger, the size of small Chihuahuas. Eve shrieked and threw herself into the backseat, slamming the door as one launched itself toward them; it hit the glass and bounced off. Claire kicked one away as she jumped in the passenger seat, and Michael locked the doors. "What the *hell*?" Eve yelled. "Oh my God, it's like Attack of the Giant CGI!"

"It's Ada," Claire said. She and Michael exchanged a look. "She's tracking me. She's got to be."

"Why?"

Symbols flashed in front of Claire's eyes, the symbols she reviewed and committed to memory every single morning. "Because I know her secret," she said. "I know how to reset her, kind of like wiping her memory. Myrnin won't do it, but I will. And she can't have that."

"Great," Michael said. "And where do you have to go to reset her?"

"Guess."

"You are just all kinds of fun right now." He fired up the engine and hit the gas. Claire hid her eyes as they drove over spiders, because that was just sick and kind of sad. The spiders chased them for a while, then milled around in the distance and one by one, turned up their legs and died.

Ada hadn't been able to keep them alive for long, which was great news for the next person in the parking garage.

"Kim first," Claire said. "Eve's right. Something could have happened to her."

"You're sure."

"I'm sure Ada would expect me to come running. I'd rather let her wait. And worry."

10

Kim's loft was a crime scene. Maybe not literally, but Claire thought if the police had roped it off, nobody would disagree.... Things were tossed everywhere, broken junk was piled in the corners, clothes were tossed on every flat surface. It smelled of old Chinese food, and the at-least-month-old trash was overflowing with cartons and pizza boxes. One pizza carton lay on the floor with a couple of slices of sausage withered inside.

"Nice," Shane said, and looked around. "Well, we know she's not a closet neat freak." There was paint all over the walls, too—not paintings, just paint, thrown on in sprays as if Kim had taken a few gallons and spun around in a circle, splashing it all over. It was probably still art, just not Claire's favorite kind.

"She's busy," Eve said, and cleaned up the pizza box and a few other Chinese food cartons, which she jammed into a plastic trash bag. "She's an artist."

"She's a slob," Shane said. "I'm not judging, though. So, what's the plan? We look around? Can I have dibs on the underwear drawer?"

Claire winced. "I can't believe you just said that."

Shane took on an angelic look. "Somebody's got to do it."

"Then that somebody will be me."

Shane lost his smile and got serious. "Hey. I'm sorry. I didn't mean—"

"I know." It still hurt. She avoided his eyes and started rummaging through things. It wasn't as if Kim actually *had* an underwear drawer—she didn't seem bothered by leaving her bras and panties all over the place. Claire grabbed a bag and started stuffing the clothes into it, just because.

"Girls," Michael said. "We're here for clues, right? Not cleanup?"

"Right." Eve took a deep breath. "I'll check the bedroom."

"Bathroom," Shane volunteered.

"You're brave. All right, you keep going in here," Michael told Claire. "I'll take the kitchen."

"Good luck." She meant it. She bet mold had formed its own civilization in the refrigerator.

That left Claire on her own in the big, trashed-out room. She had no idea where to even start looking, but when she let herself ignore the trash, strewn clothes, and general mess, she found herself focusing on the walls. One of them had a mural painted on it, creepy elongated faces and staring eyes.

Staring eyes. They glittered. For a frozen second, Claire thought there was someone behind the wall, watching her, and then she got her head together. It was just glass, reflecting; it wasn't real eyes. But why would Kim put glass on the eyes—no, on only *one* eye?

Oh.

"Guys?" Claire opened the closet beside the mural, shoved through piles of crap and boxes, and found the camera that looked out through the eyehole. It was a small high-tech thing, wireless. So there had to be some kind of receiver, somewhere. She ducked out of the closet to yell, "Any computers around here?"

"In here," Eve said. There was a Mac set up on a rickety table in the corner of the bedroom, jammed in next to a sagging, unmade bed. It had a screen saver on it, and when Claire tapped the space bar, it asked for a password. She looked at Eve, who raised her shoulders in a clear no-idea shrug.

Claire typed in Eve's name. Nothing. She tried Morganville, but again, nothing.

On a wildly unpleasant hunch, she typed in *Shane*.

The screen cleared, and Claire was looking at herself. She recoiled in surprise, and the screen image did the same, leaning back from the camera. *Oh.* The built-in camera was on. Claire clicked it off and looked at what was on the desktop, which was where she personally put things she wanted to use quickly . . . and there it was. It was a folder, marked *Reality Project Cam #72.*

There were video files there. Claire clicked one, and instantly, Kim was there, filling the screen, leaning in dramatically toward the computer's lens. "Day twenty-two of the project," she said in a loud whisper. "Still not sure whether or not any of the extra sites have been discovered, but I'll run it as long as I can. Great stuff so far. The official history project is still going, but most of the vamps won't talk. It doesn't matter anyway; this is going to be so much better. The Oscars are going to be kissing my ass." She grabbed a handy bottle of soda and held it in both hands, looking over-the-top happy. "Oh, thank you so much; I just can't believe this honor. I'd like to thank the Academy—"

Claire paused it and looked at Eve, and Shane, who'd come out of the bathroom to watch. Michael joined, too.

"What is this?" Claire asked. Eve was shaking her head, eyes fixed on the screen. "Seriously, you don't know?"

"No. What's she talking about?"

Claire fast-forwarded until Kim finished her acceptance speech, then clicked PLAY again. Kim's image was glowing with glee. Whatever she was talking about, to her, it was major.

"I can't believe it; I finally got to put some in the last Founder House. Connections look good, stream is starting up. God, why do people always fall for the stupidest things? The old bathroom trick? She didn't even worry when I was gone for ten minutes, poking around. Sweet." Kim leaned in, close and confidential. "I may have to keep some of this for myself. Shane, undressed. Oh yeah."

"Excuse me?" Shane blurted. "What the hell?"

Eve's eyes widened, and she licked her black-painted lips and said, "When was this?"

Claire checked the date. "Early last week."

"Oh God," Eve said. "I—I met Kim at the auditions. I mean, I already knew her, but not like close friends or anything, and she just seemed really—interesting. She came over after we got done. You were at school, Michael was out, Shane was just leaving."

"And she asked to use the bathroom?" Claire prodded.

Eve looked miserable. "Yeah. She was gone awhile, but you don't ask, right? You're not supposed to hover, I mean, come on. Besides, she was so *cool*."

"She is cool," Shane agreed. "She's also a raving bitch manipulator. I dated her, remember? Once. You should have asked me. And what is this crap about seeing me naked? I wasn't even there!"

Eve covered her mouth with both hands. "What did she do? Oh my God—she used me, right? She used me."

"She uses everybody," Shane said. "Twenty-four, seven. I'm sorry, but I was kind of worried when you got so head over heels with her. She's not . . . yeah. She's just not."

Claire wondered if she should feel some kind of vindication, but she didn't. She felt nervous. "What did she do in our house?"

"What do you get Oscars for?"

Shane and Michael both said, at the same time, "Movies."

And the four of them looked at one another in silence for a moment. Claire didn't know how they felt, but her stomach seemed to be in free fall, and no end in sight.

She slowly turned back to the screen, shut down the video, and looked at the folder.

"What?" Shane asked. She pointed at the screen.

"This is Kim's personal video journal," she said. "It's where she recorded all her personal stuff."

"So?"

"Look at the number."

"Reality project cam ... number ..." Eve drew in a sharp breath. "Oh, holy crap."

"There are seventy-one other cameras out there in Morganville," Claire said. "Somewhere."

"And at least one of them's in our house," Shane finished.

There was no sign on the Mac in Kim's apartment as to where the video was streaming *to*. . . . She'd need more computing power than a laptop to run seventy-one other cameras, especially if she was saving terabytes of data. "She'd need a server array," Claire concluded, after doing the math. "Or off-line storage dumps. Maybe she only records during certain hours, then dumps everything to DVD-ROM or something."

"What about the university?" Eve asked. "Plenty of servers there, right?"

Claire considered it, then shook her head. "Yeah, there's available space, but how would she get to it without somebody noticing? She's not even an enrolled student. And the TPU computer security's pretty tight—it would have to be, because the vamps monitor it to prevent anybody from sending compromising information out." That led her to another, badder place in her mind. "Kim thinks of herself as some kind of renegade indie filmmaker, right?"

"Right," Eve said. "She talks about that a lot. About TV, cable shows, all that kind of thing. She's kind of obsessed with it. The acting thing was really so she could see all the backstage stuff, the technical parts."

Shane lowered himself onto Kim's sagging bed, which gave Claire unpleasant associations she wished she hadn't made. "She's bugged the town," Shane said. "She's got it rigged up with surveillance. And she's going to cut it all into, what, some kind of über-documentary about vampires?"

"Worse," Claire said. "Seventy-two cameras, all running at once? She's cutting together episodes. She wants a reality show. A *Morganville* reality show." She spun back toward the keyboard and brought up Kim's e-mail. As far as Claire could tell, the built-in in-box had never been used. "She's got to have e-mail."

"Web mail," Michael said. "If she wanted to cover her tracks, she'd do it that way. You think she's in communication with someone outside?"

Claire brought up the browser's history, but it had been cleared. "There's some kind of maintenance app running. It wipes out her temp files and history every twenty-four hours."

"Somebody's working with her," Shane said, and shrugged when they all looked at him. "Makes sense. Webcams don't fall off trees, right? Buying that many takes funding, and Kim isn't making that off her spare-parts art."

"Somebody outside Morganville knows," Claire said. "Do you think the vampires found out? That they're behind Kim's disappearing?"

"Oliver didn't seem bothered. If we knew, I guarantee you that this wouldn't still be here," Michael said, and nodded at the computer. *We,* not *they*. Claire didn't miss that, and she saw it register on Eve, too. "We'd have taken it."

Shane exchanged a look with both the girls. He hadn't missed the us-versus-them implications, either. "What's with the *we*, man?"

"What?"

"You counting yourself on the vampire team now?"

Michael sighed. "Do we need to have this fight right now? Because I think we've got bigger problems."

"No, we don't," Eve said. "Kim's disappeared. She's doing something really dangerous, and a lot of people—including the vampires—might want her stopped, or just gone. But I need to know where you are, Michael. Are you with the vampires? Or are you with us?"

"*Us* meaning what? Humans? Eve—"

"*Us* meaning me, Shane, and Claire," Eve said flatly. "Are you? Or are you going to tell Amelie and Oliver what Kim's doing and make this an all-out witch hunt?"

He didn't answer for a few seconds. Shane got up off the bed, which groaned as the old springs adjusted. "Michael?"

"Don't do this," Michael said, straight to Eve. "It's not a choice. I don't have a choice."

"You always have one, you know that. You had one when you let Amelie turn you, and you've got one now. Sam didn't run with the crowd. You don't have to, either. You can—do good things."

"Not everything vampires do is bad."

Shane slapped his hand on the wall, a sharp gunshot of impact, and they all jumped and looked at him. "Are you going to help us stop this, or are you going to run off and snitch?" he asked. "It's a simple question, man."

"It's not about you three. This is about Kim trying to destroy all of us, make herself some kind of reality TV diva, and get rich."

"Maybe," Shane said. "And maybe it doesn't have to

be. The video's streaming somewhere. She must still be trying to cut it together. We can still find her and put a stop to it. Nobody else has to know."

"Why do you want to protect her?" Michael asked. Shane glanced quickly at Claire, just a flash, but she saw the guilt in it. "Old-girlfriend blues?"

"Oh man, you'd *better* shut up."

"Eve wants to save her because they were friends; I get that. Claire just wants to save everybody—"

"Not *everybody*," she muttered.

"But you, you hold grudges. You'd throw Monica under the bus in a hot second, but you don't want Kim to get hurt."

"Seriously," Shane said. "Shut up. Now."

"See how it feels?" Michael said softly. "I don't like people questioning my motives, either. I'm a vampire. I can't help that. I drink blood. Get the fuck over it and don't make this about me. You want to save Kim? Fine. But if we don't find her in the next twenty-four hours, I've got to tell someone, and then it's on."

"It's all on," Eve agreed. There were tears in her eyes, shining like silver, but she blinked them away. "And it's all over. You bet your life on it, Michael."

She turned on her heel and walked out, shoving crap out of her way as she went. Claire looked after her, then began unhooking the computer. "Shane," she said. "Get the camera from the closet in the next room. Maybe we can trace the IP and see where she's sending the video."

Michael went after Eve, but Shane lingered as she stuffed the computer and power cord into the laptop bag. "Hey," he said. His fingers touched her hair lightly, then her shoulder. "I'm not—look, it's not like I'm in love with her. I'm not. It's just—"

"You slept with her once. Yeah, I heard." She snapped the catches closed on the bag and slung it over her shoulder. "She makes a hell of an impression."

Shane got in her way, and despite everything, all her

best intentions, she looked up into his eyes, and the light in them took her breath away. His fingertips touched her face, and then he bent down and kissed her. "No," he murmured into her mouth. "She doesn't. You do."

Before she could think of anything to say, he turned and left to grab the camera from the closet. In the other room, Claire saw Michael talking to Eve—well, Eve's rigid back. He turned when he saw her and Shane coming.

Eve opened the front door and slammed it back, charging down the stairs and leaving them all far, far behind. By the time they caught up, she was already in the passenger seat up front, face turned toward the tinted window. If she was crying, Claire couldn't tell. She'd put on a gigantic pair of mirrored sunglasses that she absolutely did not need inside a vampire's car.

"Right," Michael said, and climbed behind the wheel. "Where to?"

"Take me home," Claire said. "I'll work on the technical stuff."

"Drop me off at Common Grounds," Eve said. "I need to talk to some people."

Michael cleared his throat. "Want company?"

"No." Her voice was flat and cool, and Claire winced and looked at Shane. In the dimness, she could only see the broad strokes of his expression, but it looked like a *yikes*. "You've got things to do, right?"

She must have been right, because Michael didn't exactly deny it.

Shane said, "So—I'll stay home and watch TV. Critical job, too. Not everybody can do that under pressure."

"You should come with me," Eve said. "I could use some help." Even though she'd just flatly turned down Michael's offer. *Ouch.*

Shane must have thought that, too; he flashed a look at Michael, clearly apologizing, and Michael nodded slightly.

"Okay, sure," Shane said. "Outstanding." Shane held out a fist, and Eve tapped it. "Claire? You'll be okay alone?"

"Sure," she said, and hugged the laptop bag closer. "What could go wrong?"

Michael's eyes flashed to meet hers in the rearview mirror.

"Besides everything, I mean," she said.

11

At home—meaning, at the Glass House; the last thing she wanted to do was put her parents in the middle of all this—Claire unloaded Kim's laptop, set up the webcam, and started trying to access the data stream. That wasn't especially hard, because she knew the IP address of the camera; Kim had helpfully put the info right on a label. The problem was that the other end was on a randomizer, a special program that shifted the signal and rerouted it across the Internet every few minutes. It was right in Morganville; it had to be, because of the packet times, but Claire had no real idea where to start looking. She wasn't especially computer savvy, although she knew her way around; Kim obviously had taken some precautions.

But Claire wasn't giving up that easily, either. She didn't like Kim, but there was a lot at stake here: the vampires' lives, including Michael's; Kim's life; maybe everything they'd built here, at whatever cost.

Michael was right: they couldn't just let Kim sacrifice it all for her own ambition. The truth might come out, but it shouldn't come out like this, as some kind of horrible exercise in voyeurism.

She finally reran the video of Kim they'd watched at her loft. *I can't believe it; I finally got to put some in the last Founder House. Connections look good; stream is starting up.*

Claire went in search of cameras in the Glass House.

She found the first one in an air vent in Shane's room, and had to sit down, hard, on his bed with her head in her hands. It was focused right on his bed.

Oh my God. Oh no. At first she was sick with the thought of Kim combing through hours of video of Shane, invading his privacy, watching him get undressed . . . and then she remembered.

We were in here. Together. And she saw it.

Claire lifted her head and looked right up at the camera. She had no idea what was on her face, but if it was any match for the rage burning inside her, the feeling of total betrayal and exposure, she couldn't imagine Kim was having any fun seeing it. "I hope there's sound on these," she said. "You *bitch.* I officially hope you rot in hell, and I swear, if you post *any* of this online, I will find you."

Then Claire dragged a chair over, stood on the seat, and yanked the vent screen out of the wall. Behind it, the little webcam blinked its light and stared at her with a glass eye every bit as emotionless as Bob the spider's.

Claire picked it up, carried it into her bedroom, and put it next to the first one they'd found in Kim's apartment. Then she started searching the other rooms. She found two more—one hidden on top of a bookshelf, barely visible, in the living room, providing a bird's-eye view of the whole space, and another in Michael's room, focused on his bed.

"Pervert," Claire muttered, grabbed it out of the fake plant on top of his dresser, and carried it back to set it with the others. The IP addresses were consistent. Claire tried entering them into the web browser, and the signal was there, but it just displayed as gibberish.

Encrypted, which went along with the randomizer program that Kim was using.

She was just starting to backtrace the signals when

she felt that familiar tingle along the back of her neck, a feeling that the world had just *shifted*.

Portal.

Claire slid out of her chair and grabbed weapons, then waited. It had felt like the portal had opened upstairs, in the attic, and as she waited she heard faint creaks and pops from the old wood floor overhead. *Not spiders*, she thought. Spiders wouldn't be that heavy.

God, she *hoped* spiders wouldn't be that heavy. That was a terrifying thought. She was already entering B-movie horror territory... alone in the house! With a giant spider!

And a vampire, maybe.

Which could be worse.

Long minutes passed, and nothing came to eat her. Claire's hand had gotten sweaty, and her muscles hurt from the strength of her grip on the silver knife in her hand. *Come on*, she thought. *Just get it over with already.* It could have been somebody with a lot of power— Myrnin, or Oliver, or Amelie. In which case she'd put the knife down and apologize.

But she thought it was probably Ada, making another run at her.

The creaks overhead paused, and she heard them retreat.

Then she felt the portal activate again, and slam closed. All her protections snapped back into place, as if they'd never been broken. If she hadn't been here... she'd never have even known someone had been inside.

Claire edged out into the hall, staring at the hidden door up to the secret room. It was shut, and she heard nothing at all. She wouldn't, of course, it being sound-proofed, but still... She felt as if she ought to be able to feel *something*... and the house usually conveyed a feeling of danger. When it didn't, it was usually because Amelie...

Amelie.

Claire opened the hidden door and went up the stairs, and found the lights on at the top. The soft glow thrown through colored glass painted the walls, and on the couch, Amelie lay full length, one white hand pressed to her forehead.

She was wearing a flowing white dress, like a very fancy nightgown, and there were flecks of blood on it. Not as if she'd been hurt—more as if she'd been standing near someone else who had been. As Claire entered the room, Amelie's eyes opened and focused on her, but the Founder didn't move.

"We have a problem. Ada," Amelie said. "You know, don't you?"

"That she's crazy? Yeah. I figured that." Claire realized she was still holding the knife, and put it down. "Sorry."

"A reasonable precaution in uncertain times," Amelie said softly. Nothing else. Claire waited, but Amelie was as still as one of those marble angels on top of a tomb.

"What happened?" Claire finally asked.

"Nothing you would understand." Amelie closed her eyes. "I'm tired, Claire."

There was a simple kind of resignation to the way she said it that made Claire shiver. "Should I—is there somebody I should call, or—"

"I will rest here for now. Thank you." It was a dismissal, one Claire was a little relieved to get. Amelie just seemed—absent. Empty.

"Okay. But—I guess if you need something—"

Amelie's eyes snapped open, and Claire felt it at the same time: a surge of power—the portal reopening.

Amelie's will slammed it closed.

"Someone's looking for you," Claire said. "Who is it?"

"None of your affair."

"It is if they're coming here! Is someone after you?"

"It's my guards," Amelie said. "They'll find me, sooner or later, but for now, I want to be here. Here, where Sam—" She stopped again, and silvery tears pooled in her eyes and ran down into her unbound pale hair. "Where Sam told me he would never leave me. But he did leave me, Claire. I knew he would, and he did. Everyone leaves. Everyone."

This time, when the portal flared, Amelie didn't try to keep it shut. In seconds, the attic door flew open, and it wasn't the guards after all, in their black Secret Service suits.

It was Oliver, still wearing his bowling shirt, graying hair pulled tight into a ponytail. For a second, as his gaze fell on Amelie, he looked like a different person.

No, that wasn't possible. He couldn't really *feel* something for her. Could he?

"You," he said to Claire. "Leave us. *Now.*"

"Stay," Amelie said. There was an unmistakable thread of command in her voice. "You don't order my servants in my house, Oliver. Not yet."

"You're hiding behind children?"

"I'm not hiding at all. Not even from you." She slowly sat up, and in the multicolored glow of the lamps she looked young, and very tired. "We've played our games, haven't we? The two of us, we've schemed and cheated and used each other all these centuries, for our own purposes. What did it bring us? Peace? There's never peace for us. There can't be."

"I can't talk of peace," he said, and went to one knee, looking up into her face. "And neither can you. Morley tried to kill you out there in the graveyard the other evening, and still you wander alone, looking for your own destruction. You must stop."

"Speaking as my second-in-command."

"Speaking as your friend," he said, and took her hand. "Amelie. We have our differences, you and I. We always will. But I would not see you suffer so. Morganville is too much for you right now—there are too many vampires here with too much ambition. Control must be maintained, and if you won't do it, you must put it in stronger hands. My hands."

"How kind of you, to keep the best interests of others so close to your heart," she said. She didn't try to remove her fingers from his, but her tone had taken on a remote kind of chill. "So what do you propose?"

"Until you can put aside your mourning, give me the town," he said. "You know I can keep order here. I'll act as your regent. When you are ready, I'll give it back to you."

"Liar." She said it without particular emphasis, or blame, and Claire saw Oliver's hand tighten on hers. Amelie smiled, just a little. "Liar, and bully. Do you really think such tactics could work, against the daughter of Bishop? You would have done well to pretend to a little more sympathy, or less. Half measures never work for you, Oliver."

"You're losing the town by inches now," he said. "Morley's only the first of the vampires to make a move against you—more will come. The humans, too; there are gangs of them attacking us in the night. I've already been approached to stop it."

"So now it's a plot. A plot to remove me from control. And you are my faithful servant, coming to warn me." Her teeth flashed as she laughed softly. "Oh, Oliver. The only reason you didn't betray me to my father when you had the chance was because the odds were even. Had he courted you for even a moment, you'd have yielded like a lovesick girl. You'd have planted the knife in my back yourself."

"No," he said, and pulled her off balance, down to her knees on the floor across from him. "I wouldn't. You're not a queen anymore, Amelie. Don't presume to sit on your throne and judge me!"

She wrenched a hand free and slapped him hard

across the face, and Claire backed up as the two vampires locked red stares. "I'll judge as I see fit," Amelie said. "And I'll have none of your insolence. Scheme all you want, but it doesn't matter. Morganville is mine, and it will never be yours. Never. I'm on my guard now. You may be assured that whatever plots exist against me will be uncovered and destroyed. Even yours."

She shoved him back, and Oliver fell full length on the floor. In a flash, Amelie reached out for the silver knife that Claire had put on the table, and before Claire could blink, that knife was at Oliver's throat. "Well?" she demanded. "What say you, my servant?"

He spread his hands wide in mute surrender.

Amelie stared down at him, then looked at Claire. "Summon my car," she said. "I believe I will go for a drive in Morganville. It's time my people see me, and know I'm not to be underestimated."

She slammed the knife into the floor next to Oliver's head, close enough that the edge left a bloody streak down his cheek, then rose to her feet and swept out of the room and down the stairs. Claire dug her cell phone out and called the number to Amelie's security, and told them to meet her downstairs.

By the time she was done, Oliver was sitting on the sofa. He dabbed at the cut on his face, looking a lot less upset than Claire expected him to be.

"Wow, you planned that," she said. "Right?"

He shrugged. "She loved Sam. She needs someone to fill the void inside her—either a lover, or an enemy."

"And you're the enemy."

Oliver dusted himself off. "Through all the long, long years, it's what we've always had between us. Anger, and respect." He smiled a little. "And sometimes a glimmer of something else, not that we would ever admit it to each other. No, enemies are easier. She likes being my enemy. And I rather enjoy being hers."

Claire really, really didn't get it, but she didn't think that either one of them would care.

"Hey," she said. "You came through the portal. Did anything weird happen?"

"Weird?" He frowned. "I don't understand."

"I mean—never mind. I'm just kind of worried about the portals. I want to recalibrate the system."

"I was planning to walk in any case. It's just as important for the residents of Morganville to see me afoot as for them to see Amelie in her queen's black coach." Oliver straightened his shirt and stood up. "It gives us . . . balance."

"Oliver?"

He stopped at the head of the stairs.

"What would happen if someone got word out about the town?"

"Out?"

"Out in the world. You know."

"Oh, it's happened before. But no one believes. No one ever believes."

"What if—what if they had proof?"

"The only possible proof would be a genuine vampire, and that will never happen. Short of that, any proof can be denied easily enough."

"What about—video?"

"Claire. You go to the cinema, don't you? Do you imagine, in this age of digital trickery, that anyone would believe video of vampires?" He shook his head. "They would believe it now less than ever. The very popularity of vampires in your stories protects us." He sent her a sharp glance. "Why?"

"Just wondering," she said.

"Stop wondering. It's not healthy."

Then he was gone. Claire sat down on the couch and smoothed her palms over her jeans.

Oliver was right; people probably wouldn't believe it. Most people didn't believe all the ghost reality shows, either. The problem was that these days, reality didn't have to be real to be a hit—and Morganville couldn't stand up to real scrutiny.

They had to stop Kim, before it all fell apart.

Plus, as a bonus, they had to really kick her ass about the cameras, because that was just *wrong*.

Eve and Shane got home first, while Claire was devouring a peanut butter sandwich. She didn't tell them about the visit from Amelie and Oliver, and besides, they looked pretty grim. She was sure they wouldn't really care.

"What?" she asked. Shane snagged half her sandwich from her plate as he passed. "Hey!"

"Worked up an appetite, watching Miss Bad Attitude's back," he said around a mouthful of bread. "She goes to the most interesting places. I mean *interesting* in terms of scary as hell."

"Do *not* tell Claire about that club," Eve said, and took off her metallic sunglasses. Behind them, her mascara was smeared, and her eyes were red—not vampire red, but more like an overdose of tears. "Besides, it's not like I just randomly decided to go there. It's where Kim liked to hang out."

"What kind of club?" Claire whispered to Shane.

"Leather," he whispered back. "She's right; you really don't want to know."

"Kim hasn't been there in a couple of days," Eve said. "But we found a few vampires who did interviews with her recently, for her history project."

From the expression on Shane's face, there was more to the story. Claire said, doubtfully, "And they just told you? Just like that?"

"I had to make some deals to get the details." Eve avoided making eye contact on that. She shed her black leather jacket, the one with all the buckles, and snagged a corner of Claire's leftover half sandwich. "Hmm, this is good; did you put honey on it?"

"You did *what*?" Making any kind of deal with any kind of vampire in Morganville was crazy. Making deals with the kind of vampires hanging out in a leather bar was ... suicidal. Claire rounded on Shane. "You let her do that?"

"Seriously, you can't even think about blaming me when she gets like this. I'm the bodyguard. Unless you wanted me to tie her up and gag her ..."

"They'd probably have gotten into it there," Eve said. "Look, I can get out of the deals. Amelie's our get-out-of-deals-free card. But I needed to find Kim, and to do that, we needed information. Unless you waved your magic techno-wand and ...?"

Claire had to shake her head.

"Okay then, quit looking at me like I broke house training or something." Eve, Claire realized, was really uncomfortable about this. She'd probably had to force herself to talk to these vamps, and the last thing she needed was the postgame analysis on what she'd done wrong.

Claire cleared her throat. "What did you get?"

"I found four vamps that Kim either talked to on camera, or set up interviews with in the next week or so, which means she wasn't planning on leaving town just yet. And a couple of human guys who, ah, visited Kim at her place."

"Hookups," Shane confirmed. "Which is Kim's style. Although I can't say much for her taste. It's kind of gone downhill."

"So, wait—what does that tell us that we didn't already know? And what did you promise these vamps, anyway?"

"Things," Eve said, without adding any details. Shane looked away. "Not important right now. The point is, two of the vamps she interviewed she filmed at Common Grounds, but the other vamps said she took them to a kind of studio."

"A studio," Claire repeated. "That sounds promising."

"Thought so. It wasn't knee-deep in crap, so it couldn't have been her apartment, right?"

"Did they tell you where?"

"No," Shane said, leaning over Eve's shoulder. "They wanted more for that little gem. And I told them to stuff it sideways."

Claire blinked. Vampires. Leather bar. "And they just thought that was okay?"

"Honestly? Not so much. They mostly decided we'd make good chew toys."

"Shane!" Claire looked at him with pleading eyes. "You didn't—"

"Fight? Didn't have to," he said. Before he could explain, the front door opened and closed, and Claire heard the locks clicking shut again. Eve stiffened and looked down, burying her black-painted fingernails in her palms as she made fists.

Michael looked—like he'd been through a rough night in a bad bar, Claire guessed. Mussed, clothes torn at the seams. Something dark on his shirt that could have been blood.

"Are you okay?" Claire came to her feet, staring at him. He wasn't bruised or anything, but he looked tired. There was a little flush of red in his eyes, and his hands were shaking.

"I'm fine," he said. "I just need—something to drink. Be right back."

He disappeared into the kitchen. The silence in the room was sharp and uncomfortable, and Claire looked at Eve, who folded her arms across her chest.

"I didn't ask him to come rescue us," she said, and looked down. "I didn't want him to come at all."

Michael came back carrying a black sports bottle. They all knew what he had in it, but nobody mentioned it as he sipped through the built-in straw.

"I had my reasons for going," Michael said. And

didn't look at Eve. And Eve didn't look at him. "Thanks for getting her out of there when you did, Shane."

Shane nodded. "No problem. What happened?"

That was a question Michael wasn't going to answer, evidently, because he just shrugged. "Fight." One hell of one, from the state of his clothes and his hunger for blood. "It was worth it. One of them told me where Kim took him to interview, and it wasn't any of the places you already had."

Eve slowly raised her head, and her eyes narrowed. "You followed us. You thought we couldn't handle it."

"I knew where you were going. And I was right, wasn't I?"

"No, you were *not* right! Michael—"

He put the bottle down, stepped forward, and caught her hands in his. Eve started to try to pull free, but he held on, willing her to look at him. It seemed really personal, somehow.

"I'm a vampire," he said. "I'm never going to be anything else. You need to decide if you're okay with that, Eve. I am."

"What if I'm not?" Her voice sounded really small and wounded. "What if I just want you to be Michael, not—not Vampire Michael of the Clan, or whatever?"

"I can't," he said. "Because I'm not just Michael anymore. I haven't been since before you moved in. You just didn't know it."

He let go of her hands, uncapped the sports bottle, and drank the blood down in long, thirsty gulps, making sure she was watching. His eyes turned ruby red, and he licked the drops from his lips. He put the empty bottle down, watching her.

She crossed her arms and turned away from him, and Michael closed his eyes in pain. When he opened them again, they were just human, and sad.

Claire wondered if she'd actually just witnessed a breakup. She hoped not.

Shane cleared his throat. "So. You turned up at a place where Kim goes, right? Let's talk about that. Please."

Michael walked over to the chair, where his guitar lay across the seat. He picked it up and cradled it in his arms, still watching Eve. After a few seconds, he began to softly play a series of chords. It was an aching kind of sound, gentle and full of emotion, and Claire saw Eve's shoulders tense and shake as she suppressed tears.

"Kim used to work at KVVV," Michael said. "She was an intern there before it shut down. The vampire said she interviewed him in a booth there at the old studios at the edge of town, by the transmission tower."

Claire couldn't help feeling a little spike of excitement. "That's it. That's got to be it, right? You said it was shut down?"

"Yeah, Amelie shut it down a few years back after—there was an incident," Michael said. "The town council decided we didn't need another radio station. It's been locked up since then."

"We need to go look!" Claire bounced to her feet, but Shane caught her shoulder and guided her back into the chair.

"Cool it. Not at night, we don't. The last thing we need to do is go poking around an abandoned building in the middle of the night in a town full of vampires."

"But what if she decides to close up shop? Cut her losses, take her goodies, and try to leave?" Eve said. "She could get killed. We have to warn her."

"Warn her?" Claire felt short of breath, ready to burst out into wild laughter. "Eve, don't you get it? She rigged our house. She was *watching us*. Watching everything, every private thing—"

"No," Eve said. "No, she wouldn't do that. You're wrong."

"I found cameras in the bedrooms!"

Eve's mouth opened and closed, and Claire didn't think she'd ever seen her look quite so devastated.

She slumped down on the couch and covered her rice-powder-pale face with both hands.

Shane was staring at Claire with a frozen expression. "Which bedrooms?"

"Yours," she said softly. "And Michael's."

For a second Shane didn't move, and then he reached out, picked up the nearest thing—a DVD case—and hurled it across the room so hard that it dented the wall. "Son of a *bitch*," he muttered. "That little—"

Michael's face had gone completely still, and he wasn't playing anymore. He held the guitar as if he'd forgotten he had it. "She was recording us. Her own little *Big Brother* reality show, with vampires."

Eve said nothing. Claire couldn't even imagine what she was thinking, but she looked utterly miserable.

"We have to go," Eve finally said. "We need to find where she keeps the recordings, and wipe them out. Every little bit. This can't happen. She can't do this."

"I just hope she hasn't *already* done it," Claire said. "She's been putting this together for almost a month. She's got to be almost done by now. If we're right about her having some kind of sponsor outside of town . . ."

"Then we *really* have to go. Now. Tonight."

"No," Michael said. "Not at night."

"She's going to *get away with it*!"

"That's a chance we're going to have to take," Michael said. "Shane's right. No charging off into the dark. It has to wait until morning." He started playing again. His head was down, as if he were concentrating on his music, but Claire didn't think he was. There was something a little wrong with the way he said it, the way he wouldn't look at them. "How about more of those sandwiches?"

Eve raised her head and stared at him, tears smearing her mascara into clown makeup. "Unbelievable," she said. "You know what's on those recordings. You *know*, Michael. You'd let her take that and sell it?"

"We need to be smart about this. If we go running off without a plan—"

"Screw your plans!" she shouted, and jumped off the couch, then pounded up the stairs, chains jingling. "Screw you, too!"

Michael looked at Claire, then Shane.

"She's not wrong," Shane said. "Sorry, man."

Michael had lied to them, and Claire caught him at it.

She was on her way to the bathroom with her tank top and pajama bottoms over one arm, thinking about curling up warm in Shane's arms, when she heard Michael talking in his room. The door was open a crack. Shane and Eve were still downstairs, cleaning up the kitchen.

He was on his cell phone. "No," he was saying. "No, I'm sure. I just need to go check it out, tonight. Make sure nobody is using the facility without—"

Claire pushed the door open, and Michael twisted around to look at her. *So busted.* He froze for a second, then said, "I'll call you back," and hung up.

"Let me guess," she said. "Oliver. You're telling him everything, aren't you?"

"Claire—"

"We asked you. We asked you if you were with us, and you said you were. You *promised*."

"Claire, please."

"No." She stepped back when he stretched out a hand. "Eve was right. You're not Michael anymore. You're Vampire Michael. It's really us and them, and you're with them."

"Claire."

"What?"

"That wasn't Oliver."

"Then who was it?"

"Detective Hess. He was going to meet me at the station and check it out, tonight. Eve was right. We really can't wait, not even for morning." Michael's expression took on a dangerous edge. "Kim crossed the line. She tricked her way in here, and she screwed us over. I can forgive a lot of things, Claire, but I can't forgive her for this."

"So you were going to leave us behind."

His eyes flared hot. "Because I care about you. Yes. Do you know how close Eve came to getting herself killed tonight? And Shane? No more. I'm not risking you guys, not for this. Not for *her*."

"Hey! You're not our father! You can't just decide we need protecting—we're all in this together!"

"No," he said. "We're not. Some of us get hurt a lot easier than others, and I love you guys. I'm not going to lose you. Not like this."

He stripped off his ripped shirt and pulled on another one, grabbed his keys from the table, and very gently picked Claire up and moved her when she tried to block his path. "Don't," he said. "Claire, I mean it. Don't tell them where I went. Let me handle this."

She didn't say anything.

She didn't want to lie to him.

Michael stared at her for a few long seconds, long enough that she was almost sure he could read her mind, and then he shoved his keys in his pocket and moved off down the stairs.

She sat down on his bed, staring up at the vent where she'd found the camera. Claire didn't actually know what she was going to do until she heard Michael's new replacement car starting up outside, and then she stood, walked down to the kitchen, and interrupted an intense conversation between Shane and Eve at the sink to say, "Michael's gone to get Kim, and we need to go, right now."

They both stopped and looked over their shoulders at her. Eve had her arms elbow-deep in soapy water. Shane held a dish towel and a plate.

"Right now," Claire repeated. "Please."

Eve yanked the plug on the sink, grabbed the towel from Shane's hands, and wiped her hands and arms. She three-pointed the towel onto the counter. "I'll drive," she said, and ran to grab her keys. Shane stayed where he was, still holding the plate in one hand, watching Claire. He opened his mouth.

"Don't you dare tell me I can't go," she said. "Don't even, Shane. I'm on those videos, too. You *know* I am."

He put the plate down. "Michael went alone?"

"Mr. Vampire Superhero doesn't need backup." Well, that wasn't quite fair. "He's meeting Detective Hess there. But still."

The kitchen door swung open, and Eve blazed back in, vivid in black and white, a mime on a mission. She tossed her keys in a nervous jingle of metal and said, "Weapons."

Nobody argued that it would only be Kim they were going up against. Shane grabbed a black nylon bag from under the counter—in other towns, people might keep emergency supplies of food and water, maybe a medical kit, but in Morganville, their emergency readiness kit consisted of stakes and silver-coated knives. "Got it," he said, and tossed it over one shoulder. "Claire—"

"Don't *even!*"

He grinned and tossed her a second bag. "Silver nitrate and water in a Super Soaker," he told her. "My own invention. Ought to be good at twenty feet, kind of like wasp spray."

Oh. "You get me the nicest things."

"Anybody can get jewelry. Posers."

Eve rolled her eyes. "Let's go, comedian."

As she tossed the keys again, Shane grabbed them in midair. "I may be a comedian, but you look like a mime, anybody ever tell you that?"

He dashed for the door. Eve followed. Claire shouldered the nylon bag and prepared to shut the door of the house; as she did, she felt a wave of emotion sweep through her. The house, Michael's house, was worried. It was *almost* alive, some of the time. Like now.

"It'll be okay," she told it, and patted the countertop. "He'll be okay. *We'll* be okay."

The lights dimmed a little as she shut the door.

Eve's car wouldn't start.

"Um ... this isn't good," Eve said as Shane cranked the engine again. There was a click, and nothing. "You've got to be kidding me. This is *not* the time, stupid evil hunk of junk!" She slapped the dashboard, which had zero effect. "Come on, *work*!"

It was very dark outside—no streetlights on, and the moon and stars were veiled by thick, fast-moving clouds. In the glow of the dashboard, Shane and Eve looked worried. Shane pulled the old-fashioned lever under the dash, and the hood of the car popped up with a thick *clunk* of metal. "Stay inside," he said. "I'm going to take a look."

"Because you've got guy parts, you're automatically a better mechanic than me? I don't *think* so," Eve said, and bailed out of the passenger side. Shane banged the back of his head against the seat.

"Seriously," he said. "Why is it always so hard with her?"

"She's worried," Claire said.

"We're all worried. *You* stay in the car."

"*I* don't know anything about cars. I will."

"Finally, a girl with some sense." He leaned over the seat to kiss her, then got out to join Eve as she hauled the giant, heavy hood of the car upward. From that point on, Claire had a limited view of what was going on—the hood, the dark night outside, some lights glowing in nearby houses....

A car turned the corner, and its headlights swept color over darkness, lighting up the Glass House in all its decaying Victorian glory, then the sun-faded picket fence, the spring crop of weeds along the curb. . . .

And then came a group of vampires out of the darkness, heading for Shane and Eve. One of them was Morley, the skanky homeless dude from the cemetery. She supposed the others were his friends; they didn't look as polished and well-groomed as most of the other vamps seemed to be. These looked hungry, mean, and dirty.

Claire lunged across the big bench seat from the back and slammed her hand down on the horn. It was as loud as a foghorn, and she heard a sharp bang as either Eve or Shane hit their head on the hood of the car as they straightened up.

"Guys!" she yelled. "Trouble!"

Shane, one hand held to the top of his head, opened the back door and pulled her out. "Door," he said. "Get back inside. The car thing isn't happening."

Claire didn't argue. She dug her front door key out of her jeans pocket as she ran, banged open the front gate, and skidded to a halt in front of the door. The porch light flickered on.

"Thanks," she told the house absently, jammed the key into the lock, and opened the door.

Shane was at the foot of the steps, but he'd stopped, looking back.

Eve was trapped between the car and the house, and she was surrounded by vampires. Claire gasped, and saw that neither Shane nor Eve had had time to grab the weapons bag out of the car.

She still had hers.

Morley lunged forward, slamming Eve against the rounded fender of her car, and Eve's scream of panic split the night. Shane rushed toward her, pulling a stake from his jacket, but it wasn't going to help. There were six of them, all with vampire strength.

He'd get himself killed.

Claire zipped open the bag and pulled out the big plastic Super Soaker. It was a totally absurd color of neon, and it was heavy with a full load of water.

God, please work. Please work.

Claire moved forward at a run, and pressed the trigger. A shockingly thick spray shot out, hit the sidewalk, and splashed; she quickly angled it up, over the fence, and sprayed it in an arc across Shane's back, the vampires turning to meet him, Morley, Eve.

Where it hit exposed vampire skin, the solution of silver powder and water lit them up like Christmas trees. The bony woman with long dark hair heading for Shane broke off with a yelp, slapped at her burning face, and then gaped at the burns on her hands as the solution began to eat away at her flesh.

Claire pumped the toy gun again, building up pressure, and put it to her shoulder as she came to a flat-footed stop. "Back off!" she yelled. "Everybody just *stop*! You, let her go!" That last was directed at Morley, who had Eve by the shoulder and was holding her in front of him. He was wearing a filthy old raincoat, and it had protected him from the spray; she could see a livid burn spreading across his cheek, but nothing that would really hurt him.

Shane backed up next to Claire, breathing hard. She aimed the Super Soaker directly at Morley and Eve. "Let her go," she repeated. "We didn't do anything to you."

"Nothing personal," Morley said. "We're starving, love. And you're so juicy."

"Ewww," Eve said faintly. "Has anybody ever told you that you smell like tombstones?"

He glanced at her and smiled. "You're the first," he assured her. "Which is a bit charming. I'm Morley. And you are . . . ? Ah yes. Amelie's friend. I remember you from the cemetery. Sam Glass's grave."

"Nice to meet you. Don't eat me, 'kay?"

He laughed and combed her hair back from her pale face. "You're cute. I might have to turn you and keep you as a pet."

"Hey!" Claire said sharply, and took a step forward. "Didn't you hear me? *Let her go!* She's under Amelie's protection!"

"I see no bracelet." Morley grabbed Eve's arm and lifted it to the dim light, turning it this way and that. "No, definitely nothing there." He kissed the back of her hand, then extended his fangs and prepared to munch out on the pale veins at her wrist.

Eve twisted and punched him in the mouth.

Morley stumbled backward against the car, and Claire triggered the sprayer, coating him in silver spray. This time, he screamed and flapped his arms and lunged away from Eve, toward the darkness. Claire sprayed the rest of his crew again as they followed, waking howls of pain and anger.

Shane dashed forward, vaulted the gate, and helped Eve stand up from where Morley had shoved her. "That went well," he said. His voice was shaking. "No fang marks, right?"

"Lucky me," Eve said, and laughed wildly. "Get the weapons bag. I can't *believe* you left it in the car; what was that? What town did *you* grow up in?"

"I was trying to help you fix the car!"

"Bozo." She hugged him, hard, and smacked him on the back of the head; then she took a deep breath as Shane left her to retrieve the black nylon bag out of the car. "And you."

Claire lowered the Super Soaker. "What? What did I do?"

"Saved my life? Redefined awesome in our time?"

"Oh. Okay." She felt a smile bloom from deep inside, and for a moment, it was all good.

Really good.

"Ladies," Shane said, and slammed the car door.

"Let's have the champagne inside, okay? And talk about who pulled the wires in the engine, and how we're planning to back Michael up with no wheels?"

He had a point. Claire covered their retreat with the Super Soaker, feeling kind of like a neon-gunned Rambo, and Eve slammed and locked the door, then put her back to the wood and breathed a deep sigh of relief.

The second Claire put the water gun down, Shane wrapped her in his arms and kissed her, really tender and sweet and a little bit desperate. Hot.

"Hey," Eve said. "Michael, remember? What are we doing for transpo, cabbing it?"

There was exactly one taxicab in Morganville, and he didn't work at night, so that wasn't much of an option. They didn't even bother to discuss it. "Well," Claire said, very reluctantly, "there's another way. But you won't like it."

"I'll like it less than getting molested by a vampire in a flasher raincoat who smells like graveyards? Try me."

"I could open a portal," Claire said. "But I've never been to the radio station, so I can't risk doing it blind. I have to go someplace close that I know. What's around it?"

"Hang on a second," Shane said, and dropped the weapons bag to the wood floor with a thump. "What about Ada? You said she was out for blood, right?"

"I said you wouldn't like the idea."

"So just to recap—Ada wants to kill you, and you're going to walk through a portal she controls?"

"Well—"

"No, Claire. Next."

"But—"

"Not happening."

She sighed. "What if I get Myrnin to open it for us? He's better at it. I don't think she dares mess with him directly."

"And tell Myrnin what's happening? Bad idea. The dude is half crazy all the time."

"So what's *your* bright idea?" Claire asked. Shane spread his hands out. "That's what I thought."

She pulled her cell phone out and checked the screen. Her battery was getting low; she hadn't had a chance to charge it up recently, although that was Morganville Survival 101. She picked up the old-fashioned landline phone on the hall table and dialed Myrnin's lab.

It rang, and rang, and rang, and finally, Myrnin picked up. "What?" he snapped. "I was in the middle of dinner."

Claire was afraid to ask who that was. "I need help," she said.

"Claire, you are my assistant. Not the other way around. Perhaps it would be helpful if I prepared an organizational chart you could keep on your person. Possibly tattooed on your arm."

He *was* in a mood. Claire bit her lip. "Please," she said. "It's a little favor."

"Oh, all right. What?"

"You know the old radio station outside of town? KV—" Her mind blanked. She looked at Eve, who mouthed the answer. "KVVV. Could you open me a portal?"

"Hmmm," he said. She heard the sound of liquid being poured in the background, and him swallowing it, and him smacking his lips. "Well, I suppose I could get you close, if not inside the building. Would that do?"

"Sure. Anything."

"And why can you not do this yourself?"

"Ada . . . ?"

Myrnin was silent for a long few seconds. "She's better," he said. "I don't know what got into the old girl. But I've had a talk with her, and really, she's much better now. Much better."

"That's good." It would be, if it were true, but Claire didn't trust Myrnin's judgment when it came to Ada. "Um, about that portal—"

"Yes, fine, coming right up. I will be there in a moment."

"No, Myrnin—"

He hung up before she could explain that she didn't actually need him to come along. Not that he was going to listen to her, anyway. Claire replaced the phone on its cradle.

"Crazy boss is coming," Shane interpreted, just from the expression on her face. "Lovely. This ought to be fun."

About five seconds later, Claire felt a psychic wave sweep through the house, so strong she was surprised neither Shane nor Eve seemed to feel it, and then a dark opening formed in the far wall of the living room, and Myrnin stepped over the threshold.

"I *so* want his wardrobe," Eve sighed. "Is that shallow, or just strange?"

"Don't sell yourself short. It's both," Shane said, and cocked his head to take in Myrnin's latest effort at blending in. It was ... interesting. Claire couldn't decide if it was some deliberate, unholy mix of Victorian lord and hippie, or just what had been on the floor of his closet.

He had on his bunny slippers.

These had fangs.

They all stared at them in silence for about a heartbeat, and then Shane said, "*That* is impressively wicked. Crazy, but wicked."

Myrnin frowned at him, then looked down at his shoes. He seemed genuinely surprised. "Oh. Those. I thought—well, they're appropriate, I suppose."

"Wouldn't want to be inappropriate," Claire said. "You really didn't have to come. I'm sorry."

"I did, in fact. I tried to open the portal to the radio station, and I couldn't do so." Myrnin's dark eyes were wide and gleaming, clearly fascinated. "Claire, do you know what this means?" He paced, the bunny slippers flopping their ears in a very distracting way. "Someone locked down the area. And it wasn't me."

"Who else could?"

"No one."

"But—"

"Exactly!" He smacked his hands together in glee. "A mystery! Thank you for calling and imposing on me for a favor; this is very exciting stuff, you know. Chaos, mayhem, someone stealing a march against me—ah, I've missed it these past few months, haven't you?"

"No," they all said, exactly together. Claire took Shane's hand and said, "Myrnin, who else could lock down areas of town and freeze out portals?"

"Amelie," he said, "but it's not her. There's a certain signature to her work, and by the way, she's been here recently, did you know? She reeks of pain these days. It's most disturbing."

"Dude, *focus*," Eve said. "Who else?" She threw Claire a why-am-I-even-asking look, but Myrnin got hold of himself and nodded as he thought about it.

"There have been a total of six others in the history of Morganville," he said. "But they're all dead. All but you, Claire."

They all looked at her. She blinked. "Well, *I* didn't do it!"

"Oh. Pity. Then I have no idea."

She cleared her throat. "What about Ada?"

"Ada is not the boogeyman behind every shadow, my dear," Myrnin said, and flopped himself down in Michael's chair, taking hold of the acoustic guitar and picking out a surprisingly competent series of chords. "Ada does as she's told. Unlike you, I might add, which is not an attractive quality in a lab assistant."

"Could she do it?"

He stilled the strings with one hand, and looked up.

His dark hair fell back from his pale face, and for a moment, he looked entirely serious. "Ada can do anything," he said. "I don't think even she understands that. But I find it highly unlikely—"

"You're a vampire wearing bunny slippers with fangs. Highly unlikely kind of goes with the territory," Eve said. "How close can you get us? To the radio station?"

"Why do you want to go there? It's hardly safe for untagged blood donors to roam around out there after dark. Even Claire would be at risk, and she's wearing the strongest protection available. I don't advise it." He put the guitar aside and steepled his fingers together. "But you're not quite foolish enough to be doing it for the thrill, I think, so you do have a reason. Tell me."

Claire exchanged a quick look with her friends, and then said, "Michael went alone out there. We need to help him."

"Michael is a vampire. Vampires go out at night." Myrnin shrugged and dusted a bit of fluff from his black velvet jacket, which was pretty elegant, if you were heading off to a costume party. "Why concern yourself, unless you think there will be trouble? Stop lying by omission, Claire. Tell me everything. Now."

Eve shook her head, a tiny spasm that was probably involuntary. Even Shane looked like he thought it was a terminally bad idea. Claire said, "We can trust him. We have to trust him."

"Oh, this sounds interesting," Myrnin said, and leaned forward in Michael's chair. "Please continue."

She did. She even brought down one of the wireless cameras, showed it to him, and explained how it worked, which was a complete delight to his obsessively scientific side. "But this is amazing," he said, turning the little device over in his nimble fingers. "This girl, she's quite the enterprising little thing. How many of these, you say?"

"We think seventy-two."

He lost his smile, focused on the object in his hand. "She can't be doing it alone, then. There must be a larger purpose. A larger plan. Still, this Kim, she may be using it for her own purposes; have you thought about that?"

"We know she's getting her own thing out of it," Claire said. "But you're saying . . . she didn't come up with it in the first place?"

"Exactly."

So, maybe Kim had been recruited to put cameras out, and then hijacked it for her own reality-show dream project . . . but that meant someone else was in charge.

Someone smart enough to not get caught. Or even suspected.

"You really should tell Oliver," Myrnin said. "I know he's not the most pleasant of allies, but he is effective in the right circumstances. Rather like one of those nuclear bombs."

"If we tell Oliver, Kim's dead," Eve said. "She may be an epic bitch, but I don't want her executed, either."

"Valid," Myrnin agreed. "However, if this goes wrong, she's dead in any case. I will come along. You need an adult chaperone."

"Once again, bunny slippers," Shane said. "I'm just pointing that out."

"I suppose they would get dirty. I'll be right back." Myrnin jumped out of the chair and dashed for the portal. It snapped shut behind him with a flare of energy.

"Do you think—"

Before Shane could finish the question, the portal opened again, and Myrnin hopped out on one foot, pulling on serious pirate boots, the knee-high kind with the cuff of leather. He finished tugging the left one on and did a runway pose for Claire. "Better?"

"Um . . . yeah. I guess." He now looked like a demented version of that pirate captain from the rum bottles.

"Then let's go."

As he turned to concentrate on the portal, Eve tugged on Claire's shirt.

"What?"

"Ask him where he got the boots."

"*You* ask." Personally, Claire wanted the vampire bunny slippers.

12

The closest Myrnin could get them was a few blocks away. Claire was glad, actually, that he hadn't warned her where they were going; she wasn't sure she'd have been able to step through if he had.

German's Tire Plant had closed at least thirty years ago, and the gigantic, multi-story facility was basically one big gold mine of creepy. Claire had been in it exactly twice before, and neither visit held pleasant memories—and those had been daytime excursions. At night, the terror level went way, way up.

The only reason she knew they were at German's Tire Plant was that the weapons bag Shane had brought contained flashlights, and one of the first things Claire's lit up was the spooky clown face graffitied around a big open maw of a doorway. She'd never forget that stupid clown face. Ever.

"Oh man," Shane breathed. He wasn't fond of this place, either.

"Buck up," Eve said. "At least you didn't get locked in a freezer here like next month's entrée. I did."

Myrnin, blue-white in the flashlight beams, looked offended. "Young lady, I put you there for safekeeping. If I had meant to eat you, I would have."

"That's comforting," Eve said. And then, under her breath, "Not."

"This way." Myrnin put out his hand to shield his eyes from their flashlights, and picked his way around a pile of tottering, empty beer cans left by adventurous high schoolers, a stained, torn mattress, and some empty crates. "Someone's been here."

"No kidding?"

"I mean, recently," he said. "Not humans. Vampires. Many of them." He sounded a little puzzled. "Not my creatures, either. They all died, you know. The ones I turned."

Back in his crazy (crazier?) days, Myrnin had experimented on some hapless victims, trying to turn them into vampires but failing as his illness took hold. The results hadn't been pretty—more like zombies than vampires, and not focused on anything but killing. Claire wondered how they'd died, and decided she really didn't want to know. Myrnin was a scientist. He was used to putting down lab animals at the end of a test.

"Are these vampires hanging around now?" Shane asked. He had a stake in his left hand, and a silver-coated knife in the other—a steak knife he'd used a car battery and a fish tank full of chemicals to electroplate. Stinky, but cheap and effective. "Because a heads-up would be nice."

"No, they're gone." Myrnin continued to hesitate, though. "I wonder. . . ."

"Wonder later. Move now," Eve said. She sounded nervous, and she kept shining the light around erratically, reacting to every rustle in the dark. There were a lot of those. Rats, birds, bats—the place was full of wildlife. Claire kept her own light trained on the path ahead of her, making sure she didn't trip or cut herself on rusty juts of metal as Myrnin led the way. Shane's warmth behind her felt good. So did the weight of the Super Soaker in her arms.

Myrnin threw open a metal door with a snap, shattering the lock and scattering links of the big chain that had secured it all over the pitted concrete outside. "There," he said, and pointed as they gathered around him. The clouds thinned a little, allowing some diffuse moonlight to paint the ground with cool blue and silver, and a mile or so away sat a concrete block of a building, and a tall, skeletal metal tower. Big white letters on the tower said KV V; one of the *V*s was long gone, and the other was tilting drunkenly to one side, not far from dropping off entirely to join its missing mate. The place looked deserted. Wind rattled over the flat landscape, whipping up dust and scattering trash, and made an eerie whistling sound through the metal of the tower.

"I don't see Michael's car."

"One way to be sure," Myrnin said. "Let's go."

The closer they came, the creepier the place was. Claire wasn't a fan of blighted industrial buildings, and Morganville was full of them—the half-destroyed hospital, German's Tire Plant, even the old City Hall had its decaying side.

This one looked so . . . grim. It was just a cinder block building, not very large, and the one window in front had been long ago broken out and boarded over. Someone had spray-painted KEEP OUT on the bricks, and part of it was heavily decorated in multicolored swirls of graffiti. Beer cans, cigarette butts, empty plastic bags—the usual stuff.

"I don't see a way in," Eve whispered.

"Why are you whispering?" Myrnin whispered back. "Vampires can hear us, anyway."

"Is there a vampire in there?" Claire asked.

"I'm not psychic. I have no idea."

"You could tell in the tire plant!"

He tapped his nose. "Five senses. Not six. It's not so easy to sniff them out standing outside the building." He gently moved the business end of her Super Soaker away from himself. "Please. I bathed already, and I'd rather not do it in the vampire equivalent of pepper spray."

"Sorry."

They made their way around the side of the building, closer to the tower, and there they found Michael's dark sedan sitting in the shadows.

Empty.

"Michael?" Eve called. "Michael!"

"Hush," Myrnin said sharply, and flashed supernaturally fast across the open space to grab the knob of a door Claire could barely see. It sagged open, and he disappeared inside.

"Wait!" Claire blurted, and darted after him. She switched on the flashlight as soon as she reached the door, but all it showed her was an empty hallway, with peeling paint and a floor covered in mud from some old flood. "Myrnin, where are you?"

No answer. She yelped when Shane's hand closed over her shoulder; then she pulled in a breath and nodded. Eve crowded in behind them.

Down the hallway was a dead end, with more hallways stretching left and right. The fading paint had some kind of mural on it, something West Texas-y with cows and cowboys, and the letters *KVVV* in big block capitals.

The whole place smelled like mold and dead animals.

"This way," Myrnin's voice said quietly, and with a hum, electricity turned on in the hall. Some of the bulbs burned out with harsh, sizzling snaps, leaving parts of the space in darkness.

Claire followed the hall to the end, which took a right turn into a small studio with some kind of engineering board. The equipment looked ancient, but clean; somebody had been here—presumably Kim—and had taken care to put everything in working order. Microphones, a chair, a backdrop, lighting . . . everything in the studio needed for filming, including a small digital video camera on a tripod.

On the other side of the room was a complicated editing console, which had a bank of monitors set up. They obviously weren't original to the setup—decades more modern than the soundboard—and Claire identified different components that had been Frankensteined into the system.

These included an array of fat black terabyte drives, all portable.

Michael was sitting at the console. "Michael!" Eve blurted, and threw herself on him; he stood up to catch her in his arms, and hugged her close. "You incredible *jerk*!"

He kissed her hair. "Yeah, I know."

She smacked his arm. "Really. You are a jerk!"

"I get that." He pushed her off a little, to look at her. "You're okay?"

"No thanks to you. You had to go running off in the middle of the night and not even say boo . . ."

"I should have known you guys wouldn't stay put."

"Where's Detective Hess?" Claire asked. "I thought you were meeting him here."

"Yeah, I did."

"Where did he go?"

"I'll tell you that in a minute." Michael seemed preoccupied, as if he were trying to figure out how to tell them something they weren't going to like at all. "This is Kim's data vault. At least, most of it. Claire, that's a router, right? I think this is her receiving station for the signals."

"She's using the tower to amplify the signals," Claire said. "Did you find—?" She didn't want to get more specific than that. Michael shook his head, and her heart fell. "What about the other ones?"

"She's been a busy girl," Michael said. "There are video files there from City Hall, Common Grounds, spots all over town. It will take hours, maybe weeks, to look at everything, but she's done a rough cut." He hit some controls, then pointed at the central monitor. "This is the raw file."

After some old-fashioned leader signals, there was a shot of the Morganville town limits sign, creaking in the wind ... and then, in special effects, the word *Vampires* appeared in bloody streaks right below the sign.

"Subtle." Eve snorted. "She's got a future in Hollywood."

Kim's voice came on, breathlessly narrating. "Welcome to Morganville, the town with bite. If you've ever driven across the barren landscape of West Texas, you may wonder why people live out here in the middle of nowhere. Well, wonder no more. It's because they can't live anywhere else without people knowing what they are."

The visuals cut to a montage of Morganville daily life—normal, boring stuff.

And then a night-vision shot of a vampire—Morley, Claire realized with a shock—sucking the blood out of someone's neck. It was an extreme close-up. His eyes were like silver coins, and the blood looked black.

Cut to Eve, working the counter at the coffee shop in all her Goth glory. Eve sucked in a quick breath, but said nothing. More shots of Morganville, some handheld. Claire saw footage of students, and remembered Kim running around the campus with her digital camera, asking people stupid questions.

It was in there, and so was Claire, saying, "I have two words for you, and the second one is *off.* Fill in the blank."

Claire covered her mouth with both hands. God, she looked so *angry.* And kind of bitchy.

It got worse, with the voice-over. "Even the normal people of Morganville aren't so normal. Take my friends who live in this house."

A shot of the Glass House, full daylight. Then some

kind of hidden-camera thing of Kim knocking on the door, Eve answering.

A shot of Shane. One of Michael.

"Living in a town full of terror doesn't mean you can't find true love—or at least, real sex."

The video morphed into Claire and Shane in his bedroom. *Oh God no . . .* Claire felt sick and hot and breathless, full of horror at seeing herself there on that screen. She stumbled away and almost threw herself into Shane's arms. He, lips parted, was staring at the picture, looking just as horrified as she felt. But he couldn't look away, while she simply couldn't watch.

"Goodness," Myrnin said quietly. "I don't think I should be watching this. I don't think I'm old enough."

"Turn it off," Shane said. "Michael."

Instead of turning it off, Michael hit FAST FORWARD. He slowed it down as the scene changed. More Kim voyeur porn, this time Michael and Eve. No voice-over. Claire couldn't imagine what she was intending to say, but it couldn't have been good.

"I'll kill her," Eve said. It sounded calm, but it really wasn't. "Why are you showing me this?"

Michael looked at her, and Claire's stomach did a little flip at the grimness in his expression. "Sit down," he said, and wheeled the chair closer to Eve. She looked at it, then at him, frowning. "Trust me."

She did, still frowning, as the scene changed on-screen.

It was some dark-paneled room, with a big wooden round table, an ornate flower arrangement in the middle. Of the several people around the table, Claire recognized three immediately, with a shock. "Amelie," she blurted. Amelie clearly had no idea she was being filmed; the camera was high up, at an angle, but it caught their faces clearly. Next to her at the table was Richard Morrell, the mayor, neat and handsome in a dark suit. At his right sat Oliver, looking—as usual—angry. Several other people around the table were talking at once, arguing, and finally Oliver slammed his hand down on the wood with so much force it silenced them all.

Then came Kim's voice-over. "Morganville is ruled by a town council, but one not like any other. Nobody elects these people. That's Amelie, Founder of Morganville. She's more than a thousand years old, and she's a ruthless killer. Oliver's not much younger, and he's even meaner. The mayor, Richard Morrell, he's new, but his family has ruled the humans of Morganville for a hundred years. Richard's the only human on the council. And he gets outvoted . . . constantly."

She cut back to the sound as Richard was saying, ". . . want to revisit the decision we made earlier, about Jason Rosser."

"What about him?" Oliver asked irritably. "We've heard your arguments. Let's move on."

"You can't execute him. He gave himself up. He tried to save the girl."

"He did *not* try to save Claire," Amelie said. "He left her to die. Granted, he did turn himself in to the police and told us about his accomplice in these murders, but we must be clear: he is far from innocent, and his history tells us he can't be trusted."

"He's still a kid," Richard said, "and you can't just arbitrarily decide to execute him. Not without a trial."

"With a majority vote, we can," Oliver said. "Two for, one against. I believe that is a majority. It won't be a public event. He'll just quietly—disappear."

Eve's mouth dropped open. She leaned forward, frantically searching the screen for a clue. "When was this? Michael? When did she record this?"

"I don't know," he said. "I thought you should know. Your brother's been sentenced to death."

"Oliver—he didn't even—he didn't say *anything*."

"Well," Myrnin said, "I don't suppose he felt it was

necessary. I expect they were planning to arrange something quiet, perhaps an accident. Or suicide."

Eve fell into the chair, and blindly reached out for Michael, who took her hand. "They can't just kill him. Not like some—rat in a cage. Oh God, Michael . . ."

"I told you Detective Hess was here. He left right after we found that. He's going straight to the jail to be sure Jason's okay. He'll put him in protective custody, okay? Don't worry."

She gave out a breathless, broken laugh. "Don't worry? How do I not worry after you show me things like this?"

"Good point," Shane said. "Michael, Kim bugged the council meeting. How could she possibly do that?"

"She couldn't," Myrnin said. "The human parts of town, yes, of course, but not the vampire parts. She has no excuse to be there, and she'd be caught if she'd gone anywhere near the official chambers. Or Amelie's house." He held up another black hard drive, which was clearly labeled in silver ink. "Or Oliver's, for that matter."

Claire caught her breath. "Your lab?"

"No. Oddly enough, nothing. But the evidence she has here is damning enough, I would say."

"But nobody would believe it," Eve said. "I mean, sure, she might get some off-brand cable station to air it, but everybody would think it was some kind of hoax."

"Doesn't matter," Claire said. "Even if nobody does, tourists will come flocking to town, and how long do you think things will hold together once that happens?"

"I'd give it a week," Myrnin said. He sounded quiet, and not at all amused. "This is our refuge, Claire. Our last safe place in this world. Don't be fooled; we might be willing to compromise, but we are territorial. Kim has violated the deepest covenant of Morganville. She can't survive this."

"She didn't do it alone; you said so yourself. It took a vampire to bug the council, let alone Amelie's house."

"And we will find them," Myrnin said. "And we will

destroy them. There are rules to Morganville, and Kim and this vampire have shattered them beyond all repair. Amelie must never know of this. I'm afraid what she would do."

That seemed a strange left turn. "Why? We're going to catch them, right? We've got the video."

"Do we?" Myrnin looked at the array of hard drives. "You spoke of more than seventy cameras, but I see only sixty or so hard drives. What's missing, Claire? You know Amelie. You know that her first concern is for her people. If she believes that we've been compromised here, she will cut our losses."

"Losses being humans," Shane said.

"She'd rather move us and destroy all evidence we were ever here. It's always been her final option. You have no idea how many times she's come close recently."

Claire swallowed. "We can't let her do that."

"We cannot stop her," Myrnin said. "Not even I can do that. But what we can do is remove the evidence."

He crushed the hard drive he was holding into junk and dropped it to the floor, then moved on to the next, and the next.

Michael helped Eve out of the chair, picked it up, and smashed it into the editing station. He ripped out the hard drive from the video editing system and smashed it against the wall.

Claire and Eve backed up against the wall, holding hands, as the two vampires systematically destroyed every bit of data storage in the place. It took a while, but they were thorough, and when the last piece of equipment was broken into random parts, Shane said, "I thought that would feel better, somehow."

"We're not finished," Myrnin said. "We need to find every camera and destroy those, as well. And we *must* find Kim and force her to tell us who helped her. This is not negotiable. A vampire traitor is far too dangerous to live."

* * *

Kim had kept records—a hard copy printout stuffed in a cabinet drawer next to the wrecked editing machine. It listed a total of seventy-*four* cameras, all over Morganville. "She must have added a couple at the last minute. This is going to take hours," Eve said. "We'll have to split up, each take ten or so. Myrnin and Michael, you've got the Vamptown cameras. Claire, Shane, here you go. Knock yourselves out."

"What about Kim?" Claire asked, taking the page of locations. "We still need to find her."

"I will ask Ada to locate her," Myrnin said.

"She can do that?" Claire asked, and then blinked. "Of course she can. *Will* she do that?"

"Possibly. If she's in a good mood, which is never certain, as you know. But I assure you, Ada is no longer angry at you, so don't be worried about that." Myrnin checked a gleaming gold pocket watch he kept in his vest pocket, some complicated dragon-shaped thing. "We must meet back before sunrise. Where?"

"Someplace deserted," Claire said. "Much as I hate it, how about German's? I don't want anybody overhearing us."

"Paranoid much?" Eve asked. "Yeah, me too. I'm never taking my clothes off again, I swear."

"German's it is," Myrnin said. "You know the portal frequency. Be there before sunrise, and do try to avoid getting yourself killed, if at all possible."

He led them out of the studio, out into the night. Michael took his car, heading off with his list of camera locations. At German's, Myrnin stepped through the dark clown-mouth doorway and was gone on his own errands, leaving Shane, Eve, and Claire standing there in the dark, in a fragile circle of flashlight.

"So?" Eve prodded. "Fire it up, Teleport Girl. I want this over with."

Claire checked the list. "Right. The first twenty are

easy—all in common areas. Eve, I'll send you and Shane to the alley behind Common Grounds. I'll take the university."

"Hey," Shane said. "Wait a minute. I don't want you out there alone."

"University," Claire reminded him. "Protected ground. Besides, I'm the one with the bracelet." She flashed the gold at him, and he didn't look happy, but he did look resigned. "Also, we've got no time to argue. Go."

Shane looked back at her before he stepped through the portal, and Claire felt a moment's sick fear that she'd never see him again. Morganville was a dangerous place. Every good-bye could be the last.

We'll get through this.

She focused on the portal, shifted frequencies, and started on her camera-destroying mission.

She hoped Myrnin was right about Ada.

Four hours later, it was approaching sunrise, Claire was bone-tired, and she'd bagged all of the cameras on her list, including the one in the football team's shower room, which was an interesting experience. Kim had clearly been combining business with personal pleasure. She took the portal back to the alley behind Common Grounds, intending to pick up Shane and Eve, but they were nowhere in sight. She called Shane's cell, and heard it ringing, but it was distant and muffled.

She found him standing braced against the wall, holding Eve's ankles as she stood on his shoulders to reach a camera set on top of the roof of a shed. "Got it!" Eve called, and nearly overbalanced. Shane staggered around, got his equilibrium again, and helped her down to the pavement. "We should totally join the circus."

"One of us already looks like a clown."

"Hi guys," Claire said, and they both jumped and turned her way. "Sorry. Didn't mean to scare you."

Shane hugged her. "How'd you do?"

"Twenty cameras. There was one missing. I think somebody found it and swiped it from the University Center. You?"

"That was the last one on the list," he said. "Guess it's time to see how Team Vampire did."

Claire opened the portal to German's Tire Plant, and stepped through, with Shane and Eve right behind her. The portal snapped shut as soon as they were inside, and Claire flipped on her flashlight.

"Um . . ." Eve turned on her light, as well. "Okay. Wrong number, Claire."

"No," Claire said. "That can't happen. I mean, it's the right frequency. I don't know what happened, but we *should* be at German's."

"Well, we're not," Shane said, and shone his light around. They were in an underground tunnel. It was damp and dark and it smelled really foul—much worse than most of the vampire highway tunnels under Morganville. This one didn't look like it had been used for a road, either. "Wrong turn."

Eve said, in an entirely different voice, "*Really* wrong turn." She pointed off down the tunnel, and Claire saw shapes moving in the darkness. Pale skin. Shining red eyes. "Oh man. Dial us out, please."

The only problem was that the portal system refused to pick up. They were locked out.

Claire looked at Shane and Eve and shook her head. Her heart was pounding a mile a minute, and she could see the light trembling from the force of her pulse beats. "We're stuck," she said.

Shane dropped the bag he was carrying, unzipped it, and passed weapons to Eve, then took out a wicked-lethal crossbow with silver-tipped bolts. "Somebody up there doesn't like you, Claire."

Claire primed the Super Soaker. "It's Ada," she said. "This time, I'm not letting Myrnin talk me out of it."

*   *   *

The vampires—well, vampirelike *things*, sort of like Myrnin's experimental attempts to turn humans back in his crazy days—hurled themselves out of the darkness with high-pitched, batlike squeals. Claire resisted the urge to scream, and let loose with the water gun. A blast caught three of them in midleap, and they shrieked even louder, hit the ground, rolled, and kept rolling. She could see the ghostly blue flare of flames around them as the silver ate into their exposed skin—which was most of it, because these things were more like tunnel rats than anything approaching human. Giant undead tunnel rats.

Only in Morganville . . .

Shane aimed and fired, taking one of them out just as it was preparing to leap, and reloaded with an ease that told Claire he'd been practicing. Eve had a handful of what looked like darts—regulation darts, the kind you threw at a target in a bar. She was dead-on accurate with them, too, as soon as any tunnel rat came within ten feet of her.

By the time Claire was starting to worry about her water reservoir, and Shane was running low on cross-bow bolts, the attacking forces were running. "Let's go," Eve said, tossing another dart that landed in the ass of a retreating vampire. "Ooooh, trip twenty!"

"You're enjoying this way too much," Shane said. "Darts? When did you come up with that?"

"I was playing with your electroplating thingy. After I did all my jewelry, I started in on pointy things." Eve held out a dart for inspection. It had—of course—a skull on the fletching. "Sweet, right?"

"Cute. Time to run now."

Claire slung the Super Soaker around her back and ran up the hill, chasing Shane, who was, as always, faster—the result of longer legs, not really dedicated practice. Shane only ran when someone chased him; he was more of a weights kind of guy.

The fact that the tunnel tilted uphill was a good sign—it was basically an entrance ramp, which meant they'd come up to ground level soon enough. Then Claire could figure out where they were, how to find a working portal, and get back to the business at hand—find Kim, beat Kim like a taiko drum to find out who her vampire coconspirator was, and then hit Ada's RESET button.

Simple.

Except, of course, it wasn't.

Shane slowed, and Claire almost crashed into him. He dashed over to the side of the tunnel, hugging the wall, and Claire and Eve piled in next to him. "What?" Eve asked around breathless pants. She wasn't much for running, either.

"Someone's coming," Shane said. "Shhhh."

Eve choked and strangled on a cough, and muttered, "Got to cut down on the cigarettes."

"You don't smoke," Claire whispered.

"Then I'm completely screwed."

Shane whirled toward them and put hands over both their mouths. His face looked fierce. They nodded.

It was dark where they were, but not dark enough. A shape appeared ahead of them, coming down the tunnel . . . then another. Then more. Six—no, ten. Claire lost all will to snark, and she was pretty sure, from Eve's wide-eyed look, that she felt the same. They'd done pretty well against the tunnel rats, but these were *real* vampires.

Hunters.

Morley stopped about twenty feet away, still facing straight ahead, and held up a hand to stop the group of vampires following him. Claire recognized some of them from earlier. Some of them were still healing from the burns left by her water gun.

"Look who's come to visit," he said, and turned his head in their direction at the side of the tunnel. "Claire and her friends. I wonder if they want to stay for dinner."

Shane snapped the crossbow up and took aim on Morley. "Don't even think about it."

Morley stuck his hands in the pockets of his dirty raincoat. "I tremble in fear, boy. Obviously, in all my long life, no one has *ever* threatened me with a weapon before." His tone changed, took on edges. "Put it down if you want to live."

"Don't," Eve whispered.

Morley smiled. "The boy's got two arrows left," he said. "You have a handful of darts. Little Claire's water weapon is almost empty. And by the way, I am aware of your strategic position. I hate to repeat myself, but I will: put down your weapons if you want to live."

"No choice," Shane said, and swallowed hard. He crouched down and put the crossbow on the concrete, then rose with his hands up.

I could get in one good spray, Claire thought, but she knew it was a terrible idea. She lifted the strap of the toy gun over her head and let it fall. It sounded empty.

"Shit," Eve said, and threw down her darts. "All right. What now? You get all *Nosferatu* on our asses? If you make me a vampire, I'll make you eat those fangs."

Morley eyed her with a bit of a frown. "I believe you might," he said. "But I'm not interested in converts. I'm much more interested in allies."

"Allies," Claire repeated. "You've tried to kill us a whole bunch."

"That wasn't about you," he said. "The first time, you were simply with Amelie. The next, well, I was doing a favor for someone else. Another ally, as it happens."

"What do you want?"

"We want freedom," Morley said. "We want to live as God meant us to do. Is that such a terrible thing?"

There were a few vampires in his group that Claire recognized with a nasty jolt of surprise. "Jacob," she said. "Jacob Goldman? Patience?" Two of Theo Goldman's family—and Theo was the last vampire she'd expect to be in the middle of this. His kids, though ... she really didn't know them very well.

Jacob looked away. Patience, on the other hand, stared right back, and lifted her chin as if daring Claire to say anything else. From her last encounter with the Goldmans, Claire had been aware the younger generation was starting to hate the whole philosophy of their parents; it made sense that they'd found someone here in Morganville more like-minded.

"Amelie and Oliver are trying to make us into something we never were," Patience said. "Tame tigers. Performing bears. Toothless lions. But we can't be those things. Vampires are not caretakers of humanity. I'm sorry, but it will never be true, however much we wish it could be."

"You're not making much headway on this *Let's be friends* argument," Eve said. "I'm just saying."

Morley let out an impatient sigh, and looked back at the other vampires. "Surely you want us out of your town," he said. "As much as we'd like to go. But Amelie won't allow us to leave. We have only two choices: destroy Morganville, or destroy her. Destroying Morganville seems easier, in many ways."

The light dawned. "You were working with Kim. She suggested the cameras, didn't she?"

"It seemed a way to achieve what she wanted, and what we wanted," he agreed. "The end of Morganville. The beginning of her career. Granted, spying is an unseemly way to go about it, but it's probably less objectionable than murder."

"Until the camera's on you," Eve shot back.

"A valid point." Morley bowed slightly in her direction.

"You're the one who put the cameras in Vamptown for her."

"Me?" His thick eyebrows climbed into his tangled hair. "No. I'm hardly welcome there, you know. Nor are any of my people. I know nothing about how she managed that."

"Then let us go find out who did."

"You know, I don't have to bargain with you. I could just distribute you among my followers as a treat if you'd prefer that."

"No," Jacob Goldman said. He and Patience exchanged a look that was more like a silent argument, and then he stepped forward. "Not her. Morley, if you hurt her, we walk away."

"Patience?"

She sighed and shook her head. "The girl helped, before," she said. "Theo wouldn't want us to hurt her."

"The girl left you in a cell to die at Bishop's hands!"

"That was my father's mistake, not hers," Jacob said. "I will do many things to get our freedom. I won't do this."

The tension was ramping up fast. Claire swallowed. "Then let's make a deal," Claire said. "We want Kim, and whatever video she turned over to you."

Morley frowned at her. "In exchange for . . . ?"

"I'll ask Amelie to let you all leave."

"*Asking* is an easy task; there's no commitment required. *Doing* is accomplishment. So you will *get* Amelie to let us leave. Here is my incentive: if you don't manage to secure her permission, your two friends here sign lifetime contracts to me." Morley turned to Jacob and Patience, who nodded. "You see? Even they agree with that."

"Oh *hell* no," Eve said.

"And you are in a position to bargain . . . how?"

Shane held out a hand toward Eve, trying to restrain her a little. "No lifetime contracts," he said. "One pint a month, blood bank only. Ten percent of our income."

"Hmmmmmm." Morley dragged the sound out, still staring through half-lidded eyes. "Tempting. But you see, I can simply insist on a lifetime contract with none of your silly restrictions, or kill you right now."

"You won't," Shane said. That made Morley's eyes open wide.

"Why not? Jacob and Patience were quite specific—they're concerned for Claire. Not for you, boy."

"Because if you kill me and Eve, you'll make her your enemy. This girl won't stop until she sees you all pay."

Claire had no idea whom he was talking about—she didn't feel like that Claire at all, until she imagined Shane and Eve lying dead on the ground.

Then she understood. "I'd hunt you down," she said quietly. "I'd use every resource I have to do it. And you know I'd win."

Morley seemed impressed. "She is small, but I see your point, boy. Besides, she has the ear of Amelie, Oliver, and Myrnin; not a combination I would care to test. Very well. Limited contract, one year, one pint per month at the blood bank, ten percent of your income payable to me, in cash. I will not hunt, bite, or trade your contracts. But I insist on standard punishment clauses."

"Hey," Eve said. "Don't I get a vote?"

"Absolutely," Morley assured her. "Your thoughts?"

"I'd rather die," she said flatly. Shane turned toward her, and from the look on his face, that was not at all what he'd expected her to say. "Don't look at me like that. I told you, I'll never sign a contract. *Never.* If Morlock here wants to kill me, well, I can't stop him. But I don't have to die by inches, either, and that's what this town does to us, Shane; it takes little pieces of us away until there's nothing left and *I won't sign*!" Eve's eyes flooded with tears, but she wasn't scared; she was angry. "So bite me, vampire. Get it over with. But it's a one-time thrill."

Morley shrugged. "And you, boy?"

Shane pulled in a deep breath. "No deals if Eve doesn't buy in."

Claire's mouth tasted like ashes, and she was trying frantically to think of something, *anything* to do. She tried to build a portal behind them, but the system bounced her back, wouldn't let her so much as begin the process.

Ada.

She took Shane's hand in hers. "You'll have to kill me, too," she said. "And you can't. Not without consequences."

Morley looked positively unhappy now. "This is getting far too complicated. Fine, then we do it this way. I give you the video you're looking for, and if you don't manage to secure Amelie's permission within, let's say, a month, your friends' lives are forfeit. Yes?" When she hesitated, he bared his stained teeth. "It's not a question, really. And my patience is wearing thin. In fact, it's positively threadbare."

"Yes," Claire said.

He spit on his palm and held it out. They all just looked at him. "Well?" he demanded.

"I'm not shaking that," Shane said. "You just spit on it."

"It's the way deals are sealed—" Morley made a sound of frustration and wiped his palm against his filthy clothes. "Perhaps not anymore. Better?"

"Not really," Shane said.

Claire stepped forward and shook Morley's hand. She'd done worse.

He turned, dirty raincoat flapping, and the other vampires fell in behind him. Jacob Goldman held back, staring at Claire. He looked unhappy and tormented.

"I wouldn't have let him do it," he said. "Not to any of you. But you understand why I have to do this? For myself, and Patience?"

"I understand," Claire said. She didn't, really, but it seemed to make him feel better.

Claire, Eve, and Shane picked up their weapons and followed them into the dark.

Morley's hideout was a series of what looked like limestone caves, hollowed out into actual rooms, with doors

and windows—a city, underground. Not fancy, but it was
definitely livable, if you were sunlight averse. There were
more vamps here, living rough, hiding out. Claire figured
a lot of those who'd decided not to take sides during the
Amelie and Bishop fight had fled down here, taken up
with Morley's crew.

"I guess this means you aren't really homeless," she
said. Morley looked back at her as he opened up the
ancient, cracked door of one of the rooms. "I'd still look
into running water." Because the place stank, bad. So
did the vampires.

"We grew up in ages when running water meant
streams and rivers," he said. "We've never been overly
comfortable with modern luxuries."

"Like baths?"

"Oh, we had baths in the old days. We called them
stews, and they caused diseases." He shoved open the
door and lit a row of candles set into a kind of shelf along
the side of the room, which gave off just enough light to
make Claire feel she could turn her own portable lamp
off. "What you're looking for is here, in the box."

The box was a rickety-looking crate with rope han-
dles. Inside were more hard drives—the ones that had
been missing from the radio station—and some DVDs.
One was labeled, in black Sharpie, MICHAEL & EVE. Claire
choked a little at the sight of it. She frantically combed
through the others, but there was nothing marked SHANE
& CLAIRE.

"Don't worry," Shane said. "The lighting was terrible
on ours, anyway."

"Not funny."

"I know." He put his arm around her. "I know. Speaking of not funny, where's Kim? I'd like to tell her just
how much I appreciate all she did to make us stars."

Morley nodded. "Follow me."

Three doors down was a much smaller cave—more
like a cell—and Morley combed through an ancient

ring of ancient keys until he found one to fit the huge rusty lock. "I keep her here for her own safety," he said. "You'll see."

He opened the door, and Kim cowered back from the wash of the flashlights—but not Kim. The face was the same, but all the Goth had been scrubbed off except the dyed hair. She was dirty, dressed in filthy clothes, and there was zero bad attitude left.

Claire had been prepared to let loose a flood of anger, but this was just ... pathetic. "Kim?" No response. "Kim! What did you do to her?"

"Nothing. She doesn't respond to her name," Morley said. "It seems she's lost her mind."

"Bullshit," Eve snapped. "She's an actress."

"I've seen rehearsals," Morley responded. "She's not that good."

Eve shoved past him to crouch down next to Kim, who covered her face and tried to curl into a ball. "Hey!" Eve said, and shook her, hard. "Kim, snap out of it! It's Eve! Look at me!"

Kim screamed, and Claire caught her breath at the sound of it; there was real terror in it, and pain, and horror. Eve let her hand fall away, and she leaned back against the nearest wall, frowning.

"What happened to her?" Shane asked. Morley shrugged.

"Something bad," he said. "Something permanent, as far as I can tell. She crossed someone who didn't take well to her initiative."

"You said you keep her locked up for protection."

He flashed Claire a dark smile. "Consider it locking up the wine cellar. The girl's still a good vintage, if not a brilliant conversationalist."

Ugh. "I need her," Claire said. "I need to take her with me."

Morley's vampire followers didn't seem especially happy about her act of kindness. "She's got no family,"

Patience said. "No one is going to miss her. No one was even looking for her."

"We were."

"To punish her! We will do that for you."

Even Shane looked a little sick at that. "We'll do our own punishing, thanks," he said. "Humans, I mean. Not me, personally."

Morley's eyes narrowed, but he shrugged as if he didn't really care. "Take her," he said. "Take the black boxes she thought were so important. Take it all, and remember your promise, Claire: you have one month to secure Amelie's permission for us to leave Morganville. If you don't get it, I'll be paying your friends a visit."

Kim was too scared to fight, but Shane took some strips of cloth and wrapped her wrists and ankles tight before slinging her over his shoulder. Eve took the box with the hard drives and DVDs.

Morley and his vampires stood in their way.

"One month," he said. "Remember what I said."

Then they parted ranks, and the three of them, carrying Kim, walked uphill toward the light at the end of the tunnel.

Ada was standing right at the very edge of the darkness, hands clasped before her, eyes like burned paper holes.

"I see you found her," Ada said. "Good. I want her."

"Why? Why did you bring us here?"

"Morley was supposed to kill you. I suppose one must do everything one's self these days."

Claire felt a sick wave of understanding flood over her. "You," she said. "You would have known all about the cameras. You probably found out the first time Kim placed one."

Ada smiled.

"You let her do it."

"Oh no," Ada said. "I *helped* her do it. The girl told me she would use the video she'd collected to rid me of

Amelie and Oliver, and I gave her access. I helped her place her cameras. But she was a liar. A cheat. A thief." Ada's image contorted, taking on a monster's shape for a flicker, then smoothed back to her Victorian disguise. "She was going to cheat me out of my revenge and destroy Morganville altogether. I won't have that. Unlike Morley and his rabble, I can't simply leave. I *am* Morganville. I must survive."

"You're not Morganville," Claire said. Kim, draped over Shane's shoulder, had caught sight of Ada, and she was thrashing wildly, screaming. It was all Shane could do to hold on to her. "You're just a science project. One that doesn't work right."

"I am the force that holds this lie of a town together," Ada said, and glided closer, so close Claire could feel the cold chill generated by her image projection. "As far as Morganville is concerned, I am its goddess."

"Word of advice," Eve said. "It's time for a change of religion."

Ada's image became distorted again, and she stretched out a hand. Claire controlled the natural impulse to flinch. *She's not real. She's just a ghost—*

Ada's fingers touched her face. Not quite real, but almost.

Claire jumped back. "Outside!" she yelled. "Get outside!"

Ada smiled. "I'll see you soon."

They made it outside, into the faint hint of sunrise, without anyone jumping them again.

Claire flagged down a passing police cruiser and got them to take Kim, who shrieked and fought so hard they had to use a taser on her. Eve winced, and so did Shane.

Claire didn't. She felt bad about it, but she just couldn't bring herself to really feel sorry for Kim. *Karma*, she thought. They'd end up putting her in a padded cell, and eventually maybe Kim would recover enough to function as a normal person. Maybe even a better one. Claire didn't even resent that, so long as she never, ever had to talk to her again.

Ever.

By ten a.m. they were back at the Glass House, and Michael was waiting. "Where were you?" he demanded as soon as they opened the door. Claire said nothing; he was focused on Eve, anyway. "I've been calling; it went straight to voice mail."

"I turned it off," Eve said. "We were kind of being stealthy."

"Since when do you turn off a phone?" Michael put his arms around her, and Eve relaxed against him, and for just a moment, it looked like everything was the same again.

Then Eve pulled free and walked away down the hall, head down.

Michael looked awful. "What do I have to do—?"

Shane slapped his shoulder as he passed. "Give her space," he said. "It's been a hard couple of days. Where's Myrnin?"

"He never showed at the rendezvous," Michael said. "I wasn't really worried about him. More about you."

"Yeah, about that—we kind of had to make a deal with Morley. You know, Graveyard Guy?"

"What kind of deal?"

"The kind where we don't want to pay up," Shane said. "Ask Claire."

She shook her head, walking on. "Ask Shane," she said. "I'm not done yet."

"What?" Shane grabbed her wrist, pulling her to a stop. His face was tense and pale. "You can't be serious. Not done with what? We've got the videos, the cameras, Kim. What else?"

"Myrnin," she said. "He didn't show up at the rendezvous."

"And? Dude's crazy, in case you didn't notice recently. He probably went off to chase butterflies or something"

"He'd have been there. Something happened to him." Claire knew already, knew it all the way down to her bones. "Ada did something. She sent us to Morley, thinking he'd kill us. She'd go after Myrnin, too. I have to find him."

"Not by yourself."

"No," Michael agreed.

"Ditto," Eve said, and picked up a fresh weapons bag from the closet to sling over her shoulder. "Definitely not by yourself."

Claire looked at each of them in turn, saving Shane for last. "You're sure. Because it's going to be dangerous."

"You're going after Ada, right?" Eve put stakes in her pockets, then tossed a crossbow to Shane, who caught it in midair. "You're going to need backup. Especially if she's got Myrnin. Besides, if we just sit here and wait, she can get us anytime she wants."

"We should take the car," Claire said, heading toward the closet to get her own weapons stash. "It's not safe now going through the portals anymore. . . ."

A black hole formed in the wall next to her, and Claire felt the storm of force rip through the house. The portal wavered as the house itself fought back, trying to heal the rift, but whatever was tearing the entrance held firm. *Ada.*

Claire didn't have time to run.

Ada's blue-white hands came out of the darkness, grabbed Claire by the shirt, and dragged her into the portal.

It snapped shut on the shocked, angry faces of her friends.

She heard Shane scream her name.

So, Ada really could touch things. Claire kind of wished she'd taken that idea more seriously.

Claire woke up lying on cold, damp stone, feeling damp little feet skittering over her arm—rats, probably. She hoped it wasn't roaches. She'd just die if it was roaches.

She was in the dark—utter, velvety darkness that pressed in on her like smothering cloth. When she moved, she heard the scrape of her shoes echo off into the distance.

Cave. Probably not Ada's cave, because Claire couldn't hear the distinctive hissing and clanking that came from Ada's gears and pipes. *It doesn't have to be her cave*, Claire reminded herself. Ada could open any portal, anywhere within Morganville—or under it. From the ragged, crude way she'd done it at the Glass House, though, she might not be able to keep up that sort of thing for long.

She was unraveling in control, even while she was getting stronger in raw power.

"Ada," a voice said in the distance—weak and faint. "Ada, you must let me go. I order you to let me go."

"No." Ada's voice came from nowhere, and everywhere; not out of Claire's speakerphone this time. Claire slapped at her pockets, but she had nothing—no weapons, no phone; Ada had taken everything. "You're going nowhere. I've waited all these years, you know. So many years for you to love me."

"Ada, please." Myrnin sounded very weak; Claire could hardly believe it was really him. "I do love you. I always have. Please stop this. You don't know what you're doing. You're not well. Let me help—"

He broke off with a strangled gasp. She'd hurt him, and it took a lot to hurt Myrnin.

Claire slowly climbed to her feet, put her hands on the nearest stone wall, and began to feel her way through the darkness.

"Going somewhere?" Ada's voice asked from right behind her, as if the computer was leaning over her shoulder. Claire yelped and flailed out a hand, but there was nothing there. "I brought you here so that I can get rid of you once and for all, and you can help me make Myrnin better at the same time. Isn't that clever of me?"

Her voice was breaking up into strange harmonics, not really a voice at all—mere noise. "How are you talking?" Claire asked. "You're not using my phone."

"Does it matter?"

"No," Claire said. She sounded a lot less scared than she actually was, which she supposed was a good thing. "I'm just curious."

"You'd be curious at your own autopsy," Ada said, and broke into distorted laughter that reeled wildly out of control. "I'd like to see that."

"Where's Myrnin?"

"*Don't you dare try to take him away from me!*" Ada shrieked. The echoes filled the cave, bounced, magnified until Claire had to clap her hands over her ears. She could feel the sound waves on her skin, like speakers booming at a rave. "He is mine; he's always been mine; I will never give him up, never!"

"I'm not trying to take him away!" Claire shouted. "I just want to be sure he's all right!"

The sound cut off, just like that. Even the echoes. Claire slowly lowered her hands and touched the wall again; she was afraid to try to move without keeping it under her fingers, because there was no possibility of seeing a thing. Not with human eyes.

"Claire?" Myrnin's voice again, coming from ahead of her and to the right. He sounded weak, and concerned. "You have to get out of here. Please go away."

"Kind of not an option," she said. "Unless Ada wants to open me a portal . . . ?"

Ada laughed softly.

"Guess not." Claire took a couple of more steps forward, but it took her off the angle toward Myrnin's voice. "Myrnin, I can't see. I'm going to try to get to you, but you have to keep talking, okay?"

"Don't," he said. "Don't try to reach me. Claire, I'm asking you, please stay where you are. Get out if you can. *Do not come near me.*"

She was ignoring that, mostly because the idea of staying alone in this darkness, listening to Ada do bad things to him, was worse than anything he could do to her himself. "Keep talking," she said. She heard him take in a deep breath, then let it out. He didn't say a word. She guessed he thought that if he didn't encourage her, maybe she'd give up.

He should have known better.

"Stop!" Myrnin's voice suddenly rang out of the black, urgent and sharp, and Claire paused with her right foot still raised. "Back up. Slowly. Two steps. Do it, Claire!"

She did, putting one foot carefully behind the other, and stopped. "What is it?"

"The floor isn't stable. If you try to cross that way, it'll break through under your weight. You *must* stay where you are!"

"So concerned for the new girl," Ada's voice said, vibrating out of the cave walls. "Never so concerned for me, were you? Even though you always knew how much I loved you. How much I wanted to be with you. I let you drink my blood, Myrnin. I let you take *everything*. And then you did *this* to me."

"Oh, stop whining," Myrnin snapped. "You were grateful enough to become a vampire, and it had nothing to do with your being a lovesick schoolgirl. You wanted a thousand lifetimes to explore the world, to discover, to learn. I gave you that, Ada."

"You were supposed to take care of me."

"According to whom?"

"According to me!" The echoes built again, bouncing wildly, and Claire crouched down in place, hands firmly over her ears again. This time, the echoes died gradually.

Once it was quiet, Claire rose to her feet and started moving carefully forward at an angle to her original course, testing the floor before putting her full weight on the stone.

It felt solid.

"Claire, please stop," Myrnin said raggedly. "You can't see. You don't know how dangerous this is."

"Describe it to me. Help me! If you don't, I'll just keep walking."

"That's exactly what she wants. She wants you to try to reach me—" Myrnin broke off with a small cry of pain.

"Myrnin?" Claire forgot all about being careful, and took a step forward. Too fast. She felt the stone snap and crumble and fall away, dark on dark, and she teetered off balance over the edge of a hole that led to the center of the world, apparently. She didn't even hear the falling rocks hit bottom.

Claire slowly shifted her weight to her back foot and stepped back to solid stone again. Her heart was pounding so hard it hurt, and she couldn't seem to slow down her panicked breathing.

"Myrnin, you have to help me," she said. "Tell me which way to go. We can do this."

"Even if you reach me, it's no help to either of us," he said. "She has me. There's no point in your dying, as well."

"Just tell me how to get there."

After a few silent seconds, Myrnin said, "Two steps to your right, then one forward." As she accomplished that, he said, "Claire, she's right. I did take advantage of her. She did love me. I used that to get what I wanted from her."

"You mean, like a guy?" Claire counted steps carefully, then stopped. "Next."

"One step forward, then one diagonally to your left. What I did was considerably worse than you think. I made her a vampire so I could have a reliable assistant, one who loved me and would never betray me. I made her a slave."

"Next. And one thing I can tell you about Ada, she was never a slave, not to you or anybody else. And you really did love her, or you wouldn't have kept her locket all these years."

"Another step straight to your left, then six forward. And don't be daft. I keep gum wrappers. It doesn't mean I love the gum that was once in them."

She counted. He didn't say anything else. Once she got to the end of the directions, she said, "Next. I'm not wrong about Ada. You did love her."

"Straight ahead, one step."

"You're not going to tell me I'm wrong?"

"What's the point? Three steps to your right."

"The point is to keep us talking so I'm not so terrified out of my mind," she said. "What are we going to do about her?"

"Nothing. There's nothing we can do."

"I'm there. Next? Also, there's got to be something. What about—" She was about to say *the reset code*, and he must have known it, because he let out a sharp hiss for silence. She swallowed the words.

"Focus," Myrnin said. "Forward three small steps. Be careful not to overshoot."

She found out why when she took the steps; her toes overhung what felt like another sinkhole.

Myrnin's voice was close now, very close. "Next," she said.

"This is the difficult part," he said. "You're going to have to jump."

"Jump?" She wasn't sure he was thinking straight. "I can't jump. I can't see!"

"You wanted to get to me, and this is what it takes. If you want to stay where you are—"

"No. Tell me."

"Two steps to your left, and jump straight forward, hard. I'll catch you."

"Myrnin—"

"I'll catch you," he whispered into the dark. "Jump."

She took two running steps and before she could let herself think about what she was doing, dug in her toes and leaped forward.

She crashed into Myrnin's solid body, his cold arms wrapped around her, and for a few breaths he held her close as she shivered. He smelled like metal. Like cold things.

He didn't let go.

"Myrnin?"

"I'm sorry," he said.

And then he bit her.

13

When Claire came awake again, there were lights in the cave—diffuse and dim, but enough to make things out. Like Myrnin, sitting huddled against the cave wall. She must have made some noise, because his head came up, and he looked straight at her.

She didn't think she'd ever seen anybody look so miserable in her life, and for a moment she couldn't think why he would look that way, and then it all came crashing back.

The throbbing in her neck.

The hollow, disconnected feeling inside her.

The panicked thudding of her heart trying to speed too little blood through the racetrack of her veins. Yeah, she recognized that feeling all too well.

"You bit me," she said. It came out surprised, and a little sad. She started to sit up, but that didn't go so well; she sank back to the cold stone floor, feeling sick and vague, as if she were fading out of the world.

"Don't move," he said softly. "Your pressure is very low. I tried—I tried to stop, Claire. I did try. Please give me the credit."

"You bit me," she said again. It still sounded surprised, although she really wasn't anymore. *You can't trust him.* Shane had said that. And Michael. And Eve. Even Amelie.

You can't trust me.

Myrnin had told her that, too, from the very first. She'd just never really, really believed it. Myrnin was like a thrill ride, one of those dark carnival tracks where scary things swooped in close but never *quite* touched you.

Now she knew better.

"I told you I'd kill you if you did that. I *promised.*"

"I am so sorry," Myrnin said, and lowered his head. "Lie still. It won't be so bad if you keep yourself flat." He sounded tired and defeated. Claire blinked back gray fog, fighting her way back into the world, and almost wished she hadn't when he shifted a little, and she saw—really saw—what had happened to him.

There was a silver bar through his left arm, driven in between the two bones. On either side of it hung silver chains that rattled on the stone and were fixed to a silver-plated bolt. The wound continued to drip red down his arm and hand, to patter into a large puddle around him.

Claire had a flash of Amelie at Sam's grave, silver driven into the wounds to keep them from closing. But Amelie had chosen to do that. This had been done to keep Myrnin here, pinned and helpless.

He shuddered, and the chains rattled. Even as old as he was, the silver must have been horribly painful to him; she could see tendrils of smoke coming from his arm, and he was careful to keep his hand away from the chains. His skin was covered with thick red burns.

"I'm sorry," he said again. "I tried to warn you, but I couldn't—I needed—"

"I know," Claire said. "It's—" What was it? Not okay, okay would be a real stretch. Understandable, maybe. "It's not so bad." It was, though. Still, Myrnin looked a little relieved. "Who did this to you?"

The relief faded from his face, replaced with a blank, black rage. "Who do you think?" he asked.

And from all around them, from the faint shimmer of crystal embedded in the walls, came a soft, smoky laugh.

"She touched me," Claire said, remembering. "She dragged me here. I didn't think she could do that."

"No," Myrnin agreed. "I didn't think she could do a great many things, although she was capable of them on a purely theoretical level. I've been a fool, Claire. You tried to warn me—even Amelie warned me, but I thought—I thought I understood what I'd created. I thought she was my servant."

"And now," Ada said, gliding out of the wall in cold silver and black, "you belong to me. But am I not a generous master? You starved me for so long, barely giving me enough blood to survive. Now I give you a feast." Her cutout image turned toward Claire, and she folded her hands together at her waist, prim and perfect. "Oh, Myrnin. You didn't finish your dinner. Don't let it go bad."

Myrnin stripped his black velvet coat off his right arm, then shrugged it down his left until it was covering the chain. He took hold of it, right-handed, and pulled. Claire tried to get up to help, but her head went weird again, and she had to rest. She rolled on her side and watched Myrnin's right arm tremble as he tried to exert enough pressure to snap the chain, and then he sat back against the wall, panting.

He stared at Ada as if he wanted to rip her into confetti.

"Don't pout," she said. "If you're good, I'll let you off the chain from time to time. In a few years, perhaps"

Claire blinked slowly. "She's sick," she said. "Isn't she?"

"She's insane," Myrnin said. "Ada, my darling, this would be amusing if you weren't trying to kill us. You do realize that if I die, you waste away down here. No more blood. No more treats. No more anything."

In answer, Ada's image reached out and grabbed Claire by the hair, dragging her up to a sitting position. "Oh, I think I can hunt up my own blood," Ada said. "After all, I control the portals. I can reach out and snatch up anyone I wish. But you're right. It would be terribly boring, all alone in the dark. I'll have to keep you all to myself, the way you kept me all to yourself, all these years." She dropped Claire and wiped her hand on her computer-generated gown. "But I can't share you with *her*, my love."

Myrnin's eyes flared red, then smoothed back to black, full of secrets. "No indeed," he said. "Why, she's in the way. I see that now. Send her out of here, lock her out of the portals. I never want to see her again."

"Easily done," Ada said, and grabbed Claire's hair again. She dragged her backward, and Claire flailed weakly, grabbing at loose stones and breaking nails on sharp edges of rock.

She looked over her shoulder in the direction they were going.

Ada was dragging her to the edge of the sinkhole.

"No!" Myrnin said, and got to his feet. He lunged to the end of his chain, reaching out; his clawing fingers fell short of Claire's foot by about two inches. "No, Ada, don't! I need her!"

"That's too bad," Ada said. "Because I don't."

Claire's hand fell on a sharp, ancient bone—a rib?— and she stabbed blindly behind her head. A second later it occurred to her that she was trying to stab an image, a hologram, an empty space—but Ada let out a yell and the pressure on Claire's hair eased.

Ada's pressed both hands over her midsection, which slowly spread into a black stain.

She was bleeding.

Where the blood hit the stone, it vanished in a curl of smoke.

But the wound didn't heal.

"Yes!" Myrnin cried out. "Yes, by manifesting enough to touch you, she makes herself vulnerable—Claire! Here! Come here!" Myrnin cried, and Claire crawled back in his direction. The second she was within reach, he dragged her toward him, putting her against the wall.

Ada was still standing where she'd been, looking down at her and the spreading dark stain on her dress. Her image guttered, flared, sparked, and then stabilized again.

She flashed toward them, screaming that awful, echoing shriek from all the walls. Myrnin pivoted gracefully and hooked the slack of his chain around her silver, two-dimensional throat. Where it touched her, it burned black holes, and her scream grew louder, until it was cracking stone in the walls. She tried to pull free, but the silver wouldn't let her go. "I've got her!" he said, although Claire could see that his whole body was trembling from the strain, and the burn of silver on his hands must have been horrible. "Go, Claire! Get out of here! You have to go!"

She was too weak, too dizzy. The room was a minefield of sinkholes and false floors, and even if she'd known where to step, chances were she'd simply collapse halfway across and disappear into one of those deep, dark chasms . . . .

And she couldn't just *leave* him.

"Claire!" His voice was desperate. "You have to go. Go *now*."

Now that the lights were on, she could see a clear trail that looked solid, leading all around the room's edge. Claire stumbled out onto it, guiding herself with both hands on the stone wall, and took one torturous step after another. The lights flickered, and the screaming suddenly cut off behind her.

Claire didn't dare look back. She was at the door, a black unknown facing her.

Portal.

She couldn't think. Couldn't get her head together.

Couldn't remember all the frequencies to align to take her where she needed to go.

Behind her, she heard Ada laugh.

You have to do this. You can do this!

Claire's eyes snapped open, and without thinking about it, without even meaning to do it, she threw herself forward into the darkness.

And fell out on the other side, into the tunnel beneath Myrnin's lab. Overhead, the trapdoor was open, letting in streams of pale lamplight. Claire staggered into a wall, bounced, and ran away from the light, into the damp chill of the tunnel.

Twelve long steps, and she heard the cavern echoing overhead. She slapped the wall until she found the lights, flipped them on, and ran toward the keyboard at the center of Ada's hissing, steaming, clanking metal form.

A cable slithered across the stone, trying to trip her, but she stumbled on, caught herself against the giant keyboard, and took a second to gasp for breath. Her body was shaking all over, cold as a vampire's, and she just wanted to fall down, fall and sleep in the dark.

Claire closed her eyes, and the symbols began to burn against her eyelids. The symbols she'd memorized every day since Myrnin had given her the sketch on paper of the order. She knew this.

She *had* this.

She opened her eyes . . . and gasped in utter anguish, because the keys were all *blank*.

Somewhere in the darkness, Ada's tinny voice scratched out a contemptuous laugh. "Surprised, little wretch? What's wrong, not as easy as you'd thought?"

You've got this. Claire chanted that to herself, and closed her eyes again. This time, she didn't just imagine the symbols she wanted to push, but with a huge effort, she imagined the keyboard as it had been the last time she'd seen it. She fixed the image in her mind, opened her eyes, and touched the first key.

Yes. Yes, that was right.

The force required to push the key down seemed enormous, like trying to squeeze a boulder. She got the first symbol pressed, then pushed her palm down on the second and leaned her whole weight against it. It slowly, reluctantly clicked and locked.

Ada's laughter died away.

The third symbol was Amelie's Founder's Symbol, the same as on Claire's gold bracelet, and Claire clearly remembered its position right in the center of the keyboard. She put her palm on it and pushed until it locked down. As she reached for the fourth key, she lost her balance and almost fell.

Behind her, Ada's voice came out of the scratchy, ancient speakers. "Stop. You're going to make a mistake."

"I won't," Claire gasped, and pushed the fourth key down. Two more to go.

She couldn't remember the fifth symbol. She knew it was there, but somehow, her mind wouldn't focus. Everything seemed blurry and odd. She closed her eyes again and concentrated, concentrated very hard, until she remembered that it had been hidden down on the bottom-left side.

When she opened her eyes, Ada was *right there*, inches from her face. Claire shrieked and jumped back, slamming her fist forward.

It went right through Ada's form. She wasn't able to stay physical anymore. Myrnin had really hurt her. She hadn't fixed the damage to her image, either—there were black wounds on her throat and hands, and a black stain covering most of her dress.

Her eyes were glowing silver.

"Stop," Ada said.

"No," Claire panted, closed her eyes, and stepped through her image. She found the key she was looking for, and pushed it.

One more.

"All right," Ada said. "Then I'll stop you."

Claire felt cold against her skin, and heard the hiss and clank of the computer grow loud, almost like chatter.

The lights went out, but the noise got louder—and louder.

Ada's cold fingers brushed the back of her neck.

Claire turned toward the darkness behind her. "So that's it?" she yelled. "That's all you've got? Turn off the lights? Scary! I'm totally shaking, you freak! What do you think I am, five and scared of the dark?"

"I think you're defeated," Ada said. "And I think I will kill you, when and how I wish." Ada had made herself physical again, but it wouldn't last. It couldn't. She was still bleeding from where Claire had hurt her, and now her neck and face were scarred and burned from the chain. Her head was at a strange angle, but she was still alive. She glowed a very faint, phosphorous kind of silver.

"You'll never find the key in the dark," Ada almost purred. "You're defeated. And now you die."

"You first," Claire said.

Claire reached behind her from blind instinct and memory, and slammed her palm down on a key. It almost went down, but then it popped up again.

Wrong.

Ada's ice-cold hands—not really hands anymore— closed around her neck. "Stupid girl," she said. "So close."

Ada's fingers squeezed, locking the breath in her throat, and Claire wildly hammered her palm down on the next key to the right.

It locked down with an almost physical snap.

As Claire's fingers slipped off the key, it clicked into place, and the clattering of the machine . . .

. . . stopped.

For a breathless second those cold fingers kept on strangling her, and then they softened, turned to mist . . .

And then they were gone.

A steady, quiet glow came up around her.

Lights.

Claire sank down, back to the keyboard, gasping in breaths through her bruised throat, and watched a silvery light flicker in midair, then take on form.

Ada, but not Ada. The same image, but immaculate, perfectly groomed, and with an entirely blank expression.

"Welcome," Ada said. "May I ask who you are?"

"Claire," she said. "My name is Claire."

"My name is—" Ada cocked her head and frowned. "I'm not quite sure. Addy?"

"Ada."

"Ah yes. Ada." Ada's flat image smiled, but it was a fake kind of smile, with nothing behind it. "I'm not feeling very well."

"You just got reset."

"No, I know all about that. I don't feel at all well, quite beyond that. There's something very wrong with my mind." Her image flickered, and a spasm of emotion flared across her perfect, blank face. "I'm scared, Claire. Can you fix me?"

"I—" Claire coughed. She was so tired, and she really, really hurt. "I don't know." She knew she sounded discouraged. "Maybe I don't want to."

"Oh," Ada said softly. "I see. I really am broken, aren't I?"

"Yes."

"And I can't be fixed."

"No," Claire said softly. "I'm sorry. I think—I think you've got brain damage. I don't think you're ever going to be right."

Ada was silent for a moment, watching her, and then she said, "I loved him, you know. I really did."

"I think he really loved you, too. That's why he tried to hang on to you all these years."

Ada nodded. "Please tell him that I still love him.

And because I love him, I can't take the risk that I might hurt him again."

Claire had a very bad feeling. "What are you—"

"Just tell him." Ada smiled, and it was a real smile. A sweet one. "Good-bye, Claire."

And the panel at the wall blew up in arcs of electricity and flames and shredded metal, and Claire ducked and covered her head.

The lights went out.

Ada's image flickered in place for a moment, and then she said, very quietly, "Tell Myrnin I'm sorry I hurt him."

Then she was gone, and the low-level hum of the computer just . . . died.

Claire crouched there, trembling in the dark for a while and listening to the escaping hiss of steam. On one of the round screens on the computer, she saw Ada's image appear. It moved to the next screen—and then to the next. It grew a little fainter every time.

Then Ada's image faded to a single dot of white, and the screen went totally black.

Silence. Real, total silence.

Claire put her head on her upraised knees.

I'll just take a nap, she thought, and then it all just went away for a while.

When she woke up, Amelie was standing in front of the silent, dead computer, one pale hand on the keyboard touching the metal and bone.

"We'll have to get this running again as soon as possible," she said, and then turned toward Claire. "I see you're awake."

"Not really," Claire said. "I don't know what I am right now."

"Your friends are coming." Amelie's tone was cool, and her face was a mask. Claire couldn't tell anything about what she was feeling. "I called them."

"Where's Myrnin?"

Amelie's gray eyes focused on her neck. "He bit you."

"Well—a little." Claire put her hand to the wound, and winced when it throbbed. "Is it bad?"

"You'll live." Amelie turned back to the keyboard. "I'm afraid Ada is beyond help. When the electrical power failed, the nutrients that sustained her organic remnants turned toxic."

"She's dead?"

"She was always dead, Claire. Now she is well beyond our attempts to revive her." Amelie looked at her with cool, calm eyes. "Did you kill her?"

Claire swallowed. "No. I reset her, and she figured out that she couldn't be fixed. She did it herself." That seemed . . . sad, somehow. And a little bit brave. "Where's Myrnin?"

"Here," he said, and crouched down next to her, all long arms and legs, awkward and graceful at the same time. He was still wearing his black velvet coat. Claire fixed her gaze on the bloodstained, ragged hole in his left sleeve. Under it, the skin still looked red and torn. "I'm all right now. Don't worry."

"I'm not," she lied. "Does it hurt?" she asked, because he was holding his arm at an odd angle.

"A little." He was lying, too—a lot. "Claire—"

"No, don't say you're sorry. I know, you had to do it."

"I was going to say thank you for stopping Ada. She always knew you would be the one to destroy her, you know."

"What?" Claire rubbed at the headache forming between her eyes. "What are you talking about?"

"She had taken it into her head that you were going to kill her," Amelie said. "She believed it. So she tried to kill you first, and in doing so, she forced you to this. Unfortunately, it is a great deal of trouble for me; Ada was very valuable. Without her, we cannot maintain many of the less scientific measures of security and travel in the town."

"No more portals," Myrnin said, and sighed. "No more barriers to keep people from leaving. And we won't be able to track those who leave, at least for now."

He turned away, looking at the computer, and for a moment—just a moment—Claire saw the agony clearly visible on his face. His hand was clenched, and as he opened it, she saw the locket she'd found in the box. Ada's portrait. "Oh my dear," he said, very softly. "What we did to each other . . . I am so very sorry."

Amelie watched him and said nothing. Myrnin closed his eyes for a moment, then slipped the locket into his vest pocket and turned toward her, clearly making an effort to make himself seem normal again. As normal as Myrnin ever got. "Right. I'll need a viable candidate to replace Ada. Do you have someone in mind?"

Amelie was still watching Claire. Claire swallowed.

"I do," Amelie said softly. "But I think not quite yet. Let's see where this takes us, Myrnin."

Myrnin said, "I believe it will take us straight into trouble, if experience is any guide at all. Ah, there they are. Claire, your friends—"

She hardly had time to turn before Shane had her and was smothering her in a hug, then devouring her in a kiss, and even though she wasn't exactly in the best possible shape, she felt a hot flush race through her veins to warm her whole body. "Hey," Shane said, then gently combed her hair back from her face. "You look—"

He saw the bite mark, and froze.

Michael and Eve were right behind him, and Claire heard Eve make a funny, strangled noise. Michael's head snapped toward Myrnin.

"I'm okay," Claire said. "A little juice, a steak—I'll be fine. It's just like the blood bank. Right?"

Amelie exchanged a glance with Myrnin, then turned

away. He said, "Absolutely," and bounced to his feet to join Amelie at the hissing hulk of the computer. "Take a few days off. With pay."

Shane's face turned red. "You son of a—"

"Don't," Claire said, and put her hand on his cheek. "Shane. I need you. Don't do that."

"I need you, too," he said. "I love you. And it is *not okay*."

Myrnin didn't look at either of them again. After a moment, though, he reached into the pocket of his jacket and came up with a small, portable hard drive.

SHANE & CLAIRE, it read in silver Sharpie.

"I think this is yours," he said.

Claire felt a wave of weakness that had nothing to do with loss of blood. "Where did you get it?"

"Ada," Myrnin said. "She was planning to do something creative with it, I expect—put it on the Internet, or send it to your parents. Her idea of a prank. You can thank me later."

She stopped, staring at his back. "You didn't watch it, did you?"

He didn't turn around. "Of course not."

It even sounded as if he might be telling the truth.

"My car's outside," Michael said. "Come on. Let's get you home."

"In a moment," Amelie said, and turned to face them. In that moment, with her hands clasped at her waist, she looked very much like Ada, which gave Claire a severe attack of the terrors. "I've made a decision. About the three of you."

That didn't sound good. They all exchanged looks.

Claire felt something odd happen inside her, like a flash of heat, followed by one of cold . . . and then the bracelet on her wrist, a constant, heavy presence, clicked, and fell off to roll away on the stone floor.

Claire cried out and rubbed at her wrist. It was dead

white where the bracelet had been, and indented with the shape of gold.

"I've decided to record you as Neutrals," Amelie said. "Friends of Morganville. You will be issued special pins, which you must wear at all times. Your names will be recorded in the archives. You are not to be menaced or hunted by any vampire from this point onward. In return, I will require services from you, as I do from other Neutrals, from time to time. You will be listed as employees of the town."

Even Myrnin seemed surprised, Claire thought. "Generous," he said.

"Pragmatic," Amelie said. "Less trouble for me. The four of them are stronger together, and less vulnerable. And I'm well aware that there are those within Morganville who would prefer to split them apart, for their own uses. I can hardly have people with such intimate knowledge of us running around without ... restrictions."

Claire licked her lips. "About that—I kind of made a deal with Morley. That you'd let him and his people leave Morganville, or else Eve and Shane get hunted."

"Why on earth would you do such a thing?" Amelie shook her head. "I can't protect you from deals made prior to the announcement. If Morley can make a claim, he can register the hunt. It would be legal, according to law. It would be up to you to protect yourselves."

"But you could let Morley and his people leave, right? That's all they want. To be set free, to go where they want."

Amelie was silent for a moment, and then she said, "No." That was all. No *Sorry* or *Hope you don't die*.

She turned back to the dead computer.

"But—"

Shane shook his head. "Let's go home. Come on, we have a month. We'll work it out."

Claire didn't think so, but she shut up and let Michael

ferry them, one by one, out of the trapdoor and up to the lab. As they headed for his car, Eve's cell phone rang.

"Hello? Oh, hi, Heather." Eve sighed. "Don't tell me, I'm fired, right?"

Heather? Claire remembered, finally, that Heather was the assistant director for the play. It was the last possible thing Claire could think of, importance-wise, but Eve's face gradually lit up with a smile. "I'm not? Seriously? He didn't—oh wow. Okay. Yes. I'll be there. Yes, of course! . . . Oh, sure, hang on." She handed the phone to Claire. "She says she wants to talk to you."

Claire carefully put the phone to her ear. "Yes?"

"Claire, look, we need a new Stella. Mein Herr says you're perfect. He's already cleared it with your boss."

"He *what*?" And how did Myrnin get to make that kind of call, anyway? "I'm not an actress! I don't know anything—"

"That's what he likes," Heather said. "You're cast. Be at rehearsal tomorrow. Eve will tell you when."

She hung up.

Claire stared at the dead phone, then handed it back. "I guess I'm in the play," she said.

"Good news," Eve said. "You've already got on-camera experience."

"Yeah, speaking of that, what's going to happen with Kim? Not that I care," Shane said quickly when Claire looked at him. "Just curious."

"I asked," Eve said. "Chief Moses says they'll keep her in the nuthouse for a while, see if she gets better. But even if she does, she'll be in jail a long time."

"You okay with that?"

Eve took in a deep breath. "Yeah," she said. "Yeah, I guess I am."

Claire looked down at the hard drive in her hand, the Sharpie-marked evidence, took it out, and handed it to Shane. "You do the honors," he said.

One smash against the bricks, and it shattered. He

kept on smashing it, just to be sure, and then tossed the remains into a handy trash can at the end of the alley.

"The end," Shane said.

It wasn't. Michael and Eve were walking together, but not touching; Claire could see the tension between them. Ada was dead, and that meant the vampires were risking everything, at least for a while. As for Amelie's "gift," Claire knew there had to be a catch, and a big one.

It wasn't the end at all . . . but Claire was content to pretend for now. With Shane warm at her side, and the future stretching out in front of them, she could pretend for today that it was happily ever after.

Of course, tomorrow was another day.

TRACK LIST

In case you want to listen along to the songs I used to help me write this book, here they are! Buy the tracks, please. Don't be a vampire preying on the artists.

"Ghost Town"	Shiny Toy Guns
"Falls Apart"	Hurt
"Under the Gun"	Supreme Beings of Leisure
"Auditorium"	American Princes
"Devil in Me"	22-20's
"John Barleycorn"	Traffic
"Glory Box"	Portishead
"The Hop"	Radio Citizen feat. Bajka
"Roads"	Portishead
"My Old Self"	Wide Mouth Mason
"I Got Mine"	The Black Keys
"C'mon C'mon"	The Von Bondies
"Every Inambition"	The Trews
"Ladylike"	Big Wreck
"Numb"	Holly McNarland
"Beauty of Speed"	Tori Amos
"Best Way to Die"	Jet Set Satellite
"Love Hurts"	Incubus
"Little Toy Gun"	HoneyHoney
"I Don't Care"	Fall Out Boy
"Many Shades of Black"	The Raconteurs
"Headfirst Slide into Cooperstown"	Fall Out Boy
"URA Fever"	The Kills
"Manic Girl"	Radio Iodine
"Take Me to the Speedway"	The Dexateens

"Alsatian"	White Rose Movement
"Poison Whiskey"	Tishamingo
"Welcome Home"	Coheed & Cambria
"Tick Tick Boom"	The Hives
"Jockey Full of Bourbon"	Joe Bonamassa
"Leopard-Skin Pill-Box Hat"	Beck
"The Ballad of John Henry"	Joe Bonamassa
"Funkier Than a Mosquito's Tweeter"	Joe Bonamassa
"Happier Times"	Joe Bonamassa
"Faster"	Rachael Yamagata
"Around the Bend"	The Asteroid Galaxy Tour
"Slow Dance with a Stranger"	Danger Radio
"Ardmore"	Cardinal Trait
"Prayer"	Lizzie West
"Bounce"	The Cab
"Time Bomb"	Jessy Greene

About the Author

Rachel Caine is the author of the *New York Times* best-selling Morganville Vampires series as well as the best-selling Weather Warden series, which includes *Ill Wind*, *Heat Stroke*, *Chill Factor*, *Windfall*, *Firestorm*, *Thin Air*, *Gale Force*, and *Cape Storm*. Her ninth Weather Warden novel will be released in August 2010. She also recently started another series, Outcast Season, with the release of the first novel, *Undone*. Rachel and her husband, fantasy artist R. Cat Conrad, live in Texas with their iguanas, Popeye and Darwin.

Web site: www.rachelcaine.com
Myspace: www.myspace.com/rachelcaine
Livejournal: rachelcaine.livejournal.com
Twitter: @rachelcaine
Look for Rachel Caine on Facebook.

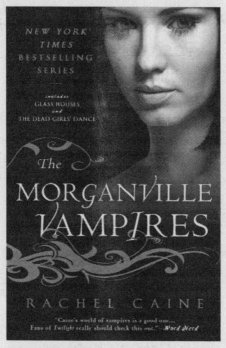

ALSO AVAILABLE IN THE
MORGANVILLE VAMPIRES SERIES
FROM
RACHEL CAINE

Carpe Corpus

In the small college town of Morganville,
vampires and humans lived in (relative)
peace—until all the rules got rewritten when
the evil vampire Bishop arrived, looking for
the lost book of vampire secrets. He's kept a
death grip on the town ever since.

Now an underground resistance is brewing,
and in order to contain it, Bishop must go to
even greater lengths. He vows to obliterate the
town and all its inhabitants—the living and
the undead. Claire Danvers and her friends
are the only ones who stand in his way. But
even if they defeat Bishop, will the vampires
ever be content to go back to the old rules,
after having such a taste of power?

Available wherever books are sold or at
penguin.com